Malicious Mischief

A Rylie Keyes Mystery

Malicious Mischief

A Rylie Keyes Mystery

Marianne Harden

Entangled Publishing, LLC
2614 South Timberline Road
Suite 109
Fort Collins, CO 80525
Visit our website at www.entangledpublishing.com.

Edited by Libby Murphy
Cover design by Libby Murphy

Ebook ISBN 978-1-62266-032-2
Print ISBN 978-1-62266-033-9

Manufactured in the United States of America

First Edition October 2013

To my mother

˜When the chips are down, the buffalo is empty˜

Am I a flake? Sort of. But I'm trying to change. My grandfather has property tax issues, and what troubles Granddad, troubles me. Good thing I've held down a steady job for months. This is a major deal. Not the getting a job part—I've had lots—but the held down aspect. Somehow, I always end up unemployed, but not today.

Today, I am Rylie Tabitha Keyes, chauffeur to the seniors at Fountain of Youth Retirement Home (FoY).

It was dawn Sunday when I eased my employer's van from one freeway onto another. After that, I concentrated on the wet asphalt up ahead. I didn't want to think about my job history or our financial woes. Instead I focused on the summery sunrise over the Cascade Mountains due east. I stared at it a moment, charmed by its contrast to the more typical Bellevue, Washington gloom brooding overhead.

I should've been asleep, but I needed to toss trash from

a fundraiser rolling around in the back of the van. Leland Rosenberg, my boss at Fountain of Youth Retirement Home, had asked me to dump the bags at his second business, Rosenberg Laboratory, as FoY's Dumpsters were full from a recent remodel. His mood had been edgy, sort of insistent I dispose of them last night. I confess, before I could carry out this task, a minor traffic accident and an all-important overnight obligation had waylaid me. I didn't bother to sigh over how blunders always seemed to pepper my work performance. Some things were fated to be. After all, I slogged at my job for money not joy. It isn't that I don't like working at FoY, it just isn't my dream gig.

Sadly, at twenty-four, I have a résumé too long to recite from memory, but not because I'm aimless. For as long as I can remember, I have yearned to be a private detective, a Veronica Mars 2.0. Problem is my grandfather is against the idea. *Dead set against it.* "Rylie, it isn't always pretty or exciting," he had said. "The hours are lousy, the pay measly, and then there is the danger." He stared at me reflectively, and I knew he was thinking of the two times he'd been shot on the force. "There is a lot of danger."

"Danger is how I roll," I said, grinning.

Granddad had pursed his lips. He doesn't always appreciate my silly sense of humor.

"Detective work isn't for you," he'd decreed.

"But—"

"Rylie." His eyes misted when he looked at me. "Do this for me, please."

Nevertheless, there was no good reason why as a grown woman I've caved to his demands, except one: I adore him. He's always been there for me—right from the beginning when he took me in as newborn after my mother ran off. And with his health in decline from a recent heart attack, I cannot—will not—risk upsetting him.

So with the stench from the trash bags mounting, I steered FoY's van onto the off-ramp and headed toward Rosenberg Laboratory just off the freeway exit. My mind was filled with thoughts of a steamy shower, maybe a few hours of shut-eye before punching the clock at nine. I stared forward, squinted due to the dimness. Then I iced over. Up ahead, traveling in the wrong direction a panel truck advanced, peeling rubber.

Faster.

Closer.

Zeroed in to hit me.

I whipped the van off the road, the red, white, and blue panel truck whizzing past. I slammed on the brakes, fighting to control the wheel. I wrestled with it, panicked, my mind flashing on one fortunate thing: no seniors were in the van.

Tons of hazards burst before my eyes. I struggled to absorb them. A mangled guardrail zigzagged up ahead, its many gaps from other out-of-control vehicles big as life. Worse was the wall of giant Douglas-firs growing beyond, lower trunks scarred, limbs low and swaying.

I was going to careen through the railing.

I was going to hit the trees.

I was going to die.

I shut my eyes, but terrified of dying in the dark, I forced them open. The van bulleted through the ruptured guardrail, shot toward the trees. I jumped when something brown hit the windshield, bounced off. Several horrific seconds passed before the van miraculously whizzed between two trees, hurdling into a shrubby field. No time to celebrate, not with a concrete wall up ahead.

The sound of steel hitting stone caught my ears, and glass shattered as the van sideswiped the wall. Then it rolled to a stop, right side billowing in cement dust.

I froze rock-solid before the shakes began. I shook in silence, a disbelieving, embarrassed silence. I wondered about having two auto accidents in less than six hours. I rejected the idea that someone wanted me dead. It amazed me how silly that sounded. No way was I important enough to murder. Sure, if I were a private investigator, killing me might make sense. After all, I may be a skinny redhead with tons of freckles, but I have a fair grasp of detective work after secretly studying on my own. So I could see me pissing off some baddy, making him snap and seek revenge. Only problem: I'm no PI, just a harmless chauffeur for a retirement home—

Or, at least I *was* a chauffeur for a retirement home. Leland would probably fire me. I'd have to stand in more unemployment lines. I'd have to schlep to more interviews. I'd have to tell Granddad I was out of work. *Again.*

The hardest part about losing this job was leaving friends. I liked the seniors, well, maybe not crabby Otto Weiner, who once grumbled to Leland about my driving. When my boss sided with me, I caught Otto draining the lizard on the van's front seats. We had a pinky tussle where one of us ended up on our knees. Okay, so I will not be wearing those tights again.

With the wrong-way driver probably halfway to Seattle by now, I searched the van in the early morning light for my cell phone, only to realize I had left it along with my jacket at the abandoned train trestle downtown. I didn't relish walking down the street in the damp to find an open convenience store with a pay phone, or calling the police once I found one. But it was necessary. I was a cop's granddaughter and had learned early the importance of laws.

Then as though the universe took pity on me, a patrol car cruised down the street up ahead. I unclicked my seatbelt as the car pulled to the curb, roof lights dark and covered. I tried for laid back but failed miserably as my stomach nose-dived to my apple-green Converse. Weird. One would think I'd be cool around police since Granddad retired after forty years on the force, twenty of those as a Bellevue detective. But I squirmed like a bucket of worms.

When the officer climbed from the squad car, my heart followed my stomach. As difficult as it was being pathetic in the job department, it was harder to love an unattainable guy. Particularly, *especially,* Officer Zach O'Neil.

About a hundred feet lay between both vehicles, but they blurred away as Zach ran toward me, calling out my name. Dang, he was hot. And reliable. That practical thought skipped into my mind, and I snorted at the silliness of it, yet there was no denying his awesomeness.

"You okay?" Vague irritation crossed his face. "Everything in one piece?"

He leaned on the window frame, his dark butterscotch hair made radiant by the rising sun, and his tender gray eyes stealing my voice. I smiled my best 100-watter to cover my silence.

I studied his face: gentle, barely a shadow of beard, and a squared-off chin. I had known him for most of my life and loved him for eons. Not only did Zach know nothing of my crush, but also after he shot and killed an armed convenience store robber several months back, he'd made it clear he wanted no long-term relationships, not with anyone. Ever.

"Right as rain." I bit my lip. Who was I kidding? Just look at him, those wounded eyes. I was a goner. "A panel truck ran me off the road."

"You aren't hurt?" He reached out and, with amazing tenderness, laid a finger on my forehead. "What's with the blood?"

"Blood? On me?" As I suffered a dogged blood phobia and certain I would faint at the sight, I fought the urge to touch the wound. "Is it bad?"

He shook his head, but he didn't smile. "I'm just kidding. It's only a small scratch."

I twisted to see my face in the side mirror. He was right— no blood, only a bit of red. I tried to grin but knew it came out a smirk. "It does hurt," I said without a hint of poutiness. I was proud of that. "Head wounds can be tricky."

He opened my door and pulled me close. "Any dizziness?"

I slid my hands inside his jacket, around his back. I felt something beyond love. I felt safe. I always did with Zach. "I'm okay, really."

Then halfway into what I hoped was a sexy look, I hiccupped. *Great.*

Zach leaned closer in a conspiratorial whisper, "You smell fishy."

Clearly, fish oil was not an animal attraction scent.

"It's Leland's new liquid vitamins. He has everyone at FoY taking them."

"Leland amazes me," Zach said. "Running the laboratory and FoY, making vitamins, and that new anti-frailty drug for seniors. The guy must never sleep. In fact, I know he doesn't.

All hours of the night I see lights on in his garage office."

There wasn't a lot of privacy on Lake Sammamish, and according to Granddad that was the beauty of our little lake, what made all us neighbors like family. Zach lived one house away from Granddad and me and my friend Solo, with Leland in between us.

"Tell me about it," I said. "Those lights shine down through my bedroom window, and Solo says he can see them from the dock."

Zach's jaw tightened. "Solo will survive. Listen, it may be a rundown sailboat, but is it not time you charged him rent to live on it? He's got a job, even if it's only part time."

"Full time," I corrected. "And he pays rent now."

Too much rent if you ask me, but he won't hear of us taking less.

"Glad to hear."

Zach was rubbing my shoulders, a new habit of his. It was both ecstasy and torture.

"So how—how have you been? It's been weeks. Two, actually," I said.

"Two weeks?" He frowned at this, but didn't look surprised.

"Not that I'm counting. I would never count." I stared at my feet. Truth was, after I'd stupidly deepened an innocent kiss between us after a small Lotto win, I worried he was dodging me. "You're busy. I'm busy. Okay, moving on."

His eyes darkened. "Better have that bump checked. You don't want your grandfather to worry."

"No, I wouldn't want *Granddad* to worry," I said, unable to squelch the sarcasm.

He frowned again; he'd heard the hurt in my voice.

I dropped my gaze, ashamed. I needed no proof of his friendship. His love? Well, that was a different story. I would do most anything to hear those words, short of revealing my feelings first. I just couldn't do that.

I looked up, a little lost. "When you got here, how'd you know it was me?"

"What else? This van, it's hard to miss the bright orange color." He stepped back, making more distance between us. "And the airbrushed seniors playing guitars are a dead giveaway."

"I like it," I said. A tiny lie, the flashy paint played havoc with my goal to appear older than twelve. "Leland says the color makes people remember FoY."

"I'll bet." Abruptly he reached inside the van and turned off the ignition. "You know better than to leave a damaged engine running—" He broke off, shaking his head.

"I guess in all the excitement I forgot."

He grabbed me by the shoulders. "Forgot? Rylie, you could have blown up."

I caught the terror in his voice. Resolute, rebounding, like an echo from the night of the convenience store shoot-out when a stray bullet had ignited his squad car's gas tank.

"You could have blown up," he said again, softer this time, heartbreakingly so.

I wanted to ask about the Post-traumatic Stress Disorder he now suffered. But I knew better. He always got angry, except once during a weak moment when he'd revealed his fear of hurting somebody during one of his many flashbacks. "I'm not in danger anymore, Zach. The engine is off."

There came a pause, a long sigh. "You've gotta learn to be more careful—" When his voice broke, he looked away.

"A lot more careful."

"There's no chance of an explosion," I said.

"Now," was his only comment.

"Everything is fine."

"Is it?" He paused again. "Don't you realize it took me several minutes to notice the van's engine was still on? Christ, it's up to me to take care of you. I screwed up."

Though his anguish made my heart skip, I shook my head. "It's not your fault. I screwed up, not you. I forgot to turn off the engine."

He made a noncommittal sound. "So why are you up so early?"

"Ahhh." My Saturday night routine annoyed him, so I sidestepped. "Why are you?"

He narrowed his eyes, but didn't push. "A quick break from the department's information and complaint desk. First year on the force and I'm already ferrying squad cars." He rotated his right shoulder—another injury from the shootout. "The good news is I'm done with physical therapy."

"Then you're better?"

"Yeah…yeah, I am…better." He stared over my shoulder as early rising bees buzzed nearby in a clump of shrubs. "Much better."

I decided to take a chance. "And the flashbacks, have they gone away?"

Those tender eyes of his locked on mine. "I'm not crazy. Killing a man changes a person, even when the shooting was justified."

I drew in a bolstering breath, ready to broach another sore subject. "Talk to a department counselor again, and this time tell him the truth."

"And risk being kicked off the force? Nothing has changed since the last time you brought this up. I know you're worried, but I'm fine. The flashbacks are gone. Trust me, Rylie. They're gone. Vanished. Nowhere in sight."

He was trying too hard.

"That's good," I said, unconvinced.

"Paperwork is in, awaiting the captain's signature. Soon I'll be back on the beat."

"Nice," I said with a smile that felt almost natural.

"Nice? It's freakin' awesome." His gaze slid to the van's passenger seat where I had left the blanket, Thermos, and flashlight I had used overnight. He shot me a slanted look, paired with a faint frown. "Dawn Sunday. Overnight gear. Christ, not again. How many times must I tell you Suicide Trestle isn't safe?"

I took a careful breath. "As it happens—"

"Suicidal jumpers need professional help," he said. "Not amateurs."

"Have you forgotten my suicide prevention training?"

"Two weeks preparing for the hotline doesn't make you a professional."

I caught his tone: frustration. "But you said I was perfect for the job."

"And you're the one who messed up your first call by answering '*Poisons to go*. At the end of your rope, we got your dope,'" he sing-songed.

"That is not fair, Zach." Shame and irritation swamped me. "You of all people know that's just not fair. I made a mistake. I accidentally leaned on the *live* button. I thought the incoming call was a practical joke, not the real thing."

"You should have known," he said simply.

I opened my mouth, closed it. It was all fine and good for him. He hadn't been there, hadn't been swept up in the staff's amusing stories. He hadn't heard about their pranks on rookies with phony emergency calls to soothe their nerves. I had just been going along. I'd wanted to fit in, be needed. Even so, his words made me realize something.

"You're right," I said. "I need to work on my observation skills. I'll need those as a detective."

He shook his head.

Seeing where this was going, I held up a silencing hand. "Whether you support me or not, I'm going to be a PI someday. Sheesh, why are both you and Granddad against me on this? Never mind. You're entitled to your opinion, as mean as it is."

"That's me, a big meanie." And for the first time this morning, he smiled.

I felt a flicker of guilt, knowing he was never mean and that like Granddad his resistance was out of concern. "I need to check the damage to the van." I skirted around him, only to have him keep pace as we walked to the front bumper.

We took a good look. The right side mirror was gone, the corner of the windshield scrunched, and the right side dented and scraped.

"Tell me one thing," Zach said, straightening. "You did take Solo with you last night?"

"Of course. Solo always comes along."

My friend Solosolo Namulau'ulu is Samoan, but his shortened nickname is the only thing small about him. He is huge. And strong. Truth is I'm a little scared to patrol Suicide Trestle without him. Sure, I've taken a course on negotiation, and then there is my hotline training, but I have never actually used any of it. Whereas Solo muscles people into seeing things his way. Solo has lots of muscles, but inside he is a pussycat, one with a body like a Mack truck.

"Solo gets me," I said.

Zach smirked. "Meaning I don't?"

"I didn't say that. But you could support me. If we save only one life, then all the sacrificed Saturday nights in the world will be worth it."

"What if a jumper takes you with them over the edge? What then?"

"That's where Solo comes in. Not many can overpower him. We're a team."

"A team of trouble." He typed a text message on his phone. "I just let your teammate know you'll be a little late getting home. Last thing you need is Solo waking up your grandfather, wondering where you are and why you're not home yet."

"Good thinking. We left the trestle at the same time, but he detoured to get something to eat." I shifted my gaze to the van then back again. "Could Bondo fix this damage?"

Zach's deepening grin raised a hint of dimples. "I have a theory, no proof, but it just might take more than bodywork to fix this mess. And two accidents in only a couple of hours just might be a record."

"How'd you know about the other one?" Then I remembered the message I had left on his cell after the first accident, a call he hadn't returned. I wanted to ask why, but couldn't. His pledge had not been to avoid all hook-ups, just the permanent kind. If he'd been with another woman, I didn't want to know.

"Has it occurred to you that you're a magnet for trouble?"

he asked.

"Neither accident was my fault. The delivery truck last night came out of nowhere. I'm lucky the truck just dinged the bumper." I sighed, gave in. "Okay, I'm a magnet."

He unlatched the hood, tugged, but when it rose only inches with a dismal moan, he let it drop. "The right fender took the main hit. Right hinge is crumpled." He peered beneath the bumper. "Reserve tank is crunched. No obvious leaks, though. You got lucky."

"Lucky for me, you showed up." Even to my own ears, I sounded stupidly girlish. "What if Karl Lipschitz had driven by? He'd have arrested me on the spot."

Zach straightened. "On what charge? Not been drinking, have you?"

Plaeezzze. I rolled my eyes.

He raised his brows.

"I drank way too much beer the night of the convenience store shooting, and because of that you feel the need to ask me that question?"

"Not your finest moment," he said, chuckling.

I only groaned as the mist thickened around us.

"How was it you described time that night? Something Shakespearean about a bloody tyrant devouring our love."

To his credit, he'd left out the part where I upchucked on his shoes. "Not love, silly. Life. Never love." I angled him a look. "Why would you think love? Sheesh, that's crazy. Can we never bring it up again?"

He was still grinning. "Sure. Anything you say." He grabbed the side mirror from where it had rolled beneath the bumper. It was mangled, with the orange paint scratched off, and the gray primer beneath pockmarked and angry.

"This isn't good."

My lips tightened. "Leland is going to fire me, isn't he? We'll lose our home. The tax assessor will auction it off if I miss another payment." I took another deep breath. "I can't let that happen. It would kill Granddad—"

Just then, a kickass red Vespa sped through the same gap in the trees as the van had earlier. Solo was at the helm and swatting the air with one gigantic hand. "When you texted Solo, did you tell him where we were?"

"Uh-huh," Zach said, which explained how Solo had found us. "What's he doing?"

Solo batted the air with both hands, and braced both feet on the handlebar to control the Vespa, balancing it over all the dips and bumps.

"If you think that's wild, you should see him flip off the handlebars," I said.

"He's insane."

It was true enough that most would think it took a few loose screws for someone to give up an NFL offensive lineman position in order to pursue a dream of riding a circus bike for Cirque du Soleil. But that was Solo, and the reason his mother had kicked him out last year. After that, he came to live with Granddad and me.

Zach grabbed my hand and pulled me behind him. "Something's wrong."

"Nawgh—" Then I saw it. The Vespa was traveling too fast, on dead aim to hit the rear of the van. "Uh-oh."

Solo launched from the bike, shrieking as his hulking frame took wing. At least it sounded like shrieks over a strange buzzing. He howled one last time, hit the ground, and rolled to his feet. The buzzing went on, as did the Vespa, straight toward the van, Zach, and me.

I yelped as Zach pushed me down on the dirt and dropped down beside me.

I lifted my head for a look-see, only to have Zach drag me closer.

"Keep down," he said.

A split second later, the Vespa rammed into the van and pushed it forward. When the license plate missed my ear by millimeters, I gasped, my jaw dropping. A risky position as the reserve tank picked that moment to burst. I tried to scramble back, but Zach's arm trapped me. Warm, sweet liquid drenched my face, flooded my mouth, and closed my throat.

"Spit it out!" Zach roared.

I coughed out some of the radiator fluid, drew in a gasping breath, and spewed the rest. "Geez, are you serious? I wasn't going to drink it."

He gave me a half-hearted grin. "You almost did, admit it."

When I squinty-eyed him, he only mussed my hair.

I strained to see beyond him to Solo. Big as Sasquatch, Solo was cursing a Cat 5 as he ran around thrashing the air with his ham-like paws.

"Get 'em off. Get 'em off," he shouted.

A busy black ponytail snaked from his helmet and his arms were the size of respectable tree trunks. Beneath a brown leather vest, he wore a screaming yellow shirt and a brown sarong-like skirt called a lava-lava.

Zach jumped to his feet, pulling me with him.

"What's he swatting?" he asked.

I angled my head, focused on the buzzing. Then I

remembered the brown thing that had bounced off the van's windshield. How it might have been a beehive. "Oh, no, I think they're bees!"

"Help me!" Solo yelled as he neared, his cries of pain fracturing across the field, deadening all other sounds. I started toward him, but he waved me off. "Wait. I was wrong. You'll get stung. Stay back!"

Ignoring his warning, I searched the ground and grabbed a branch. It was light and full of dried needles. I wondered if swatting the bees would chase them away or enrage them even more. Frantic, frightened, tormented by his unrelenting screams, I closed the distance between us and went after the bees with the branch.

He tried to push me away, but his hands met with only air as I twisted and swooped down on the bees. The rough bark dug into my palms as I circled him, ineffective, and spinning my wheels.

"It's no use. We need smoke," I said.

"I have matches." Solo knifed a hand into his vest pocket, missed, and snagged his lava-lava instead.

"I have another idea." Zach said, and rushed toward the van.

Solo ran around in more circles, swapping, howling, and tossing his helmet aside.

I ran after him, slapping him with the branch. "Stop moving!" I cried.

"But I'm dying. *Dying!*" He found his pocket finally, hauled out a book of matches and—after a grab for the branch—he lit it.

"Wait—" I screamed, concerned by the chance of a wildfire, but it was too late.

Fast flames ignited the needles into a fiery ball. Solo and I jumped back, the branch dropping to the ground, the tall grass bursting into an instant inferno. Stunned, we gawked at the blaze for two seconds then got busy kicking dirt on it.

Zach appeared at my side, stomping his big ol' size elevens on the flames as well. Smoke engulfed us, stealing our air, making us cough. Through the haze I checked around, the fire was beginning to wane. The buzzing was also fading. Solo paused, appearing to notice it, too. He let out a whoop of joy and, pirouetting like he does in his circus clown act, he whirled around in an enormous circle.

With two left feet, I shared in his joy by stomping a barn dance on the smolder. *Almost out* was all I had time to think before Zach took me to the ground. *Again.*

"Your skirt is on fire." He rolled me once. Then twice, before he flipped me onto my stomach and patted down my backside, his hands firm but gentle as they stroked my bare legs.

I groaned, wondering the likelihood of being turned-on and terrified at the same time. "Should I roll over?" I asked like a lovesick fool.

His narrowed eyes met mine. "Rylie, we need to talk—damn!"

He grabbed my arm and yanked me to my feet.

"What's wrong?"

"The fire, it's back!" His panic lashed out, frenzied. "Go to Solo. Stay with him."

"But—" It was all I said before his arms—strong and quick like a snake attacking prey—seized me about the waist. Air whooshed out of my mouth as he carried me to Solo. He dropped me there, where my ankle gave way, and I tumbled back.

I righted, looked around. My knees weakened at seeing the flames whipping up, strengthening as it ignited the grass again. I started raving, wanting a fire extinguisher, unclear about whether one was in the van.

"Rylie." Zach's irritation showed only briefly. "Stay here with Solo."

"But I can help," Solo said.

Zach grabbed him by his vest. "Do as you're told. Keep her safe."

Solo didn't struggle, he didn't resist, but there came a tense moment while they stared at each other, when his face cemented at being roughhoused. Though he had Zach by a hundred pounds, he would not challenge him or fend him off. People assumed his massive bulk equaled violence. Not true. Not with tenderhearted Solo. He was more boy than man, more jester than warrior. As expected, his expression softened, and his dipped is head in agreement.

Zach's fingers flexed and released his vest, but the sudden guilt in his expression stayed. "I'm sorry," he said and took off in a run.

A blast of panic had me reaching for Zach. "Don't go—"

But he left me standing terrified next to Solo, my arms out.

Gasoline. My mind noticed the smell, but not the source. The fire was guzzling a long line of grass and headed for the crashed vehicles. The flames looked to be thriving on a stream of leaked fuel from the Vespa.

Zach was sprinting to the van, possibly for the extinguisher. He wasn't going to make it in time. Fear for him sliced through me, a cry to retreat strangling in my throat. He took a moment to glance sideways, toward the fire. Veering—thank God, he was veering away.

The Vespa exploded, sudden and deafening all at once, with flames and metal shooting skyward. Charred remains rained on the ground like black hail.

Zach was on the move again, skirting the burning patches and yanking one of the van's rear doors open, only he had used too much force. I saw it immediately when the door hit the chassis, whipped back, and whacked him in the back of the head. He bent at the waist, grabbing the fixed door for support, shaking his head, his knees buckling.

I took off in a run, the fire swelling around me in a wide circle. As I drew near, Zach recovered enough to fish out the fire extinguisher from among the trash bags. He stumbled back, pulled the safety pin, and squeezed the handle. The force threw him to the ground.

I tried to grab the extinguisher but he fought me off. "Get the hell out of here."

I tried again. This time I managed a better grip and yanked it free. Budding raindrops had me scanning the sky as I smothered the fire with dry foam. I barely took in the wet against my skin as the rain swelled to a downpour. Then out the corner of my eye, I saw something unbelievable: Zach shaking with laughter. I blinked, turned. His eyes were glued to my backside.

My mind was already shrieking when I twisted for a glimpse. The fire had left my skirt a no-show over my ass, and the scarcity of my pink thong made it a shiny moonbeam.

Arrgh.

Zach climbed to his feet, shrugged off his jacket, and tied the sleeves around my waist.

"Could this morning get any worse?" I asked, sighing.

Bad thing, questioning fate. I heard a loud gasp. My lifting gaze tracked Solo's raised and pointing finger as he drew near in hurried steps. A hairy forearm hung out of the van. By the age spots, I knew it was a senior, almost certainly male. A round scar, silver dollar size and ugly, marred the back of his hand. It was familiar, yet no other thoughts gelled together.

Zach rushed to the van. Solo froze, his finger still suspended. My head filled with a boatload of promises to God as Zach lifted the man's limp wrist. I started praying big time, pondering and zeroing in on my worst habit. I mumbled bargaining words about not screwing up at work for a day, maybe two days if the G-man needed a bigger carrot. Please don't let the guy be dead.

"Alive?" I didn't blink, couldn't.

Zach shook his head, pushed aside the trash bags, and leaned in. "He's an old dude, small and bald. He has a mustache and white beard. And he's very dead."

My mind clicked. A Nazi bullet had caused the scar. "It's Otto Weiner, isn't it?"

"The Jewish guy from FoY?" Zach asked. "The one who wears the beanie?"

"Kippah," I said, and drew his puzzled gaze. "It's called a kippah."

"He isn't wearing one now, but it's him. It looks like he suffocated. A plastic bag is taped over his head."

I stared blindly at the ground. I heard a squeak like a chew toy and cut my gaze to Solo. His eyes were bright like doppelganger comets.

"I've heard baking soda helps with bee stings, or rubbing alcohol." Not only could I not bring myself to believe Otto

Weiner was dead in the van, but I was babbling like a stooge.

Solo wagged his finger. "Rylie, this is bad, really bad. What if they think you did it because of that fight?"

I sucked in air; it froze in my throat.

"That's ridiculous," Zach told him. "What fight? Rylie never fights."

I inched my eyes his way. "I might have once."

"With who?" Zach wanted to know.

My ears rang so loud they ached. "Otto Weiner."

~Just when you think life's a bitch, it has puppies~

T ypical for the Pacific Northwest, the rain rushed away as quickly as it came. Zach was on his cell, notifying police dispatch and calling my boss. Dazed and numb over Otto's death, I shuffled like a zombie to the driver's side mirror to check out my bare behind. My skirt had flamed up like a small weenie roast, yet only a bit of red marred my skin. And my pink thong looked okay, too, but no such luck with my butt, little firmness there. It looked like a deflated beach ball. Time to hit the gym.

I readjusted Zach's jacket around my waist, rummaged in the van for edibles to calm my nerves, and dug up some red licorice and a Thermos of coffee. I joined Solo a few yards away. His eyes shifted to mine, held. A muscle twitched under his right eye, but he never ceased to hold my gaze.

"What the hell just happened?" He tugged nervously on

the tip of his ponytail. "My God, Otto was murdered. But why?"

We looked over at the van, at the arm still hanging out the back, and we knew that Otto Weiner was the only person the seniors at FoY collectively loathed. "Which senior do you think did it?" I asked.

He turned my way with colorless cheeks, crushed eyes. "You can't really think one of them did it."

"Hard to say," I said, shrugging. "But someone killed him."

We both fell quiet, brooding. As I looked around, I remembered the Thermos and licorice in my hands. At this moment, I'd have paid a hundred dollars for a beer, but sweets and caffeine would have to do. "Want some Twizzlers?" I asked Solo.

He frowned, then grabbed several sticks from the bag. After wolfing them down, he sighed and took another handful. Food is medicine. Medicine is food. More than ever at a murder scene.

"Did you know that if you eat too many Twizzlers you'll poop candles?" he asked, his voice slow as though halfhearted.

My colon twitched over the bag of licorice I'd devoured last night. "Sorry about your brother's Vespa."

"It's insured, but my cell phone was in the cubby."

"Dang. I'm sorry."

"No worries. It was acting kind of crazy, probably time for a new one."

That was Solo, always looking on the bright side, if one could actually find a bright side when someone has been murdered. "This is all my fault," I said. And then told him how the van had knocked down the beehive when it had shot through the trees. "I wish Zach hadn't texted you. You'd be home in bed."

He looked beyond me, back to the van. "We can't control life, only how we deal with it."

"I suppose."

"FoY's van is messed up," he said.

I didn't whimper, but wanted to. "Yeah." Then a wave of nausea slid through me at the welts on his arms, all red and angry. "Do those stings hurt?"

He shrugged again. "A little."

I cut my eyes to a piece of broken off beehive in the grass. I wondered if the hair-of-the-dog worked on bee stings. "Maybe honey will help the pain." I dabbed some on his rain-wet welts. "Better?"

"Awesomely better, mawn," he tossed back. "Did you know honey doesn't go rancid?"

"True story?"

He nodded, getting some of his color back. "I read it earlier on a Snapple cap at 7-Eleven. Fire away, ski daddy, I studied hundreds of them nailed up on the wall behind the Slurpee machine. Try to stump me. Come on, give it a shot. What? I thought you drank Snapple."

"I do. Diet peach is the bomb. I just don't read the caps."

"Crazy, mawn. Interesting facts, free for the taking. You know how I like to stay informed. It's primal. What are the chances, huh, of lover-boy being the first cop to show up on the scene?" He nodded to Zach. "If I've said it once, I've said it a hundred times: you two look good together, like steak and potatoes."

Zach was definitely steak, lean and rare with his perfect

blend of strength and vulnerability. "Don't we, though?" I exhaled a long breath. "We're still just friends, though." I looked back and caught Solo's weighty gaze. "What?"

"Coward," he said. "Bad way to start the day, huh?"

"No joke. It's like a wide-awake nightmare."

"Thank God you didn't kill Otto Weiner." He relieved me of the bag of licorice. "I couldn't take food from a murderer," he said, chuckling, but it was a grim sort of chuckle and his cheeks were pale again.

"Want some coffee?" I gave the Thermos top a quick twist. "It's still warm."

"I'm good," he said.

From across the field, Zach called out, "Head to the squad car. We need to stay clear of the scene, not destroy anything, or remove evidence."

I stared at the Thermos. "Uh-oh."

Solo stuffed the licorice inside his vest before he grabbed the Thermos from my hand. "Tell him it's mine."

Was he serious? "I can't let you do that."

"But you could get in trouble."

"It isn't like this coffee is evidence."

"Not unless Otto was poisoned first, then suffocated. Are you sure you didn't poison him?" he asked with a wink. "By how much he barked orders at FoY, it was only a matter of time until someone bumped him off. You know I'm getting all happy when I think of about it, a fun filled workday without grumpy ol' Otto Weiner."

"Wow, I know, right?"

"Um, Rylie, better not say that to the cops. Big mistake, saying things they can misconstrue. Just play it cool and hold a tight rein on anything they could take wrong."

We fell silent, neither of us wanting to admit that my recent dispute with Otto, along with his body being found in the van, kind of made me a good suspect. Finally, Zach reached us.

"Let's go," he said. "It's going to rain again. That isn't from the van, is it?" He nodded to the Thermos. "You could get jail time for tampering with evidence."

I froze.

Solo snorted. "Of course not. We're not that stupid. I had the coffee with me."

Zach eyed the Vespa ditched in the field, and turned back to Solo. "With you? Where?"

"In my vest." He tugged it open to show the stowed licorice. "I could fit a whole meal in here. It's my brother's vest, actually."

"Oh yeah, which one? Big, Bad, or Beastly?" Zach asked in reference to the three oldest Namulau'ulu brothers who play for the Seattle Seahawks.

Solo let out a half laugh. "No way could I wear their stuff. They're way too small. No, this here is my little brother Atomic's vest. He let me wear it on account of it matching my lava-lava." He patted a hand to his sarong-like skirt. "I like to match."

Confusion sparkled in Zach's eyes. "Why haven't I heard of this younger brother before? Don't tell me he's also in the NFL."

"Guilty as charged," Solo said. "He just got drafted. Went in the first round. He's going to tough it out as a Packer, on account of how he hates snow."

"And here you gave up all of that to someday be in the circus."

"Roger, that." Solo tucked away the Thermos.

"Wake up, man. It's the NFL," Zach said.

"And give up my circus dream? Are you kidding?"

"Sorry." Zach shook his head. "Stupid of me."

Wishing to end this ongoing disagreement between them, I touched Zach's arm. "What did Leland say? Am I fired?"

"I left a voicemail and text message," he said. "No reply yet."

"That's odd. Where could he be at this hour?"

We settled inside the squad car, me in the backseat, Zach and Solo up front. Outside: sloppy drizzle. Inside: Solo whistling, Zach drumming his fingers, me riled with nervous tension.

Falling into a brief account of last night, I steered clear of reasoning why someone would want to kill Otto Weiner. Fact was I found his murder sad—I did—but not shocking. As Solo had said, the man was super nasty.

"So the fundraiser was like all the others?" Zach asked. "No arguments?"

"None that I noticed. People checked out the donations and made their bids. We ate, then most everyone left. Only a small crowd stayed for the bonfire, mostly seniors."

"And Otto was there?" Zach asked.

"No, he stayed back at FoY. It was the Sabbath."

"Then you drove the seniors back to FoY? One trip or two?" Zach asked.

"One," I said. "The van holds fifteen. Like I said, we had a small group."

"And the trash bags, when were they loaded into the van?"

"Toward the end of the night, Leland did it. He asked me to dump them in the laboratory's Dumpsters. I tossed in the last bag while he stood guard."

"Guard over what?"

"Two seniors, Elsa Utterback and Gilad Kupper."

"Gilad Kupper, as in Leland's uncle, the retired Nazi hunter?"

"Not to mention a germaphobe," Solo said. "You know, when I spot him in weight room, he sanitizes the bar afterward. Like I'm a leper, or something."

"That's Gilad, all right," I said. "Elsa and he were arguing. Elsa threatened to walk home. Leland calmed her down. She falls sometimes, balance issues. Inner ear problem, I think."

"Did you look inside the van before Leland loaded the trash?"

"No. Not that it matters. Otto wasn't at the fundraiser."

Zach appeared to reconsider. "So you left the van for how long at FoY?"

"I never left. The night staff helped the seniors inside. I waited behind the wheel. Then I drove to Suicide Trestle."

Solo shot me an anxious look over his shoulder.

"Zach already knows," I assured him. "I spilled the beans earlier."

"How long you two going to keep that up?" Zach asked.

"We're doing a good thing," Solo told him, "And it's a karma lift. You gotta rally behind anything that saves lives."

"Save anyone yet?" Zach asked, with a hint of mirth in his voice. "Or even see a jumper?"

"Nope," I said, sighing.

Zach grinned. "I know that sigh. You're thinking of

quitting. Good. I see a chocolate moment coming up."

I swallowed hard. Trust Zach to realize I'd been struggling not to give up my Saturday night routine.

"So before you reached the trestle, you were rear-ended, right?" Zach asked.

"Uh-huh, but I was never more than a foot from the van. We exchanged information, made sure the back doors opened, then we left. I know what you're thinking, but I stood at the bumper the entire time. I'd have noticed if the guy tossed in Otto's body."

Short pause. "You said the accident happened on Lake Hills. What part?"

Had he returned my call last night, he would have known. "Just before Richards," I said.

"Scary place," Solo said. "Like I told Rylie earlier, my friend ran his car into a culvert there. He almost died."

Zach said nothing, his mouth tight. "What kind of deliveries?" he asked.

"Food, Dragon Fresh," I said. "The guy's truck broke down. He worked late to finish up."

"Sounds to me like that was the first attempt on your life," Solo said.

My eyes bugged. "That's crazy talk."

"Yeah, you're probably right," he said in a feebly agreeable voice.

"That's everything, the entire night?" Zach asked.

I nodded.

"Hey," Solo said. "I read that murder often comes down to love or money. Trace those things, you'll find the killer."

"Those are good places to start," I said, brightening.

"Oh, hell no!" Zach said. "Leave this to Homicide. This

is not Suicide Trestle, where jumpers rarely show. A man has been murdered."

"Two jumped last year," Solo reminded him.

Zach was not amused, his lips thin, eyes hard. "Listen to me. There is a murderer out there. Not only is it ridiculous, but insane to think you'll do more than just make yourselves targets by asking questions." He shot me a narrowed look, then moved to Solo and back to me again. "Let this go, both of you."

We fell into silence for a second time, Zach once again drumming his fingers, Solo chomping on licorice, and me staring out the window. I wanted a licorice stick, too, but held back. The thought of a wax-plug clogging up my colon creeped me out.

The early morning traffic was light on the nearby freeway. The rain, now the usual Seattle spit, was hardly noticeable, yet drab and crushing. In the distance, Rosenberg Laboratory still looked dim and vacant.

"Holy crud, what's that smell?" Solo rummaged around. "Never mind, it's me."

"Come on, man, light a match. Forget it, you've done that already. I need air." Zach climbed from the squad car.

"It was only my shoe. It slipped off my foot," Solo said nonplussed, but grinning.

That got a laugh out of me as I joined Zach outside. With our backs against the car, we waited. The last vestiges of streetlights were blinking off in the full morning light when several squad cars arrived, followed by a fire engine and an EMT wagon.

Fire Engine #16 bumped over the curb and drove into the field with its diesel engine rumbling. I had gone to middle school with the firefighter riding shotgun. Curtis Hobbs had been my first kiss. Tranquilizing warmth had flowed over me the moment our lips touched, while he'd asked me to open up my mouth more. *Everyone is a critic.*

"Showtime," Zach said and headed to meet the gathering officers.

I climbed back inside the squad car, surrendering to a fistful of licorice as the crime scene took shape. The ME's wagon finally arrived, bringing with it a big-ass tow-truck. I had expected to see Granddad's old partner Detective Alistair Barclay inspecting the scene. What I saw was Officer Karl Lipschitz playing detective in street clothes, a badge clipped to his belt, a notebook in hand.

At twenty-seven, Lipschitz wore his whitish hair like an overturned salad bowl and was a sick piece of work, vengefully speaking. After I'd repeatedly turned him down for a date in high school, he'd dogged my every move until his graduation that same year. To date, things have not improved between us.

A young, unfamiliar detective probed the scene alongside Lipschitz. The guy was definitely a newbie to the Bellevue Police Force. I would have never forgotten a face like that. I tried not to look at his strong jaw, not stare at his amazing dark hair, or his sexy shoulders. I knew guys like him, stayed clear of guys like him. Players. The road to find a decent man, one destined never to ditch me—something my mother never found in my love 'em and leave 'em dad—was not paved with players.

Both detectives headed our way after ducking under the yellow police tape. As they drew near, Lipschitz beamed me one of his famous leers.

"Here it comes," I said.

"Be optimistic," Solo replied.

I rolled down my window. Lipschitz leaned in close. The unfamiliar detective stood several feet away, watching us.

"Hey, Sweet Cheeks," Lipschitz said against my hair. "This is going to be fun."

Sheesh, if he got a hairball, I wouldn't gripe. Probably it's mean to enjoy the image of him hacking and gagging on hair like a pack-a-day smoker, but given that it was Lipschitz, I made an exception. "When did you become a detective?"

He made slurpy noises in my ear. "That's the sound of me getting promoted. It was nice to go before an all female review board. There is always time for a Lipschitz break."

Yuck.

Solo's eyes rounded. "I'm losing my optimism."

"I'm losing my licorice," I said.

"I guess you want our statements," Solo said.

Lipschitz ignored him and gave my barely visible cleavage a cheesy brow lift. "You must be wearing the all new Miracle Bra. Anything else you're faking? Hey, Talon," he tossed over his shoulder to the player. "She's hiding something. We'll interrogate her at the station."

"You mean interview her," Zach said on his approach. "What's wrong with you, Lipschitz? Rylie isn't a suspect."

Lipschitz worked up a wintery smile. "So, Zach, how's it been on the information and complaint desk? Mollycoddle any bad guys lately?"

When Zach tugged at his shirt collar, a heavy crucifix that once belonged to his late father popped out. "Stalk any women lately?" he asked Lipschitz.

"Ah, that's right," Lipschitz said, staring at the cross. "You Catholic boys swing a different way. Boys will be toys, huh?"

Zach's eyes darkened.

"I never stalked Rylie," Lipschitz went on. "Though I bet she likes to think I did." Lipschitz shot me a sour smile. "See you at the station, Sweet Cheeks. And you, Island Boy. We'll need your statement, too." He turned and left.

Solo dribbled a little licorice spittle on his vest.

Lipschitz's partner started to follow, but paused. Our eyes caught, held long enough to suffer both pleasure and guilt. I considered his name: Talon. Not too friendly, yet he wore a classy gray woolen jacket with darker suede elbow patches, black pants, and a white shirt. Comfortable country chic. In contrast, his eyes were the sharp-edged blue of glacial ice.

"Careful." Zach lifted my chin with a finger. "You'll catch flies."

Seagulls squawked in the awkward silence. Zach was brooding over something. What, I couldn't tell, but—shamefully—I hoped it was jealousy. *Purgatory, here I come.*

"Who is he?" I asked with forced blasé.

"He's part of the Sister City Exchange Program. Name is Thad Talon. He's Scottish." He stared at me. "And he's not your type."

I laughed. "How come?"

But he didn't reply, only peered over the top of the car at someone calling his name. The tow-truck was making a grinding noise and the driver was waving for Zach to help. "Give me a minute. I'll take you home first to change clothes, then to the station." He settled his hand at the base of my neck, left it there. "Wait for me."

"Forever," I said absently.

Again, he said nothing, only captured me with those gentle eyes of his. Then he walked into the field as the ME wagon drove past with Otto's body in the back.

A minute later, Solo asked, "Are you thinking what I'm thinking?"

"That this field is a great place for a Porta-Potty."

He cracked up; he had a great laugh, just like Santa Claus. "Seriously, that Lipschitz has disco Twinkies on his mind."

I rested my arms on the seatback. "I may be nodding, but I don't understand."

"Hooking up with sister. Booty with Rylie. Aren't you worried?"

"He's a sleaze bag for sure, but I'm having trouble working up a real panic about him." I dropped my head to my arms, then raised it again. "There are no witnesses to the truck running me off the road. No way to prove I didn't fall asleep at the wheel. Leland is going to fire me. The tax assessor will auction off our house. Granddad will have another heart attack. Solo, I cannot lose him. I just can't—"

He patted my hand. "Then grab the reigns, mawn. Do what you're destined to do, investigate. No time like the present to start. Find the guilty driver and you'll probably solve Otto's murder. My gut says the two crimes are related."

"Granddad is so against me having anything to do with detective work."

"Aren't you curious? Why did someone involve you? Why did they stash Otto's body in your van? Looks to me like they wanted to frame you. I don't mind saying, I'd be pissed."

"I'm guessing you want to help me investigate," I said, amused.

"Come on, you're lips say no, but your eyes say pissed off."

"That's low blood sugar, so unless you've a cookie handy, you'll need to ignore what you think is interest."

"But—"

"Listen," I said softer than the word implied. "I can't take the chance—"

A sudden squealing drew my attention. I looked around. Passing by was a taxicab with FoY's associate chef scowling out the back window.

Booth Jackson's flashy attire always struck me as over-the-top for a cozy retirement home. Out of keeping with his smooth appearance, he ambled like an old Chevy with a bad wheel, or in Booth's case a bad hip. He was a black man with an unshakable glower and twitchy eyebrows.

The taxi stopped a few feet ahead and its reverse lights snapped on. When the cab backed up alongside the squad car, I greeted Booth warily out the side window.

"I saw the wrecked van from the freeway. Couldn't resist detouring to see what's up," he said above the engine squeal, his eyes wide, and his brows lively. "I don't usually do sympathy, but I'll give it a try. Oh darn, Rylie, looks like you screwed up another job."

"You're too kind," I said, my arms crossed.

"And don't think I'll cover for you and drive around those blue hairs." He smiled unpleasantly, the mega diamond studs in his ears glistening. "I don't drive, remember? Bad hip."

I nodded. He hardly talked of anything else.

"I'm guessing no one let you save their sorry life at Suicide Trestle last night. The weak always crack under pressure, see, you should just let them jump."

"Nice," I said.

"I don't do nice, see," he said in a voice as dark as his

skin.

"How do you know I—we…" I glanced at Solo. "…patrol the trestle?"

"I got ears, don't I? The boss likes to talk while she cooks," he said in reference to Tita Iglesias, FoY's head chef. "Tell me, what kind of losers help out depressed people?"

"Don't let me keep you, Booth," I said, wanting him gone.

"You aren't helping anyone by getting arrested," he said.

What an odd thing to say. "How would my arrest help anyone?"

He said a bland and overdue hello to Solo before he shifted back to me. "I'm not judging, see," he said. "I guess being involved in Otto's death blows your shot at keeping a job longer than—what is it now—four months you've been at FoY?"

Heavy moment of silence. I wondered how he knew Otto was dead. I opened my mouth to ask, closed it, deciding to try to make him slip up. "What makes you think I'm involved?"

"I know he wanted you fired, see. I know you would lose your home. Many homeless old people die from the elements. I figured duty called. No way could you let your grandfather die on the street."

I had heard enough. "How do you know Otto is dead?"

He raised a hand—quite a feat in view of his countless gold bracelets—and waggled a cell phone. "It's Leland's. I read a text message from that cop friend of yours, Zach O'Neil."

"You have Leland's phone, why?" I asked, surprised.

"He left it at a mutual friend's place."

"What friend?" Solo asked, piping in.

Booth ignored him. "Death waits for no one." He looked

strange, pleased, relieved. Sparkling. "Absolutely no one."

"You sound like you're glad Otto is dead," I said.

"I won't dance on his grave if that's what you mean. I got a bad hip." He faced forward and signaled the East Indian driver to leave. The taxi took off.

"It floors me how he can afford all that bling," Solo said.

"Tita says a jeweler friend sells to him at cost," I said. "Well, one thing is for sure, Leland forgetting his cell explains why we haven't heard from him. Though he had it last night. I heard him pleading with Nava to take him back."

"That Nava is a piece of work. Bat crap crazy," he said, doing finger circles around his ear. "Leland can do better. She's so mean."

"Yeah, but he's desperate to reconcile. He loves his wife," I said. "I wonder who this mutual friend is. Booth and Leland usually don't hang out together."

"It surprises me that Booth even has a friend," Solo said.

Just then, a tatty red, white, and blue panel truck sped past and pulled into the laboratory's parking lot. To all appearances, it matched the one that ran me off the road. I was already out of the squad car when it disappeared behind the concrete wall. I considered calling for Zach, but he had his hands full with the malfunctioning tow-truck.

I leaned back in. "That looks like the truck that ran me off the road. I'm checking it out."

"Not without me." Solo rocketed from his seat and rounded the hood. "I knew you wouldn't roll over. Judging by the look on your face, you're hot on the trail of a murderer."

"Whoa." I held up a splayed palm. "A confession to running me off the road, that's all I want. If Leland gets that, maybe he won't fire me."

We hoofed down the street and circled the building. We found the truck nosed into an upward-sloped spot across from the delivery entrance. I signaled for Solo to follow me into the bushes. There, we flattened against the bricks. Well, as much as Solo could flatten—he was the direct opposite of flat. We peered around the corner.

Up close, the panel truck was more rundown than I first realized, a bit like a decaying American flag. The rear was medium blue with pale splotches, the front dirty white with horizontal rust streaks. Inside a light blinked on. The shotgun seat was empty, so I figured the unseen driver must be opening their door. The light blinked off. Still no sign of anyone.

Then a gray-haired woman rose in the passenger side and settled in the seat. I relaxed a bit. Granddad said I have a knack with seniors; he called me a senior whisperer. My plan was to confront them about the accident and try to reason out a confession. Here's hoping the driver was also elderly.

"I'm going in," I told Solo.

"Want back up?" he asked.

"Nope, this is a job for the senior whisperer." I stepped from the bushes, adjusted Zach's jacket on my hips, and climbed the steep incline to the panel truck. The woman now appeared to be rummaging through the center console. She was bent, her back to me. I knew it wasn't wise to startle the elderly, so I paused a few feet away until she straightened again. When she did, I approached.

As I neared, she rolled down her window and beamed me a toothless grin. "Where's the cheap bastard who usually meets us?" Her breathless voice held a rough English accent. "That Jew."

I killed my smile; I found her tone insulting. "Leland Rosenberg?"

"That's him, Duckie. You and Leland in cahoots? Looky here." She punched the man at the wheel in the shoulder. "Leland's business is booming. The tightwad has himself a helper."

"And because of us he won't get his nuts ripped off through his nose." The man flicked an annoyed finger to a note taped to the dashboard.

"You got that wrong, love," she said. "That comedian bloke said wallet, not nose."

"What's it matter? We should've demanded more money," he said.

The woman looked back at me. "Where's your cart?"

"Cart?"

She blew out a huge breath, her lips flapping. "We haul this flippin' shit, not unload it."

Her skin was specter white; her grizzled hair pulled tight with a barrette atop her head. Both sides were teased out like elephant ears. The man was refugee thin and sunken, an air hose snaking from his nose to a nearby canister.

"I'm Doris. This here is Cokey Bill. He's got black lung from the coalmines. We're the Oleys. We do odd jobs. You need something done, odd or otherwise, you call us."

Cokey Bill Oley barked a laugh. "Odd or otherwise. Good one, Doris."

Contemplating the best way to bring up the accident, I nibbled my lower lip.

"Not so good at small talk, huh?" Cokey Bill opened his door, hocked up a loogie, and spit it out. "Well, don't just stand there, then. Go get the cart, girlie. And don't forget our extra cash. We did as we was told; we always do as we was told, week in, week out. We're like trawlers or trollers, only we got no poles."

Doris Oley beamed. "He's saving to buy some of those new extra-long ciggys, the ones with the nic-out filters. My man is trying to quit."

I eyed his air hose. "It's never too late, I guess."

"Blimey, you sound like my pecker-headed doctor." Cokey Bill settled back in his seat and gave me an impatient gesture. "Now beat it. And don't come back until you got our lolly and the cart. Come on, Doris, get back at it." When I didn't move, his head snapped around. "Go on, girlie. We're busy."

Doris massaged her wrist. "Busy, my ass. There ain't nothin' busy around here but my hand. I'm done wankin' that thing."

"The hell you are!" Cokey Bill snapped.

"The hell I am!" She grabbed a half-eaten muffin from the dash, pitched it, thumping Cokey Bill on the shoulder, gobs of poppy seeds scattering.

My eyebrows went up, froze there.

"Well, you better get to it," he howled at her. "That little blue pill don't last forever."

"It don't last at all," she said. "You need one of them penile implants, you limp dick."

"I'll show you limp." Cokey Bill wormed an arm behind her seat, pushed aside several orange and black boxes, and pulled out a fat fish. Rearing back, he pitched it at her.

Doris cried out, ducking. The fish sailed through the open window and plopped at my feet. Two seconds passed while I stood there, staring at it, its cloudy eye and shiny skin. I turned to look at Solo for help, but he was nowhere in sight.

"So you wanna play rough?" Doris scrambled into the back of the truck and started pummeling Cokey Bill with a slew of fish and fish guts.

I rushed forward, hands out. "Stop it. You'll hurt him."

"Shut your cakehole," she said, lobbing fish my way, breathing hard, arms robotic.

I leaped clear of the muck, ducking down at the front bumper. The quantity of fish hitting the pavement dropped off, so I peeked up over the hood to see if Doris was running out of steam. She was indeed. In fact, she was stock-still. Then she teetered. Swayed back. After several seconds of whirly eye rolls, she wilted forward like a stream of hot summer taffy.

I yanked open the door and jumped inside. "Doris?"

No sound. No movement. Nothing.

Cokey Bill tossed a fish tail at her head. "Now there's a decent stiffy. Must be the aneurism the docs warned about."

I lifted her wrist. No pulse. "Do you know CPR?"

He tapped his canister. "I got no air."

"How about a cell phone?" I grabbed his arm, shook it a little. "Call 911."

He stared at his wife. "How about that, my Doris is a fine specimen of a dead gal."

Crimony. I scrambled into the back to give CPR a shot. Way out of my league, but I had to try. Blind to everything, I flipped Doris onto her back.

Cokey Bill wheezed. "Holy cow, look how much color has come to her cheeks. She don't look like a ghost no more."

I couldn't stop myself from looking. Her face was indeed colorful. *And bloody*. My eyes popped wide at the sight of all that red. Gulping breaths, I told myself not to faint.

"Hey, girlie, you think I should tell Maybelline about fish blood? Might be a little lolly in it for me—" Cokey Bill broke off with a gasp. "Blimey, look at that, your arse is bare."

I managed to look down. Froze. Zach's jacket had somehow twisted to the front, leaving my butt out in the open. I started to tug it back into place, spied a huge pool of blood nearby, and keeled over. *Splat.*

"Isn't that somethin', you're wearing a pink thong." Cokey Bill's voice sounded distant. "Doris won't wear one, on account of her incontinence."

Dizzily, I struggled to my knees, staggered a little, then righted with a hand to one of the orange boxes for support. "Mr. Oley—we need to get—help. Doris needs—help."

"Ah, that's the sweetest thing, you moving over like that. I got a nice view now."

I lapsed into a moment of stillness, hand to my heart. I had a strong feeling nothing could be done for Doris, so I wanted to give Cokey Bill a moment with his wife.

"Rare and beautiful thing, a nice ass," he said.

Omigod! "Are you kidding me? You pervert. You're looking at my butt!"

"I'm a simple man," he said.

"You should be ashamed—" I broke off when his eyes went glassy. "Mr. Oley, are you all right?"

He sunk lower in his seat, grinned, and sagged against the steering wheel, making the horn blare with his pointy nose.

I couldn't move, couldn't blink. This wasn't happening.

Solo popped his head inside the open passenger door. "Holy crap!"

"Where have you been?" I managed.

"Watching some bunnies in the bushes." He looked from Cokey Bill to Doris and back to me. "What did you do, whisper them to death?"

"No!" I said, gulping air. "Check his pulse." Then I closed my eyes to the blood and straddled Doris to do my best with CPR. It didn't matter that I thought it was useless, I couldn't give up on her or Cokey Bill. A minute later, I eyed Solo. "How's he doing?"

He shook his head, shoulders slumped. "Dead."

The blood left my face, I felt it go, drip by bloody drip. "You sure?"

He nodded. "Pretty darn."

I dragged my eyes off Cokey Bill and went back to work on Doris. The shock and effort made me woozier. My panting and the footsteps outside sounded as one. When the truck's rear doors flew open, my heart skipped a beat.

"Holy Mother Mary!" Zach said.

Fish and guts streamed out in a silver wave. Zach leaped back. I grabbed for something, anything, but my hands were slimy. The truck's sharp angle made it worse. I missed a hand strap, but fisted some of Doris's shirt. She wasn't moving, probably caught on something. I heard a ripping noise. Ack! She was on the loose.

A jaunty slippery-slide over the rear bumper whipped me higher than a bucking horse. We bounced onto the pavement, bounced again. It turned out Doris was kind of springy. Even so, we went splat, a bouncy splat that whipped me onto my back, my knees heavenward, and my arms above my head. I opened one eye, peered up at Zach; his eyes were steely.

"I can explain."

~The truth will set you free, but first it will piss you off~

Listening to me explain away the best part of a half hour had worsened Zach's mood. He scowled as the ME wagon departed with Doris and Cokey Bill's bodies in the back.

The ME observed no outward signs of foul play (*as if*), but an official verdict would come after an autopsy. Upon hearing what happened in the panel truck, the ME had grinned as though wanting a peek of my butt. Pathetic as it sounded, I smiled a little.

Nearby in an unmarked car, Detective Alistair Barclay was on the phone with his wife. His teeth were clamped on a licorice stick and he talked around it. "You should've seen it, Trudy. A truck load of mackerel and smack-dab in the middle was Rylie Keyes. You know, Hawthorne's granddaughter. Yes, yes, that's her, the one who can't hold down a job—" Our eyes met through the passenger window. He looked at me apologetically for a long moment in silence before going on to discuss dinner plans with his wife.

I admit to hear others talk of my flakiness shook me. I was now convinced that I had to investigate Otto's murder to prove myself, but I had to do it without Granddad knowing until after I'd solved it.

"Look, Trudy, I've gotta run." He disconnected. "Rylie, I'll have your statement ready when you get to the station. Stop by and sign it." Another moment of serious quiet ensued. "And don't let Lipschitz rattle you. He's a punk."

I forced a smile at his sweet attempt to cheer me up. He had once saved Granddad's life during a bust gone wrong. I had never come close to thanking him enough.

"Lipschitz a punk. Tell us something we don't know." Zach slapped a farewell hand to the car as Alistair drove off.

I adjusted Zach's jacket at my waist and glanced at my watch. I wanted to change clothes. I wanted to get away from this place. I wanted to forget that three seniors died here, or in Otto's case was found dead here. And I wanted to be alone with Zach. Maybe it was being this close to death that made me feel the click of time, but I was ready to tell him how I really felt.

"Zach," I said. "Can we leave?"

Brief pause. "Leave?" he repeated. "Leave for where?"

"My house. Changing clothes. The police station."

His eyes went to my waist. Then he laughed. "Oh, yeah, sorry. But we can't leave just yet. I have to help with some last minute evidence. I won't be long, promise."

I looked at my watch again. "Go ahead, take your time. The longer it takes the more pissed off Lipschitz will get. And, of course, a girl wants the detective investigating her pissed off. It adds to the thrill."

"I know this isn't the best time to mention this, but you're a nut," he said and left.

After helping a second tow-truck driver hoist the panel truck onto the flatbed, Solo strode over. "That sure was a load of mackerel. It's weird, but I could have sworn Leland's vitamins say Peruvian fish oil? It's the best but expensive."

I caught the worry in his voice. "Maybe there's a temporary shortage or something."

"Maybe," he said unconvincingly. "False advertising and good sales don't always mix. It smacks of bad business. It doesn't take much to lose customer loyalty. One scandal can bring a company to their knees."

"That would be really bad." I looked around and found Zach beside the tow-truck. Another officer approached him, held out a clear bag, and Zach dropped in what appeared to be a piece of paper.

"Don't tell anyone, but I got a look at that note," Solo said. "It was in the panel truck—"

"Taped to the dashboard, right? I saw it. What did it say?"

"Sunday at dawn. That's the time of your accident. Creepy, huh?"

"Totally creepy," I said. "Pretty thin, though, but it could spell intent."

"Intent?" Solo asked.

"Meaning Doris and Cokey Bill planned to run me off the road."

"You think?" he asked.

"I think."

"But why would they come back later on this morning? Wouldn't they worry you could identify them, or at least identify the panel truck?"

"Good point," I said. "Maybe the note had nothing to do with me."

"You're sure this panel truck is the same one that ran you off the road?" he asked.

I nodded.

"Then the note must be about you," he said.

"Or it could be about the fish delivery. Perhaps there were two deliveries scheduled for this morning, one at dawn, and one a little while ago."

"Sure, why not?" he said. "After they dropped off the first load of fish, they left the laboratory and entered the freeway the wrong-way and ran you off the road. Considering their age and health, they probably never got more than a quick look at FoY's van, or your face. So they wouldn't worry about being identified."

"True, they didn't act like they knew me. Not that I could tell at least," I admitted, and then gave him a puzzled look at a sudden thought. "Uh-oh, I see a flaw in our theory."

"Sing away."

"Before Zach opened the back doors, the asphalt was wet but clean, no fish or guts. Solo, there were no signs of an earlier fish delivery at daybreak, only the one when I showed up."

"Well done, mawn. You're right. Only now, we've hit a speed bump. If there was no earlier delivery, then the note and running you off the road must have been on purpose. Then, as if nothing was out of the ordinary, they came back here for their usual fish delivery, drawing all suspicion off themselves."

"You make it sound like they were hired to kill me," I said.

"Blame the evidence," he said. "But why would someone want you dead?"

"Well, I guess if dead," I said, thinking, "I couldn't defend myself, couldn't deny having something to do with Otto's murder."

"Ah yes, the perfect scapegoat. The big question is who hired the Oley's?"

Two jigsaw pieces from my conversation with them teamed up. "I remember Cokey Bill saying, 'We did as we was—were—told.' Then he demanded their extra cash. At the time I thought he was referring to the fish delivery, but now—"

"You think Leland hired them?" he said. "They do deliver fish for him. It'd be easy enough to ask them to do another job as well."

"Are you saying Leland wants me dead? That's insane."

"Well, he might have killed Otto and just wants you blamed for it."

"You can't really think that," I said. "Solo, you know Leland. He's good people."

"In moments of insanity, good people do bad things."

"Not this time. Leland practically ordered me to dump the trash from the fundraiser last night. He said he wanted it done before I went to Suicide Trestle. But I got rear-ended and was running late to meet you, so I blew it off until this morning. No way did he know that, though."

Solo chewed on that. "Why did he want the trash dumped at the laboratory in the first place, why not at his house or FoY?"

"It was too much for residential pick-up. You know how

picky they are. And the Dumpsters at FoY have been non-stop full since the plumbing overhaul began."

"Oh yeah, the new low-flow toilets. They're awful. Nothing worse than having to flush more than once," he said.

Zach came up and announced it was finally time to leave. Together, we three walked to the squad car. Solo started to open the rear passenger door, but I stopped him. "Go ahead and sit up front. You'll be more comfortable."

Solo thanked me in Samoan. "*Tulou.*" He slid into the front seat, then closed the door.

Zach smoothed a stray hair from my face. "You worry me, Rylie. You need someone to take care of you."

Inhale. Exhale. "Do I?"

He seemed to weigh his words. "I think I'm seeing my future."

This blindsided me. Giddy romantic thoughts spun in my head as a diesel engine approached. A whistle sounded. I thought it contained more come-on than greeting. I looked over as Fire Engine #16 rumbled by again, only this time from the laboratory parking lot.

"Hey, Rylie, what's crack-a-lackin'?" said a male voice. Curtis Hobbs was again riding shotgun, but now his big puss was hanging out the window. "Has your mouth gotten any wider?"

I am often reminded that I haven't always chosen winners when it comes to men.

"Why did he say that?" Zach asked, leaning in.

I ran my tongue over my lips. "No idea."

With our faces near enough to tangle breath, we shyly

grinned at each other. He brushed his lips to mine, drawing a thumb along my cheek. This took me back to his comfort when we were kids and I'd tumbled down a ravine in the woods. He had soothed away my tears then, as he had countless times. There had always been Zach to count on. *Always.*

I peered into his soft gray eyes, the shade of clouds whispering with rain. When his mouth found mine again, my lips parted. A lingering pause came before he joined me, discovering—reassuring. Nothing sounded but the subtle moan in my throat.

Then as sudden as it began, he pulled back, his narrowed gaze fixed on my chin. He blinked, but didn't meet my eyes. "I better get you home," he said and opened the car door.

We inched through construction and arrive at the Overlake area uphill from Lake Sammamish. I spent the time in a daze, my mind teeming over Otto's murder and Zach's kiss.

From the backseat, I studied his profile. The tension was still there, over me, over his life. Strong in my heart was the feeling that he needed more time to get over the convenience store shooting, the guilt, the sadness, and the fear of flashbacks. I confess this didn't sit well with me. I tried to tell myself that knowing the truth about how I felt might help him heal, but I found even I didn't believe that. Almost certainly, it would only confuse the issue. So I was feeling a bit down when I made up my mind to be patient, to wait a little longer to be honest with him.

Zach bulleted the squad car down my steep driveway, the sharp hairpin turn forcing him to bump over the edge of a flowerbed crammed with foxgloves in order to park. I looked to the spot near our garage where Granddad usually parked his ancient Jetta. Empty. I mentioned this to Solo.

"Remember?" he said. "He's going to a craft show in Portland this afternoon."

Granddad had taken up glass blowing after retirement to earn extra money. "Slipped my mind, I guess."

Solo had his door open. "I'll check to see if Leland is at home. I'm headed that way." Solo lived down the hill, on Granddad's old sailboat tied up to our rickety dock alongside Leland's new dock and beachside home. "I won't be long."

"Good idea," Zach said.

As I climbed from the squad car, I heard an angry outburst from my neighbor's garage. Lilith and Paul Desmont's striking house was downhill by the lake, but their garage/office was uphill beside our tiny house, adjacent to our shared driveway. Lilith was a romance author who penned stories about women battling demons and falling in love bondage style. Paul was a self-made real estate millionaire who flipped houses until the economic downturn.

I spotted Paul standing by his over-the-garage office window. Seeing him, this gentle man who was a caring father to his daughter Mackenzie, always triggered a childish longing. It seemed to me, rather enviously, that Mackenzie Desmont was a very lucky girl. Paul returned my wave, an ever-present tissue ready to wipe tears from his sun sensitive eyes in his hand. As always, he wore a pair of sunglasses.

More curses spewed from the garage. I veered toward it, noticing as I went a familiar fisherman casting a line below on the lake. I opened the side garage door and stepped inside, the many bright lights making me blink.

"Stay back," Lilith screamed, spraying the air with spit. "Or I'll kill you."

She had the facade of a middle-age hippie in her tie-dyed caftan, flowing red hair, and dangling earrings. At five-eight in stocking feet, she was imposing. And as a habit, she tucked a flower behind her ear. This morning's choice: Shasta daisy.

"Who's in there?" Zach shouted.

I leaned out the door. "It's Lilith Desmont."

"Back off!" Lilith yelled. "I want to spill blood."

"Why is she yelling?" Zach called.

"Don't know, but she's hitting a punching bag," I said.

"She's at it again?" he said. "Tell her to go easy. She broke a finger at Christmas, a thumb last summer, and a knuckle a while back," he said and slid behind the wheel.

I slanted Lilith a look. "Geez, maybe you need some calcium."

"You just wait," she snapped. "My critics will blog about me on the web tomorrow. Readers love to find fault. They adore ripping a poor writer to shreds."

"Your readers love you," I said.

"Tell that to Wicked Spirit. She wrote on Dragon.com that my latest book wasn't even good enough to slobber out a demon's mouth."

I had read that book. It was pretty much what I would expect a demon to slobber. "That's horrible."

"Well, I showed her," Lilith said. "A friend at Dragon removed the review. Insult one of my books, I think not."

My gaze strayed as she laid into the punching bag again. I spied a nearby rack of domination clothing. I would not let myself smile at the wrist restraints, whips, leather jumpsuits, and masks. Where Paul Desmont usually kept his vast array of pricey golf equipment, the racks were oddly empty.

I started to ask why when Lilith shrieked and cradled her quickly swelling wrist. I remembered the fisherman on the lake. Probably there to see a nearly naked Lilith prance around her all-glass house, a regular thing for her, or Solo had once told me, blushing profusely.

"There's a fisherman near your dock," I told her.

"Really?" She brightened and rushed outside to the railing. "Ahoy there, have you caught me a trout yet?" There came a minute of sultry chatter between them before Lilith threw me a blushing look of her own. "I guess you can tell. He's smitten with me. Most men are."

"Nice," I said, holding back a grin. "Well, I need to change clothes. I had a little accident."

"At Suicide Trestle? Oh, don't look so surprised. It isn't like you had a date."

She had a point. "No, the accident was after, in the van."

"Did a senior get hurt?"

"No one got hurt—exactly."

"Oh God, you killed them? You braked too fast and smashed their brittle skulls."

I blew out a breath. "I didn't kill anyone. Two old people ran me off the road. I made some bees mad. Solo catapulted off his Vespa. There was this strange episode with fire. His Vespa blew up. And bam, Otto Weiner's lifeless hand popped out."

She gasped, fumbling with the daisy at her ear. "How'd Otto die? Was it his heart?"

"Suffocation, I think."

Her uneasy expression changed to shock. "How awful."

"I didn't know you knew him."

"I didn't, really. We met at a fundraiser a while back. So he suffocated…how?"

"Someone taped a plastic bag over his head," I said. "Did Otto have heart problems?"

"I think he mentioned heart business once. Everyone dies of heart failure, you know. Physiologically speaking. Writers know these things. And?"

"And what?" I asked.

"Did you kill him?"

"Of course not!"

"If someone peed on my car seats, I'd kill them." She pointed to the Mercedes Coupe in the garage. "They're of the finest leather. Then again, the van's seats are probably Naugahyde. Oh my, I cannot believe you're going to muff dive in prison over pee-stained Naugahyde." She scratched her chin, thinking. "Hmm, there's a book in there somewhere. Lesbian love stories are so hot right now."

"Geez, this isn't complicated. I didn't kill Otto—or those two other seniors."

Lilith's eyes popped wide. "Three dead seniors? Rylie, we need to talk. Sure, you normally bore me to tears, but there is a dark side to you I'd love to explore."

Kill me now.

"We'll start tonight," she said, patting my arm. "At Leland's birthday party. Did you get something nice to wear, dear?"

Silence.

"A dress or suit?" she asked. "Tell me you bought something to spruce yourself up."

"I found a dress at Ross, but a woman in a burka grabbed it from me."

"And where may I ask is she going to wear a dress? Sure, she might sneak out and club, but if caught, she'll face a firing squad of her brothers. You should've fought her for it."

"I'll try harder next time," I said, eying her injured hands. "Those bruises look painful."

She shrugged. "I have pain meds. What's that fishy smell?"

I checked Zach's jacket over my backside. "It's fish oil for Leland's vitamins."

"Those vitamins exhaust me. It must be all that oil. Fat takes more energy to digest, you know. I've heard others complain."

"Really? Who?"

She shrugged again. "Oh dear, I do hope Leland is happy with his birthday party tonight."

"It's nice of you to throw it for him."

"But I must. I mean, if things go south for you, then your grandfather will sell Leland your property. Leland will then build Nava her dream house—"

"Mansion," I said absently.

"Right you are. It is going to be huge, I mean *huge*! And only yards from my house. So I must make every effort to become the best of friends. And with Nava and him getting back together—"

"Are they?"

"Oh yes, very soon I suspect. He's decided to do things her way." She said it with such raunchiness—despite her frown—I had to smile.

"Her way, how? What do you mean?" I asked.

"It's nothing. Salacious stuff, that's all." She looked at me with troubled, almost loving pity. "Too much for your virginal ears."

"Wait a second—"

"Do you know the parable of ten virgins?" she rushed on. "Never mind, you probably don't read much. The point is you need to stay alert. Your time will come."

I just stared at her.

"Now what was I saying?" she asked through a puzzled frown. "Oh yes, Leland's party. Well, I simply had to host it. Not to mention the points I'll make with your grandfather for being neighborly." She gave me a sugary wink. "After all, everyone knows Leland has a lot of money tied up in his anti-frailty drug. So if things turn south for him, my offer to beat his price for your property stands. You'll remind your grandfather of that, won't you, dear?"

I paused a moment to absorb her heartlessness, trying not to cry out, "Hell no, you can't have our home." I knew I was being grumpy, but our humble abode—craftsman, olive green, dark brown trim, and super modest in size—had been built by my great-grandfather, Hamilton "Handsome Ham" Keyes, and I loved it. Four generations of Keyes had lived inside those crooked walls. Sure, our home was rundown, but it would kill my Granddad to lose it.

Zach climbed from the squad car. "Rylie, hurry up, Lipschitz is waiting."

"Probably choking the chicken," I said louder than I intended.

"No doubt," he said.

I laughed, my ears burning. "Zach must have sonar hearing," I told Lilith.

She grabbed my wrist. "Does he really have demon powers?"

"Wish he did," I said. "Then he'd know who killed Otto Weiner."

"Do you think he knows?"

I shook my head. "Pretty bad demon, uh?"

She nodded. "I expect more of my demons. Then again, maybe I should check him out. I'm sort of a demon divining rod."

I wondered if insanity was contagious. "I need to change clothes."

"Oh, look." She pointed a finger southward. "Mount Rainier has escaped the clouds."

I turned to the volcano peek-a-booing through the trees in the distance.

"It feels close enough to touch," she said wistfully, then beetled her brows. "Why don't you cut down your trees? They ruin your view."

"But they keep our house from sliding downhill to the lake," I said.

She shrugged. "That's the distress of living on a hillside. As you know, I have the finest beachside view on the lake. It's worth billions."

"Billions, huh?" I said a bit sarcastically, even though a Mt. Rainier view was kind of prized in Washington.

"Do not mock me, Rylie. Sure, the real estate people might say a million, or even two million, but in my heart, I know our view is priceless. After all, we have no obstructions, not a single one," she added, her voice haughty.

Zach came up behind me. "We've got three dead seniors, no answers, and a detective eager to proposition you for God knows what. I know we're partially late because of me, but if we make him wait much longer, he'll throw you in jail just for kicks."

"Zachy," Lilith said, playing with a button on his shirt. "For research purposes, would you let me study your demon staff?"

Omigod. "Not a good idea." I angled my body between them. "What would Paul say? You two are so good together."

"Oh yes, smart women do marry the well-to-do. Remember that, dear. Of course, my sweet Pauly also has his frisky moments. And, purr, last night was one of them." Yet incredibly, she trailed a finger down Zach's arm. "I wore my sex-executioner cat suit."

"The one with the tail and whiskers?" I asked, not looking at her face as my eyes were on her fingers tickling Zach's palm.

"That's the one." She laughed huskily; it was an alluring laugh, creamy and cloying with no naïveté in it. "One must never underestimate the power of a titillating whisker. And I do apologize for leaving the bonfire early."

"I hope you got a chance to grab a s'more before you left," I said.

She looked at me. "Ah, yes, two in fact. Chocolate sex." Out came that laugh again. "My Pauly likes his chocolate melted."

I stayed exactly where I was, between Zach and her. "Thanks for your generous donation. Leland plans to use the money to buy Wiis to help Solo exercise the seniors."

She waved a blasé hand. "We won't miss it."

The Desmonts' twenty-five-year-old daughter reached the top of the staircase from the top floor of their lakeside house down below. Sure, it was a redundant means to go up and down the hill since they also had a tram, but the city required a second way up in case of fire or a power outage. Mackenzie Desmont wore her reddish-brown hair straight and blunt cut to the shoulders. One side—the side with a long black streak at the temple—she'd tied back with a tiny black bow. Black eyeliner and near-black shadow called attention to her nearly violet eyes. The result was stunning, yet I thought she looked sad and lost.

"Hi, Mackenzie," I said.

She sneered at Zach's jacket around my waist. "Cute. I suppose you will be at tonight's chaos, the party for Leland, I mean. It's a chance for you to meet lots of potential employers, I suspect." She slapped a strained smile on her dark lips. "It must take hours to make sense of that crazy quilt you call a résumé."

I would have thought that comment was funny normally, but now I found it bitchy. She liked to make me look bad in front of Zach. It was no secret she wanted him for herself. Well, I was thrilled to see her expensive leather jacket had a gooey stain near the cuff.

"Mother dear," Mackenzie said to Lilith. "Fat chance, I know, but how about having lunch with me today? It's my last day at Starbucks—"

"Starbucks?" I said. "I thought you were doing filing at Leland's lab."

"I quit weeks ago. You try working with all those chemical smells. And don't get me started on those nasty germs and diseases burning up in their incinerators."

"So how come you're leaving Starbucks?" I asked. She had an employment track record about as dismal as mine.

"The commute," she said. "I thought I'd like working in Seattle, so much more urban than boring old Bellevue, but it turns out I hate it. And then there are the hordes of tourists at Pike Place Market. They're so demanding." She focused on Lilith. "So are you up for lunch?"

"I'll have to pass, darling. I am rather tired today. I must get my beauty rest."

Mackenzie barked a bitter laugh. "And why not, you put everything else before me, why not your beauty rest?"

"Nonsense. Have you forgotten all the sacrifices I've made for you? Inches to my waistline, several sleepless nights before your nanny arrived. And how can you forget all those vile months as your Girl Scout leader—"

Mackenzie brushed past her, drew near the squad car, and paused. Solo, a piece of licorice between his lips and just returning from his sailboat, shook his head when Zach asked if Leland was home.

"Are those Twizzlers?" Mackenzie asked him.

Solo smiled, held out several sticks, and opened the passenger door to the squad car. "Take 'em. Rylie's got a big bag."

"She would. Have you gotten a look at her fat ass?"

Zach whispered into my ear, "It's been a hit with two men today."

Despite my best effort not to, I giggled girlishly.

"Where are you guys headed?" Mackenzie asked Solo.

"To the police station." He settled in the car, then told her about the accident.

"So what senior kicked the bucket? One of Leland's?" she asked him.

"Someone killed Otto Weiner."

"Really? I heard Leland threaten a guy named Otto last night."

Zach stepped closer. "Leland threatened Otto?"

Time appeared to stand still as she stared up at him. "Well, not threaten exactly. He told a black guy that he couldn't wait for Otto to get what he deserved."

Zach's gaze met mine, all serious now. "Black guy?"

"Booth Jackson," I said. "You've met him. He's FoY's associate chef."

Lilith grabbed my arm. "I knew there was something suspicious about Booth. All that glitz." Her voice was hushed, but there was a tone of incredulous disbelief. "How can anyone working for Leland afford Armani?" She eyed my casual clothes as though to prove her point. "And Leland and he both acted strange last night. Writers notice these things."

"Lilith, believe me. Leland isn't involved in this." I shifted to Zach just in time to see Mackenzie smooth a stray hair from his forehead.

"Nice one, Rylie, protecting your boss." Mackenzie tossed away a half-eaten stick of licorice. "Of course, by nice I mean pathetic. What you won't do to keep a job."

"This isn't about keeping my job." *It was a little.* "It's about supporting a friend."

"Don't you mean protecting a friend?" she said.

"Mackenzie, let's get back on topic. What else did Leland say?" Zach asked.

"I'm no snoop or eavesdropper," she told him pleasantly enough. "I overheard them as they built the bonfire. Then Leland took off."

Zach looked at me. "Leland left the fundraiser?"

I nodded. "Particulate matter gives him asthma. He heads inside once the fire gets going."

"What time was that?" he asked.

"About nine thirty."

"How much staff did that leave?" Zach asked.

"Three. I made s'mores while Tita and Booth packed. Then Booth left shortly after. He took the Desmont's tram. I remember because he said he had a cab waiting."

Lilith tugged on my arm. "Who's Tita?"

"She's FoY's head chef," I told her without turning my head.

"Oh, that little shit. She had a fit when I asked for a virgin Bloody Mary."

Now I did look at her. Lilith dearly loved her full-throttle cocktails. "Virgin?"

"Yes, I planned to write later. I wanted a clear head," she said. "Last night I chatted with her assistant—Booth is it? He also adores Mt. Rainier and he also thinks Leland's vitamins cause fatigue."

I shifted to see Zach staring at his cell phone. He looked up and faintly smiled at Mackenzie, whose thumbs were on her cell. When he swung my way, his face fell. "I need to call this in." He stepped away.

Mackenzie snorted, hands on hips. "Really, Rylie, who taught you how to make s'mores? You skimped on the marshmallows. I had to add more myself—*myself*."

This explained the sticky stuff on her cuff. She had worn the same jacket to the bonfire last night. "Oh yeah?" I feigned some goggle-eye awe. "All by yourself?"

"I like lots of marshmallows. So does Zach. Don't you, Zachy?"

This angered him; his eyes were unsmiling when they met hers.

"Yes, very stingy of you, Rylie," Lilith piled on.

"See?" Mackenzie said.

We frowned at each other, a foul duo of rivals. Then at the sound of a passing truck uphill on the road, her chin shot up. "Shit. My bus will be here soon."

"Don't pout, darling," Lilith said. "You can't blame your father for making you use mass transportation. Two cars totaled in six months. Tsk, tsk. But I will keep working on him. He'll buy you an admirable one soon, maybe a nice BMW."

"Damn it, Mother." Mackenzie's eyes, her voice were pissed. "How can you be so—?"

"So what, darling?"

"Mackenzie!"

All eyes turned to Paul Desmont at his second floor office window. His neck was craned outside, his face creased with a frown, and his eyes still unseen behind dark glasses.

"Lilith, shouldn't you be writing?" His voice had regained is usual softness. "You have a deadline, remember?"

"Deadline, smeadline," she said. "My publisher hearts me."

"Two years to finish a book is absurd. You need to write faster," Mackenzie said.

Paul smiled dolefully, giving his daughter a disappointed look. "Mackenzie, shouldn't you be leaving for work? And, Lilith, turn off the lights when you're done in the garage."

Zach touched my arm. "I need to get something from my apartment. I'll be back in a minute," he said and started uphill.

"Wait," Mackenzie said, catching up. "I'll walk with you."

Zach gave me a long look. "Okay, sure."

Together, they climbed the driveway and veered toward the woods between houses.

"Don't cut through Leland's property," Lilith yelled after them.

Mackenzie raised an open palm. "Talk to the hand."

Lilith shrugged it off and jumped on their nearby tram to descend the hill.

Zach reappeared from the woods a moment later. "Rylie, over here."

With Solo at my heels, I broke into the small clearing.

"Take a look at this," Zach said, pointing to a black satin cap discarded on the ground. "Isn't that a Jewish kippah?"

I nodded.

"Maybe it means something, maybe it doesn't," he said, "but Otto was missing his."

"It's Otto's," Solo said matter-of-factly. "I'd recognize it anywhere."

"It is," I agreed, though my mind reeled with the fact that this discovery suggested Otto had been killed only twenty feet from my bedroom window, which just might implicate me even more. So armed with this newest discovery all lingering doubt about investigating his murder vanished with a *poof*.

"See the clip?" I pointed to the silver fastener dangling from the edge of the kippah. "Even though Otto was bald, he always wore that same hairclip. I heard him once say it had sentimental value. I never saw him wear another."

"Never," Solo confirmed.

"See the star on the tip?" I went on. "Normally it's blue, or at least that's what I've seen on others, but on Otto's the enamel is worn off. Just like this one, nothing left but silver."

"So Otto tried to go to the fundraiser, but never made it," Zach said, looking uphill.

My gaze followed his, trailing up the support columns to Leland's home office and the street level garage above it. The towering height made me dizzy. "I wonder why the kippah is here and not on his head."

"Maybe the killer knocked it off when they smothered him," Solo suggested.

"Don't touch," Zach warned Mackenzie as she started to reach down. "It's evidence."

The kippah was a yard away from a crushed rhododendron and in the middle of a dirt trail that twisted the two hundred feet from the street above to Leland's lakeside house below. Clear to see were drag marks across the trail, through some stinging nettles, around a stack of firewood, and into the woods to my driveway, where I had parked the van last night.

"What are you looking at?" Solo asked.

I considered. "Maybe Otto was killed up there," I said, eyeing the balcony outside Leland's street-side home office.

"You think someone threw him over the rail," Solo said, staring uphill, too.

"Possibly," I said. "Otto was a small man, way too small to tumble over a large rhododendron like this one and crush it. No, he had to drop on it from above."

"Oh, get real, Rylie," Mackenzie said. "How do you know that rhoddy wasn't already like that? It's not like you walk this way a lot to Zach's place, not like" —her eyes met his— "others."

They were involved. The thought struck me that they had been for some time, even though Zach often insisted since the shooting he didn't want long-term relationships. I dropped my gaze, in a moment of hopelessness. Mackenzie was so dynamic, so self-assured, and not for the first time, I resented that everything I wanted—parents, stability, *Zach*—she possessed.

"This is now a crime scene," Zach said.

Mackenzie curled into him, her eyes on me. "Hold me, Zach. I'm frightened."

He wrapped her in his arms, shifting his gaze in my direction, a sliver of sorry in his eyes.

I looked down again, thinking, wondering, how I could ever compete with her.

~Life is short. Don't be a dick~

I felt better after I had showered and changed and eaten a cheese stick. There was a quiet peace about our little home, as though family long gone watched over me. Still, another five minutes of my own pity party must have passed before I was able to grab a pencil and scribble a note to Granddad. No vivid exposé on this morning's accident would do, nor would a barefaced fib. I may not be completely up-front with Granddad on all the goings-on in my life, but I don't like to flagrantly lie, either. Plus, with Leland as my neighbor, there was zero chance of this disaster staying hush-hush for long.

I decided to carry on Joe Friday-like, "Just the facts, ma'am." I stared at what I had written before I erased the part about finding Otto Weiner dead in the back of the van. Naturally, Granddad would never leave town with me involved in a murder, and in order to investigate this case, he had to be gone—*had to be*! I ended with "See you tomorrow. Love, Rylie."

Next, I called Leland's house from the landline Granddad refused to give up. It was an added expense to our budget and hard to remember the last time I'd used it, but with my cell phone AWOL at Suicide Trestle, I was happy to have it. The phone, meanwhile, was still ringing in my ear. Five rings later, I stood blinking in the sunlight glancing off the lake and into the windows.

There came a squeak of the front door, and Solo with a heaving chest and gasping breath appeared. "There are way too many steps to climb up from the dock."

"Granddad says that if he ever wins the Lotto he's gonna buy a tram like Leland's."

"It's a lemon, that tram," he said. "It's always breaking. And it squeaks. Stick with the Desmonts' brand. It's ironclad. Who are you calling?"

"Leland. But there is still no answer, so I'm calling Tita now."

The instant I uttered her name, Tita answered, "What!"

Typical Tita. Gruff. "It's me, Rylie."

"I noticed," she said. "But more importantly, how come you're not at work?"

Tita Iglesias, head chef at FoY and a former gang member, was the sole breadwinner in her family, supporting two kids, overbearing parents, and a moocher ex-husband. Sort of like a Latina Britney Spears.

"I had an accident in FoY's van," I said. "It's totaled."

"Not a surprise. You've been with us, what, four months? It's fate."

"I'm okay, though. Thanks for asking. The bad news is, Otto Weiner is dead."

Long silence.

"Let me get this straight," she said. "You not only totaled the van, but you killed Otto?"

"Yes to the first question and no to the second. Someone suffocated him. They stashed his body in the van," I said.

"That's it then, it's over."

"What's over?"

Another pause. "You know? Otto, his bad temper."

As soon as she spoke, I knew she was hiding something, but over the phone was not the time to question her. "Hey, listen, Karl Lipschitz is making Solo and me go to the station to give our statements—"

"I have an idea. How about you never call me again?" she said. "I frown on having guilt by association linked to my name."

I groaned. "Ah, come on, I really need you to drive Gilad and Elsa to their Sunday services. No other seniors signed up for rides, so they would be your only two. Pretty please."

"*Gracias a Dios*," she said. "You still gonna make your shift at the marathon? We need every able body we can get to man FoY's tent. It's gonna be crazy busy."

"Sure thing. We'll walk over after we're done at the station. By the way, since you'll be in the area dropping off Gilad at temple, would you mind swinging by Suicide Trestle and picking up my jacket? I hung it on the rail at the north end. My cell phone is in the pocket."

She said a four-letter-word—also known as excrement used to fertilize crops—and agreed to retrieve my things, then hung up.

Solo and I jumped into the squad car and Zach took off. At

the top of the driveway, my across-the-street neighbor was about to drop a letter into my mailbox. When elderly Mrs. Bebitch looked up, she demanded we stop by flailing her garden trowel. Zach pulled up alongside, Solo rolled down the passenger window, and she leaned inside.

Zach and Solo greeted her. I, on the other hand, tried to be inconspicuous in the backseat. The woman freaked me out. She was never without that stupid trowel, which she wheeled freely at any hapless stupido who dared park on her private lane.

"So, Rylie," Mrs. Bebitch said. "The tax assessor wants his money. What is that look for, Zach O'Neil? I don't check the addressee on envelopes. How could I have known I was opening Rylie's grandfather's mail? Oh, that reminds me, I saw your mother last night, Zach. I don't mind telling you, it was hard to see her looking so miserable after you shot and killed that poor man last winter."

Zach grimaced, but she appeared oblivious to it.

"Well," she said. "Your shoulder must be better as your mother looks years younger, or maybe it's having Father O'Brian from St. Patrick's to cook for when he visits us. I will tell you this. I tasted her beef stew last night, before five o'clock Mass. Bland. Very bland."

"Father O'Brian watches his salt. He has high blood pressure," Zach said.

"I guess you heard he's retiring," she said.

Zach nodded.

"What we will do at St. Mary's without a priest, only heaven knows. There is a serious shortage. Young men these days don't want to make the sacrifice. Sex, sex, sex, that is all they think about. I ask you, what about my mortal soul?" She glanced at the letter in her hand and thrust it toward me. "Here."

"Thanks," I managed as Solo relayed the letter. I tucked it away unread. It hardly mattered. I knew how much we owed the taxman.

"Five minutes it took me to walk down here, Rylie Tabitha Keyes. Five minutes of my life, I'll never get back. All thanks to your grandfather's negligence. Imagine a man of his age not able to manage his money."

Grrrr. "Thank you, Mrs. Bebitch. Don't let me keep you from your post." I nodded to her hillside home. "It's a terrific thing you do, keeping your private street free of trespassers."

My sarcasm was not lost on her, a plump gray-haired woman with trifecta chins. "Afraid I'll see what you're up to, are you?"

"Up to?" I said. "How interesting."

"What I saw from you last night wasn't interesting, but — well, I suppose it isn't my place to say, but a man's apartment. Really, Rylie. And you." She waved her trowel at Zach. "I expect you're encouraging her. Don't all men. Sex. Sex. Sex, that's all you think about."

I made a wild guess since I knew she could see Zach's street-side apartment from her house. "Do you mean when I knocked on Zach's door?"

She shot me a pitying look, sniffed, and strode off, her trusty towel swaying at her side.

Explaining quickly, I gave Zach a brief account of how I had stopped by to ask him to the fundraiser, only to find his car parked outside but him not at home.

He eased out a long breath. "I was…was sleeping. I picked up some extra hours last night, starting at nine. I got some shut-eye before."

It occurred to me that he looked oddly annoyed. "God, I hope I didn't wake you."

"Don't worry about it," he said.

The edge to his voice proved my suspicion. "I did wake you. I'm sorry."

He turned to stare at me. "Rylie, I said it was okay. Just drop it, all right?"

Solo's gaze flicked over then quickly away.

"Sure," I said, realizing the root of his anger. He hadn't been alone and wasn't comfortable with me knowing.

After a quick detour due to today's Bellevue Marathon, we pulled into the police station with me feeling like a condemned woman. Not that I was dressed like one. I had done my best to look confident and professional by power dressing in an outfit I reserved for job interviews: off-the-rack suit, black and old school, everyday pumps, simple white blouse. And just in case I needed to flash a provocative ankle, I added back-seamed stockings.

Oh yeah, avoiding jail was not a spectator sport.

Zach parked and looked over the seatback. "Lipschitz is gonna give you a hard time just for kicks. Maybe you should get a lawyer."

"That makes me look guilty," I said.

"And you look so innocent now," he said.

"I resent that."

"I'm with ya, girlfriend." Solo reached over to pound fists. "Stay tough."

A shallow victory, but I wasn't greedy.

"Look on the bright side," Solo said. "You might've saved

them old folks from a stroke or cancer. And don't get me started on the horrors of Alzheimer's."

"I didn't kill anyone."

"I dunno," he said. "With those last two, you might have been a factor."

Solo said it with a laugh, which told me he had meant it as a joke. Problem is it was the truth, the sad truth, the unvarnished truth. I was partially responsible for two deaths. And for the first time—delayed by shock or disbelief, perhaps—I was flooded with what I suspected was the same gut-wrenching guilt Zach had been experiencing these past months. I almost fainted under the emotional onslaught. I closed my eyes.

"Rylie?"

Though Solo's worried tone made my stomach tighten, I couldn't lift my eyelids, couldn't risk what it would do to me to see the blame on his face.

"Rylie," he said again. "I just meant—"

Zach cut off his clarification. "Listen to me, Rylie." His voice was low and tender, the voice he had used for over twenty years to soothe me. "You are not to blame. Three coincidental deaths? Something here isn't right."

"Not to mention how they tried to kill you," Solo put in.

"Pure speculation," Zach said.

"Credible theory," Solo countered.

"Maybe," Zach said. "But you didn't hear that from me, got it?"

"Would it have killed you to say please?" Solo asked.

"Say please for what? I didn't say anything," Zach said, his voice sheepish.

"Oh right. Murder? What murder?" Solo asked, playing along.

"Exactly," Zach said.

Some of my misery dissipated at their playful banter. I opened my eyes. "Really? I'm having a moment here. This is no time to make fun."

Zach sighed. "Just relax and tell Lipschitz the truth. And remember people do a lot to cover up murder, even risk their lives to throw off suspicion." He stared at me and I stared at him, and I knew he was warning me about a line of attack from Lipschitz. "I'll be at the other side of the station if you need me, at the complaint desk. Don't let him put words in your mouth. Be brave."

I was bleeding bravery by the minute. "What's to tell? I don't know anything yet."

"Yet? Yet! Oh, no you don't. No. No. No." He narrowed his eyes. "And if that isn't clear enough, no!"

"Did you just tell me no?" I fell back against the seat.

"I'll do more than that. I'm ordering you not to get involved in this investigation. Look, it's looking real bad for Leland. And who do we know that is desperate to keep her job? Listen, desperate people make good scapegoats. You'll do as you're told."

"Do as I'm told?" I repeated, bamboozled.

Then I did one of those childish moves where I crossed my arms over my chest and stuck out my bottom lip. I had no idea what came over me. It only made me look more juvenile than usual, but I was insulted. And crushed.

"That's what I said," Zach confirmed.

"I'm not a kid," I said.

"Then stop acting like one." He nodded to my crossed arms. "It's time to grow up."

Be livid or even hysterical, anything but hurt.

"I don't need to tell you how serious this is," he said. "Stop acting cute."

He thinks I'm cute was all I could think, which only proved his point. I did act immature and it was making him nuts. It didn't take a genius to realize that to compete with Mackenzie for his affection I had to improve his poor opinion of me, which oddly enough would begin when I solved Otto's murder.

I folded my hands in my lap. "I'll do what you say," I said, my fingers crossed.

Bright sunshine streamed in through the police station windows. Zach had left us to resume his duties at the information and complaint desk and Solo stretched out in a lavishly carved, upholstered chair. Good job, Bellevue. Few cities considered the posh taste of crooks and felons. I sat down beside him, spied a run in my seamed stockings, and sighed. *So much for armed and dangerous.*

"These Buddhist guys are the bomb." Solo tapped the cover of a local magazine. "They're Tibetan monks. And that's a mandala, or sand drawing. It symbolizes the fleeting nature of material life."

I knew zilch about Buddhism. "Pretty."

"Pretty!"

I smiled at his look of indignation.

"They're wicked cool, mawn. And guess what? They're making one right here, in the front lobby."

"Good to know," I said, spying Officer Yancy Quirk scribbling on a notepad as he hung up the station desk phone. I waved when he looked my way. I knew he was gay, a secret between us since high school, and I believe so far unknown to anyone on the force. Serious acne scarred his spray-on-tan face and his muscles bulged like rock-filled socks, all the results of years of steroid use in the hope of disguising his sexuality. I stood and went to say hello.

"I hear your butt gave an old dude a heart attack," Yancy said as I drew near.

I made a noncommittal sound.

He touched my arm. "Hey, don't beat yourself up. It wasn't your fault."

I gulped, but no words came out.

"Don't be an asshat, Yancy. Of course it was her fault," a male voice said.

I turned my head.

Karl Lipschitz approached. He stopped barely a foot away. He was over six feet, nearer to six four, with slim shoulders and waist. Pale stubble as sporadic as caterpillar hair dotted his jaw. "Sweet Cheeks," he said, his lips hard. "I'm gonna need a picture of your ass for evidence."

"Hilarious." I moved around him. He moved with me and blocked my way.

"Fair warning." He licked his lips. "When I'm finished, you're gonna beg for mercy. I'm hard just thinking about it," he whispered.

I ignored the hunger in his eyes. "So much for professionalism."

"What I have in mind is anything but professional," he said.

Yancy cleared his throat. "Lipschitz, a message for you."

Lipschitz grabbed the note. Color drained from his face. I craned my neck for a look-see: *Life's short. Don't be a dick. Lay off the girl. Bintliff.*"

I read it again, after which I wondered—feared—I was the girl it referred to. And if so, it had to be a ploy to make me appear even guiltier of Otto's murder. "That's a lot of drama," I said with feigned airiness. "What does it mean?"

"Acting the innocent?" He raised his head, met my gaze. "You're gonna have to work harder than that."

I drew in a determined breath. "I asked you a question." It was not that I wanted to make him angrier, but I refused to show fear. "Well?"

"Good try." He'd seen through me. "After your statement, you'll be free to go." He tucked a hand at my back, nudged me forward. "This way."

I refused to move. "Who's Bintliff?"

He crumpled the note and tossed it in a nearby wastebasket. "Like you don't know."

I looked across the desk toward Yancy.

He shrugged. "Sounded like Marlon Brando in *The Godfather* to me."

"Run that by me again," I said. "*The Godfather*?"

"Yeah," he said, and then he treated us to a rather spiffy Marlon Brando rendition. "Make him an offer he can't refuse."

"Would you say the voice on the phone was natural, or was it disguised?" I asked.

Yancy looked up, thinking.

"Enough of this." Lipschitz grabbed my arm. "Nice to see you rub elbows with the common man."

"Nice tone," I said. "You feeling hostile?"

"I don't like being muscled."

"That makes two of us." I yanked my arm free. "That

note is a mystery to me—" I had a sudden thought. "Bintliff has something on you, doesn't he?"

His eyes were frigid cold. "I knew it was a mistake to drag your ass down here."

"Why did you, then? It was easy enough to take my statement at the scene."

"Looking at you now, I have no freaking idea," he said.

Just then, a man wearing a scruffy bomber jacket walked in, dragging his feet, mumbling nonsense. He fell silent, seeming uncertain of what to do now. He gave Yancy a long glance, then shifted to me and scowled. Mumbling again, he hauled out a small spray bottle from beneath his copycat Indiana Jones hat and sprayed a mist around his head and neck. The sterilizing smell of bleach reached me.

Lipschitz shot the man a pitying look. "Walter! You know the drill, no complaints here. Go to the front desk. Go," he insisted when Walter did not move. "Or I'll lock you up for vagrancy."

Walter ignored him again and fished out a red toy whip from his over-the-shoulder satchel, and watched it snake to the floor. "Officer Lipschitz, see my new sidekick. Cool, huh?"

"Yeah, cool. Now get going." Lipschitz stepped away to use his cell phone.

Walter assumed a sulky posture, shoulders low and bent as he crept to the doors. When he inched around for one final look, his eyes were jumpy and roving. Snapping the whip against his thigh, he whirled to leave. He was smiling.

I shot Yancy a wide-eyed look. "You realize there's something off about that guy?"

Yancy nodded.

I turned at the sound of footsteps.

Detective Talon strode into the lobby, making a beeline for Solo. A faint moan echoed behind me. I shifted. Yancy's mouth was open, his eyes moony.

"Fine place, Scotland," he said.

"Not so loud," I whispered, boosting my words with a nod toward Lipschitz.

Yancy nodded, but never took his eyes off Talon.

Talon and Solo fell into conversation, with Talon's Scottish brogue resonating throughout the room. Mellow. Smooth. *Dreamy*.

Yancy moaned again.

I leaned over. "Cover your ears," I told him.

"But that accent," he said, breathless.

"I know," I said. "It makes me all tingly."

"Talon," Lipschitz called out. "Take a quick statement from Island Boy, then drive to the Rosenberg residence. I'll meet you there." His cell phone rang, so he answered it.

When Talon shifted his eyes to mine, and his lips curved into a killer smile, Yancy blubbered out, "Omigod."

Lipschitz came back and cupped my elbow. "Let's go."

"What?" I said, brows quirked. "No Miranda rights, thumb screws?"

"Next time, Rylie. Bank on it."

I ignored his fingers digging into my skin as I walked down the hall in what I hoped was dignified grace. I was thinking about this Bintliff character. Who was he, and what was I to him? That's assuming I was the referenced girl. My little voice told me I was, especially since Lipschitz had cleaned up his act a split second after reading the note.

I sat at a spectacular black walnut inlaid table. Good to

see our tax dollars at work. Knowing we were being taped and possibly watched through the two-way mirror, I forced myself to relax. Inhale through the nose, exhaled through the mouth. Scrub. Rinse. Repeat.

Lipschitz sat across the table from me, folded his hands. Several moments passed before he spoke. "You've been up all night?" he asked.

"Maybe."

"Is it yes, or no?"

"Yes."

"And?"

"I'm not sure I know what you mean," I said.

"Where were you?"

"Suicide Trestle," I said.

"Why?"

"I'm hoping to help someone considering suicide."

"Fascinating," he said blandly. "When did you last see Otto Weiner alive?"

"Yesterday"

"Care to elaborate?"

"FoY's dining room. Dinner, around four pm," I said. "Or supper as people called the evening meal for centuries."

His brows rose, dropped. "Did you kill Otto Weiner?"

"No."

"Did you have anything to do with his death?"

"No."

Deadpan stare. "Do you have information shedding light on his murder?"

Where to start? "I don't like to speak ill of the dead, but Otto was cranky."

"Cranky," he repeated. "Have you ever had a disagreement

with Mr. Weiner?" He leaned in. "Perhaps one involving the little finger?"

"Pinky wrestling over piddle and killing a man are two different things."

He leaned back in his chair, grinning, but his eyes still challenged. "Let me guess, you got nothing but sunshine hanging over your head."

I decided to use my gift horse. "Back off, Lipschitz, or I'll tell Bintliff."

He clenched his hands on the desk, knuckles whitening. "I'm guessing you also know nothing about the letter found in Otto Weiner's pocket."

"That would be a good guess. What'd it say?"

"Apparently the way you drive pissed him off. Seems you cannot keep off the center reflectors. Driving by Braille, it's called."

I laughed. "Sounds like Otto. You're enjoying this, aren't you?"

"I take my kicks where I can get 'em. How about s'mores — do they do it for you?"

"So liking s'mores is illegal now?"

"I'm sure we can find some law against eating them while killing an old man."

The wheels of intrigue spun faster. "S'mores are connected, how?"

"One was plastered to the back of Mr. Weiner's head."

All the air left my lungs. The killer had been someone at the fundraiser. "Damn," I said.

"Easy on the swearwords. I might fall in love."

"You did that once already," I said absently.

His features hardened. "Don't worry. I have better taste

now."

His nasty response defused some of my shame for bringing up our painful past, but only some, yet still I could not bring myself to apologize. "Is that why you're doing this, out of revenge?"

He ignored me. "Did Leland Rosenberg have reason to kill Otto?"

"Not to my knowledge— No, he didn't."

"Then you are unaware of a threatened lawsuit by Mr. Weiner? Something about a fountain, citing negligence against FoY."

"Pleeeezzze, there are at least a dozen witnesses who saw Otto splash the water from the fountain, set off in a jog, and slide on the puddle. Otto wanted the fountain gone."

"Why?"

"It was a painful reminder of the Holocaust. He was imprisoned at Auschwitz."

He grunted. "Leland Rosenberg lost family at Auschwitz?"

"He erected the fountain as a memorial to his great grandmother. She died there."

Another grunt. "Have you a connection to Doris and Cokey Bill Oley before today?"

"No, never."

"In your statement to Detective Barclay, you said Doris Oley asked whether you were in cahoots with Leland Rosenberg. In cahoots is an odd term to use in reference to a legitimate acquisition of fish, is it not?"

Hell, yes. "The Oleys were…eh, colorful."

"And they said they did as they were told, yes? Maybe by Leland Rosenberg?"

"Listen, the details may be sketchy—"

"No, you listen. There is no proof Cokey Bill Oley said those words, other than your say-so. And—" He hesitated a moment. "There is no proof you were run off the road either. Might be you just fell asleep at the wheel. It's as easy as ABC to see that staying up all night has made you tired."

I looked tired. "Karl, be reasonable. Why would I lie?"

"You tell me," he said. "Can you think of any reason why Leland Rosenberg would want you silenced, or dead, other than the fact that you're irritating as hell?"

"Good one," I admitted. "Is this about Cokey Bill's extra money comment?"

He didn't answer, just nodded.

I stared at him, outraged at first, then sick. My statement had only fueled their case against Leland. "He isn't a murderer. I'd stake my job on it."

"Hope you have your résumé polished."

"What's your problem?"

"What did you expect, roses?" he asked.

"Damn it, Karl. If you have a beef with me, keep it with me. Don't take it out on Leland. He's innocent. And I can prove it. He wanted me to dump the trash from the fundraiser last night. He insisted on it."

"You should give some thought to buying a watch. Last I checked sunrise this morning isn't the same as last night."

I raised my hands, let them drop. "How many times do I have to tell you? I had a fender-bender last night."

"Mind your attitude, Rylie. Your nerves are showing."

I drew in a breath and decided to take the lead. "Have you a list of others the Oleys did odd jobs for? Would you let me see it?"

He laughed so hard he fell into a fit of coughing. "I

wondered when you were going to try and turn the tables. So annoying how you used to yammer on all the time in high school about wanting to be a PI. Well, you know what? I'm kind of digging it, you pretending to be an investigator. It gets me hot."

Now it was my turn to ignore him. "I've a right to know what's going on. Someone—someone not Leland involved me in this. They almost killed me."

"What are you saying? You want to work together on this?"

I didn't laugh, but I was wary. "Maybe."

"Well, forget it," he said. "And if I get even a whiff that you're looking into this case, I'll arrest you for obstruction."

No shocker. I had expected it. "Oh, about that old PI daydream nonsense," I said lightly to divert him. "It was teenage stuff, nothing more. But permit me to point out that you wanted to be a chemist in high school. Something about making targeting pesticides to rid the world of butterflies. Funny, you don't look like a butterfly hater, Karl."

"Butterflies," he said with a barely visible shudder. "Back on point. How about Booth Jackson? Have you ever witnessed tension between him and Otto Weiner?"

"Once. They argued about which was better, collard greens, or gefilte fish."

"Was the argument heated?"

Everything involving Otto was heated. "A little."

"Anything else you wish to disclose?"

I shook my head.

He asked me for a detailed timeline from last night. When I wandered off point on how Elsa Utterback had blamed Otto for tossing her cane into the bonfire, only to have Gilad

Kupper remind her that Otto had been too chicken-shit to come to the fundraiser, he yawned.

A loud rap sounded and the door flew open. "Officer Lipschitz!" a man yelled. "I want to make a noise complaint. The voices in my head won't shut up."

I turned to see Walter, the Indiana Jones wannabe, staring at me. His restless eyes were jumping even more now. After a frantic search beneath his hat, the spray bottle appeared for a second time. His manner was nervous, his appearance horror-struck. With all the flourish of a Shakespearian actor, he sanitized the air with another round of disinfectant.

I was about to tell him to cut it out when I caught sight of someone running up behind him. As though feather-light, Yancy grabbed Walter from behind and lifted him off his feet. "Now, you're just being silly," Yancy said. "Too much disinfectant only makes germs immune."

Walter squirmed, wagging his head. "I got rights, don't I? Don't I? Let me go!"

"Sheesh," Yancy said, nose scrunched. "When was the last time you brushed your teeth?"

"Take him to the front desk," Lipschitz said. "Zach is a sucker for whack-jobs."

Half carrying, half pushing, Yancy hauled Walter away, leaving us alone again.

"Lipschitz—" I broke off as our eyes locked. I saw disgust in those mean blue orbs. Over the years, I had seen many things there: desire, frustration, anger. But never disgust.

"Save it, Rylie." He pushed back his chair where it hit the wall with a *bang*. "You wanna know what I think? I think Leland Rosenberg killed Otto Weiner and recruited you for help. Only you had an accident before disposing of the body."

I had to swallow. "Really? Disposing of the body, how?"

His pastel eyes blinked, not twice, but three times. "The laboratory's incinerator."

Gulp.

~Don't worry, ladies. There's plenty to go around~

I lost no time in getting away from Lipschitz, slowing only as I entered the rear police lobby. There, I spotted Solo sleeping in the same chair as earlier, his head back against the wall, mouth wide open, snoring like a kitten. The lobby hummed with activity, though neither Yancy nor the bleach wheeling Indiana Jones wannabe was anywhere in sight.

As I stood there, my grandfather pushed through the outside doors. Not the best situation, but not a surprise either. I had left a note and he was very familiar with police procedure. At sixty-four, his full head of rich pewter hair meshed great with his rosy skin. His eyes were more teal than Leprechaun green like mine. Clamped in his hands was his most recent masterpiece: a beautiful blown glass Chinook salmon in shades of amber, gray, and gold. It glittered in the sunlight when he placed it on the coffee table to greet an officer walking by. Then he rushed over to me. "Are you all right?"

I nodded.

"And Solo?" he asked with a glance his way.

I nodded again.

When Granddad smiled behind his bifocals, I experienced one of those wonderful moments of childlike joy followed by gloom. I had to tell him I might soon be unemployed.

"You didn't answer your cell, so I called Alistair," he said. "He told me the details on the accident, and about those vile people, the Oleys. You sure you're okay?" After I reassured him that I was fine, he asked, "Have you any idea who killed Otto?"

"Not a one." Poor Granddad, he still looked worried. "I'm okay." I pulled him into a hug.

"Thank the Lord." He clumsily patted my back with one hand. It was a genuine hug on his part, I knew that, and his worried words and anxious tone of voice were heartfelt, but I couldn't help wanting more. It was as though he needed a protective wall between us, maybe in case I ran away like my mother, leveling the final blow to his already bruised heart. No way would I ever do that. I felt guilty just thinking about it.

Granddad pulled back, his eyes not leaving my face. "It's awful, just awful someone involving you."

"My guess is that I was supposed to be found with the body," —I left off "dead" on purpose; I did not like his pallor— "and unable to defend myself."

Nevertheless, more fear crept across his face. "That settles it. I can't leave, can't go to the craft fair."

"Granddad." I grabbed his wringing hands, held them in mine. "The danger is over. Their plan was foiled."

"But—" He broke off when another officer paused to

say hello, then turned back to me. "Rylie, I don't know—"

"We need the money." I squeezed his hand, prepared *again* to tell him how another job might slip away from me. "Because of the accident, Leland may have to let me go. The insurance company could insist on it."

He opened his mouth, closed it. With the area humming with more officers waving or stopping for a moment to greet him, I fell silent. He was going to the craft fair, period. I just had to convince him.

"It's only for a day," I said once we were alone again. "Go sell your work. I'll be fine."

He nodded. He knew I was right. "How did the interview go?"

"Not bad. He took my statement. No fuss, no muss," I said, steering clear of Lipschitz's accomplice theory in order to not worry him even more. I looked over at Solo, whose eyes were blinking open. "Good nap?"

He rose and joined us. "Epic. I feel like a new man."

"Don't let yourself get too tired, son," Granddad said. "You could make a mistake and get hurt on that circus bike of yours. We would hate to lose you. You're family now."

Solo smiled. "Thanks, mawn."

"Did you hit your head in the accident?" Granddad pointed to my temple, his finger close but not touching. "Looks like you have a small bruise."

"It's nothing. I'd already forgotten about it," I said.

"So have you heard from Leland?" he asked.

"Not a word. It's crazy. He's just vanished," I said.

"Maybe Nava and he patched things up," Granddad said. "Maybe they've gone off together to be alone."

Why would Booth have his cell phone, then?

"Maybe," I said, as I knew Granddad wanted those two back together. He always said, "A happy man marries the girl he loves. A happier man loves the girl he marries." This sentiment, of course, explained why my mother refusing to marry—or even reveal—my father's identity before she took off, further crushed Granddad.

"Rylie—"

I blinked at him. "Sorry, you were saying?"

"I was just telling Solo about your interview with Detective Lipschitz," he said. "He seemed surprised it went so well. Why is that?"

"Nothing, really. We've just never liked each other much ever since high school."

"Good heavens," Granddad said. "He behaved himself, I hope. Acted gallant."

I tried not to, but I laughed at the word gallant. "He was fine," I said.

"And Suicide Trestle," Granddad said. "How did it go?"

"A total bust," I said.

Solo nudged me. "No worries. Winter is coming. Jumpers come out in droves then."

I brightened, even though it made me feel like a ghoul.

"So are you all ready to leave for Portland?" Solo asked Granddad.

His lips tightened and he cast a worried glance at me. "The Jetta is all packed, jammed with over a hundred pieces, but—"

Solo seemed to understand. "Don't worry, sir," he said. "I won't let Rylie get hurt. She'll be fine. Reason says the danger has passed with the discovery of Otto's body. But still, you can count on me to protect her."

A relieved smile lit up Granddad's face. "You know if I sell all my glass pieces at the craft fair, we should be able to manage this month's tax payment."

"Halleluiah!" Solo said. "And if I sell my back-up circus bike that should give us a good start on next month's, too."

I touched his arm. "But you need that bike for when the other one breaks, which if the last year was any guide, that's *all* the time."

"But I wanna help," he insisted.

"You're sweet, but we can't let you do that. Can we, Granddad?"

"She's right, son. Plus, what am I going to use once you teach me how to do some of those fancy moves of yours? I'm anxious to learn. It looks like fun."

I doubted riding a circus bike counted as fun for seniors. More like exercise for those with nothing to live for.

"Over my dead body," I said and watched the happiness drain from Granddad's face. I was not sure I could ever find the words to express how much I feared losing him, so I forced a laugh instead. "Don't mess with me. I'm a Girl Scout."

"You quit Girl Scouts," he said wearily. "Remember?"

I could only nod.

"Yancy told me that Lipschitz got a note that upset him," Solo said.

I blinked. "Note?"

"Yeah, before he interviewed you. He said it was from some mafia dude and it was about you." Solo swung an arm around my shoulder. "Girlfriend, hasn't anyone ever told you not to associate with the mob? Prison time, mawn, that's all those dudes bring. Not that you wouldn't look nice in jailhouse orange." He lifted a chin-length lock of my red hair, and let it fall. "You are an autumn after all."

"Where this all fits in, I don't know, but it seems I'm in debt to a man named Bintliff," I said and relayed the details of the cryptic note.

"Crazy, mawn. A tricked out Godfather in your corner," Solo said.

"Ever heard the name Bintliff?" I asked Granddad.

"No, not that I can think of. Very strange, that note."

"Very strange," Solo repeated.

Granddad checked his watch. His face wrinkled as he stared at it.

"Something wrong?" I asked.

He looked up, and seemed to think a moment longer. "I want to say hello to Alistair before I leave, show him how I've been keeping busy since retirement." Though he loved glass blowing, his tone hinted at sarcasm. In his heart, nothing could take the place of detective work. He picked up the gleaming Chinook salmon from where he had placed it on the table, and cradled it in his hands. "Rylie, why don't you call a few friends, have them over for pizza. The company would be good for you."

Safety in numbers was what he really meant. "Sounds fun," I said in lieu of actually saying, "No can do, I have a murder to solve."

"Great," he said, "but make sure everyone stays off the deck. Without railings, it's too dangerous to stand on. Hopefully, we'll be able to replace it soon," he added and strode away.

Once he disappeared down the hall, I turned. "Go ahead, confirm what I'm thinking."

Solo's teeth flashed in a smile. "Two things come to mind. Your grandfather is worried, but knows he has to go to Portland. And—"

"He's going to ask Alistair to keep an eye on me," I finished.

"Roger that," he said. "You know whatever Alistair sees or learns he'll pass on to him. He might even figure out that you're investigating this murder. What are you going to do?"

"I don't know," I said. "But I'll think of something."

Nearby, the restroom door opened. Yancy rushed out, fluttering a hand to his flushed face. Troubled by it, I watched him hurry to the station desk.

I took a step to see if I could help when Solo exclaimed, "Great Scott!"

"A wee *bairn,* I was, when last I heard me *mither* call me that pet name," a voice from behind said.

I whipped around. Detective Talon approached. As he did, his amazing azure eyes roamed our faces, but lingered on mine. I had the sudden and foolish urge to tidy my hair.

"My apologies," he said at my side. "'Twas a tasteless thing to utter. As I live and breathe, ye must be Rylie Tabitha Keyes."

Our eyes met again, locked. He was even hotter close up. "Nice to meet you."

He caught my hand, held it. "The pleasure is entirely mine."

His wooing tone surprised me. "That's generous of you, being that Lipschitz is your partner and I'm practically at the top of his most wanted list."

"Right list, wrong guy," he said.

I was startled. "You think I killed Otto, too?"

He glanced at Solo, laughed. "Wordplay is lost on some people."

Now I got it. He was toying with me, but that was cool. Two could play at that game.

"It's so funny how your accent is stronger than before," Solo said.

Talon's smile was slow and easy. *Devastating.* "Aye, lad, a wee bird told me Rylie finds a Scottish brogue a might tingly. I aim to please ye, lassie."

Cheeks burning, I leaned back to eyeball Yancy. He ducked under his desk.

"Don't blame the lad." Talon's eyes twinkled. "He was splashing his face in the men's room. I do believe he is coming down with something. He was quite flushed."

"Yeah, a blabbermouth virus," I said with a healthy drip, drip, drip of sarcasm.

"Be aware." He stared at me. "Only owls hunt in silence."

My awareness was focused on only one thing: my weakening knees. "Your point?"

"Owls are solitary creatures, Rylie. Something you're not."

I had to grin. More wordplay. "Oh, I dunno, some say I do my best work at night," I said, toying with him right back.

But he didn't react, only turned to Solo, waved good-bye, then turned back again to me. "A moment of your time, please, in private."

I bit my lip. "Sure," I said finally.

He led me to the door. There, he pushed his card into my hand. "Don't hesitate to call if you need anything. My cell number is on the back."

I glanced around, expecting to see Lipschitz laughing at their practical joke. Instead, I met only Talon's serious blue eyes. "All right, if you tell me what this is all about."

He pushed open the door, but didn't move to leave. "An old Scottish proverb foretells that a bad penny always returns." He caught my wrist, holding it long enough to show his sincerity. "Have a care, lass."

My skin burned beneath his touch. "You're warning me? About who?"

"I've questions for you as well, but now is not the time," he said. "Dinner tonight?"

My head was spinning. "Not a good idea, I'm a suspect, remember?"

"It wouldn't have been much of a test if I hadn't remembered." And on that unhelpful, enigmatic comment, he strode into the parking lot, climbed into an unmarked squad car, and drove away.

After several long breaths, I returned to Solo, who was back in the chair reading another magazine. "Mind-boggling," I said, shaking my head.

"All things considered he just might be."

I shoved my hands onto my hips. "More riddles? Really?"

"Rylie, have you ever wondered why you've never told Zach how you feel?"

"I know it's hard to understand, but he and I have been friends a long time," I said, knowing that was an exhausted cop-out. "Look, what happens if he doesn't feel the same way as I do? How would it be possible to go on as before?"

"True," Solo admitted. "Things would change."

"I would hate that."

"In other words, you want things to stay the same."

"Yes," I said. "I mean, no. Oh, hell, I don't know what I want."

"Exactly." He tossed the magazine on the table and rose. "Detective Talon seems like a good guy."

"Yeah, well, maybe, but I'm thinking he's more a player, and I'm not into them. Players are like empty calories. Taste good, but come with a hefty price."

"Like Twinkies, those little creamy devils," he said. "But you'll never know what's inside until you take a bite. Rylie, what if you're wrong? You don't even know him."

"Maybe," I said, but the gamble wasn't for me, nor was the sadness I had seen many friends suffer with *bad boys*. The ups and downs. The cheating, the regrets, the aching heart. "Let's not get into this now. We have a murder to solve."

"All right," he said, his tone a mix of amusement and exasperation. "What I started to say earlier was there's a restaurant on Lake Union called Great Scott Café. And guess what? It's on Bintliff Pier."

I stared at him for a moment. "Ah-ha."

"Ah-ha, what?"

"No idea. I just always wanted to say that. But seriously, you might be on to something. Talon just warned me about someone."

"Who?"

"He didn't say—wouldn't say. Maybe there is a connection between Talon, the café, and the pier. And if so, who is Bintliff to Lipschitz, and why is he afraid of him?"

"Sounds like one of life's little mysteries. And you know how we like mysteries."

"Oh, yes we do," I said, smiling, "But you realize we have only twenty-four hours to solve Otto's murder. Granddad will be home by lunchtime tomorrow. And with Lipschitz threatening to charge me with obstruction—"

"Obstruction, really? That's hardcore," he said.

"More like two shots, close range. And it would be the end of everything: Granddad accepting me as a PI and paying our back taxes."

"Not to mention possible jail time."

"Solo, we can't drag this out. We have to—no, we *will* solve this case in one day."

"Well, look at you. Miss Confident. And I know just the thing to get us started."

"What?" I asked.

"Buddhist Monks," he said.

"And we're talking about monks because?"

He blew out a breath. "Earlier, me, telling you a sand drawing was in the station's public lobby to celebrate the marathon. Trust me it will bring us good Karma."

"I dunno. We're burning daylight as we speak."

"Come on, it's barely nine am. And let's face it, to solve this murder fast we are going to need all the good karma we can get. Ten minutes, that's all I ask."

He grabbed my arm, and humoring him, I let him drag me toward the exit. We were about fifteen feet away when the doors opened and a young police officer hauled inside a handcuffed teeny-tiny Asian woman. She wore a black leather jumpsuit, spiked dog collar, and on her feet were silver pumps tall enough to lift Faye Ray into King Kong's paw. A fierce look—one I could never hope to equal—twisted her Chihuahua-size face as she sputtered out a boatload of foreign words.

Solo nudged me. "Those are Korean swear words."

"I didn't know you knew Korean."

"I don't, but I watched a marathon of Korean movies

on Netflix last month when I had the flu. Oooo, what's that smell?"

I took a whiff. *Bleh.* "I dunno."

"It's really gamey."

The officer dragged the woman to the counter, told the booking cop her name was Happy Hye, and that he'd picked her up for solicitation.

Two more police officers barreled in from outside. Because his head was wagging, the handcuffed man between them was hard to see. Though from what I could see, he looked like Woody Allen in leather and chains: sandy blond hair, enormous horn-rimmed glasses over a black mask. Dragging his feet, he forced the officers to lift him by the arms.

"I couldn't even get the handcuffs to work," the man said, head down, whimpering.

Solo and I exchanged a wide-eyed looked, sighed in unison. It was our boss, Leland Rosenberg.

"I never do this sort of thing," Leland said to the officers. "It's my birthday. I'm having a big party tonight. How about letting me off with just a warning?"

"Birthday party!" Happy Hye yelled from the booking desk where she stood ready for a mug shot. "So I'm good enough to have sex with, but not invite to your party?"

"Geez, I'm trying to save my marriage, not make new friends," Leland said as he and the officers paused several feet away from the booking desk to wait their turn.

I inched up, angling closer. Solo mirrored me.

"How's banging me gonna save your marriage?" Happy Hye screamed.

Leland craned his neck, the chain fixed from his collar

to waist straining. "My wife says nothing screams sexy like a dominated man. I'm a perfectionist. I had to practice."

"And you made me talk nerdy to you, too," Happy Hye said, glaring at the camera as the officer snapped the shot. "Broke ass or not, I should have demanded more money. Enzymes, proteins, acid, or race. What dung."

We inched even closer.

Leland looked at the ceiling, sighing. "Now I've heard everything. It's base, not race." Then his eyes fell on me. "Oh, hello, Rylie." He did a good job of sounding normal. "She got that last part wrong. When you think of acid, don't you naturally think of base? That's the way my mind works anyway."

I blinked, taking in the full impact of his clothing, recognizing them as part of Lilith's domination collection. "Leland, what's with the sunglasses?"

Solo leaned in. "You look at those threads and sunglasses are what you're nosy about?"

"I thought it best to start at the top, and then work my way down," I said.

"This is really rather embarrassing," Leland said. "The sunglasses are camouflage, in case someone from my synagogue sees me. Shlomo's Deli is next door. They make the best cheese blintz."

Solo took in a big sniff. "Boss, is it my imagination or do you smell like venison?"

"Yeah, I reek of the stuff. She made me eat before we had—" Leland lifted his shoulders, then let them fall. "She said it would give me a robust—" He blushed crimson. "But I don't think it was venison. Horse, maybe. You know how well they're—"

"Gifted," Solo suggested, grinning.

Leland nodded, looking wistful. "Must be nice to be a horse."

"Oh, pleeeezzze," Happy Hye wailed from the booking desk. "It was dog meat, dork!"

"What?" Leland said, his eyes wide open. "Dog meat is forbidden under Jewish law. Oh, God! What will my mother say?"

"Time to see a man about a mug shot," the officer said, grabbing Leland by the arm.

"Oh, why not?" he said. "I'm broke. How bad can jail be?"

"For real, broke?" I asked, my eyes bulging now.

"Yeah, but I want to keep it a secret," he whispered. "The FDA suspended trial of my anti-frailty drug, something about liver damage. Go figure. Kidneys, we got two, but my drug puts holes in a solitary organ. I can fix it, though," he said, "but not from jail. Rylie, without this approval, I'll be forced to sell FoY."

No FoY, no job, no money for back taxes, no affordable housing for the seniors. *Uh-oh.* "Not to worry, Leland," I said. "Just post bail and you'll be out of jail in an hour."

Solo nudged me. "Tell him about Otto being murdered."

"Huh?" Leland said. "Otto Weiner was murdered?"

I quickly related the details of how the body was found.

"Holy cow," he said. "How did he die?"

Happy Hye being led away from the booking desk interrupted my answer.

"All right, lover boy," one of the officers said to Leland. "Mug shot time."

Happy Hye dug in her heels as they passed each other.

"Hey, dork," she said to Leland. "Maybe you not so broke ass. Maybe you buy my client list real cheap, ten grand maybe. It full of big business honchos, real estate moguls, and even billionaire Dilbert Bates's bodyguard."

"The one who let a pie hit Bates in the face?" Solo asked.

"That's the one," she said testily and turned back to Leland. "Some might pay a little something to keep their names a secret. What do ya think, huh? We got a deal, dork?"

"Oh, that's a good idea, boss," Solo said with enthusiasm. "The extra money will come in handy, especially since they think you killed Otto. You're gonna need a high priced attorney."

"What?" Leland stared at me in what appeared to be a shocked stupor as the officers dragged him to the desk. Once there, he snapped out of it enough to mouth my way, "Help."

I pointed to the phone on Yancy's desk and mouthed back, "Call me."

He looked confused, so I rushed over and lifted the receiver.

After he hesitated for a beat, he nodded. "Officer," he said to the booking cop, "I get one phone call, right?"

"Yep."

"Can I call any phone?"

"Yep."

"If you don't mind me asking, what's the number for the phone on the desk over there?"

If there was one thing I hated more than waiting around, it was waiting around a police lobby in fear of running into Lipschitz again. Some might say I'm chicken. They would be right. It wasn't that booking Leland was taking longer than usual. Nope, he was cooperative and uncomplaining to the officers, but his restrictive get-up made removing his belongings from his pockets difficult. Add to that how his black leather mask got stuck on his head. It was tight and almost tore off an ear when the officers tried to help him take it off.

Solo and I were sitting on the floor, eating licorice, two cowering figures huddled in the corner behind Yancy's desk, our backs to the wall, and our legs out straight.

"Is he almost done?" Solo said, turning to me as I had a better view. "I have a wedgie beyond belief, or at least I think I do. My ass is numb."

"That can be a mixed blessing. The numb ass," I said, "not the wedgie."

"Ssshh," Yancy hissed down from his desk chair. "Here comes trouble. Lipschitz just left the men's room."

We fell silent. Yancy was great to hide us. There was something awesome about him fudging the rules to let two suspects talk. Done, I suspected, out of our long-lasting respect and appreciation for each other.

"Thank all that is good and holy, Lipschitz is gone," Yancy said after a moment, "but it's a safe bet he'll be back."

Some minutes later, the desk phone rang. Yancy answered it then covered the receiver as he held it out for me. "I'm on marathon duty in ten minutes, so hurry."

I nodded, took the phone. "Leland, we gotta make this quick. Can you talk freely?"

"God, no, but I'll do my best," he said. "What's this all about? Who killed Otto?"

"I don't know, but I'm going to find out. And I've got

only one day to do it, so tell me everything you know."

"Rylie, I have two doctorates. That could take some time."

I rolled my eyes. "Listen, did you tell Booth last night that you hoped Otto would get what was coming to him?"

"Sheesh, I wasn't referring to murder," he said.

"What then?"

"Otto lost his watch to Booth in a late night poker game last week, only Otto threatened to file a complaint accusing Booth of stealing it."

"Did he? Steal it, I mean," I said.

"It was a fair game. Otto threw the watch into the pot once he ran out of money."

"What's the watch worth?" I asked.

"Twenty grand."

I whistled. "That's a lot of scratch. How come I never saw Otto wearing such an expensive watch?"

"He never wore it. Said it irritated his psoriasis," Leland said, sounding unconvinced.

"And you didn't believe him?"

Silence. "More important is that Booth is worried because it's his word against Otto's."

"Weren't there other players?" I asked.

"Two, but Wally dozed off and the Colonel had to leave for a swig of Pepto-Bismol."

I paused when Solo whispered a question in my ear. "Leland," I said finally, "why does Booth have your cell phone?"

"That's a story that isn't mine to tell. Ask him."

I thought about Booth's mutual friend comment. "Are you saying he has a history with Happy Hye?"

"It's complicated, but don't worry. It has nothing to do with Otto or his murder."

I looked down at the questions I'd scribbled on a scratchpad while waiting for Leland to call. "Did you meet Doris and Cokey Bill Oley at the laboratory on a regular basis?"

"Every Sunday morning, six thirty sharp. I'd have been there this morning if the cops hadn't arrested us at Crossroads Park."

"It's only ten. What took you so long to get here?" I asked

"It was totally weird, they cordoned off the area, no traffic in, none out."

"Why?"

"Dogs were everywhere. Seems they escaped from Crossroads Animal Shelter. I was handcuffed in the back of the cruiser, but Happy Hye was outside stomping her foot in a blind furry at a little dachshund. It was awful. The poor thing had only three legs."

"Oh, no," I said. "Did she hurt it?"

"Don't think so. It ran off."

I refocused on my list. "Did you schedule two fish deliveries for this morning, one at daybreak, and one later?"

"Nope, only the one. Why? What's happened?"

Long silence. Then. "I met the Oleys this morning. At the laboratory, in the back parking lot. We talked a little. Tossed around some fish. Leland, I swear to God, they were both living one moment then *bam* they were dead the next."

Even longer silence.

"And you wanna know what's funny?" I chuckled, but it came out as a squeak. "The police think you convinced me to get rid of Otto's body in the laboratory incinerator. Only they think you wanted to frame me by hiring the Oleys to kill me so I couldn't talk."

Long drawn-out silence.

"But don't worry. I don't believe it for a minute. Leland?" I said, peering around the desk. "You still there? I can't see you. Leland? Leland?"

I heard a thud, followed by the booking officer shouting, "Man down!"

˜Come to the dark side. We have cookies˜

Alistair was slouched across the desk from Granddad when Solo and I entered his office after a quick knock. Both men were cackling. Granddad's eyes were bright. It was great to see.

"I know what's going on here," I said, my cheeks burning. "You told Granddad about what happened in the panel truck, about Cokey Bill Oley seeing my bare behind."

Alistair fell into a deeper fit of laughter.

"Rylie." Granddad lifted his bifocals, wiped his eyes. "Life with you is an adventure."

Is that a good thing? "What a horrible morning. Nice sunrise, though," I said, checking my watch. "Shouldn't you be leaving for Portland? It's after ten."

Granddad bolted up to his feet. I immediately regretted asking, as sudden movement was not good on a damaged heart. "Goodness," he said, appearing all right. "I forgot the time. The fair is in three hours."

"Wish you didn't have to rush off," Alistair said. "We could have breakfast."

"I'm back tomorrow," Granddad said. "How about lunch?"

"That works," Alistair said.

Granddad looked at me. "You'll need a ride home. I can drop you both off."

"We're good. Solo wants to check out the sand drawing in the lobby."

"You'll need to go outside, around the building," Alistair said. "The cleaning crew broke the glass door that connects the two lobbies."

I remembered something. "I also have to put in an hour at FoY's booth at the marathon."

"Yeah, Tita will chap our asses—sorry," Solo said, two dots of red rising on his chubby cheeks. "I mean, her blood will boil if we don't make it."

"We'll catch the bus after," I said, and he started to leave but I called, "Granddad," and he looked back. "I love you."

He flashed a small uncomfortable smile. "Me, too. Be careful."

I planned to be and told him so. "See you tomorrow," I said, as he closed the door behind him. I turned back to Alistair. I didn't know the wisdom of my next action, but it was all I could think of. "Granddad is worried about me."

"That his gut is twisting would be a fair statement," he said.

"For the sake of argument, let's assume he's asked you to keep an eye on me."

"For the sake of argument," he confirmed.

I thought it a good time for barefaced honesty. "You

know how I've always wanted to be a private detective, and how Granddad is against the idea?"

I received a nod in return.

"And your opinion on this is what?"

"Mixed," he confessed. "Healthy birds leave the nest. Who's to say, you might soar."

So sweet, this one.

"But it can be dangerous, Rylie. No man wants his loved ones in danger."

"Alistair, how long have you and Trudy been married?"

"Forty-one years—" He stared into my eyes, and from what I could see, he got my point loud and clear. "Sneaky."

I smiled. "A little information wouldn't hurt, would it? I mean, if the tables were turned, you'd want to know, right?"

"I would," he said. "But it begs the question: what will you do with the information?"

I shrugged, put on my game face. "It might spark some memory that could help the investigation. And I know it would be a good investigative exercise, pondering possibilities, coming up with theories. Then if I think of anything solid, I could pass that onto to you or Lipschitz."

Alistair's expression hardened. "Lipschitz a detective. How do you like them apples?"

He didn't, by the look on his face, which surprised me. It was most unusual for one cop to malign another cop, even subtly. All in all, it was a brotherhood thing, one not taken lightly. Still, there was no denying it, Lipschitz wasn't the favorite son in this department.

"Alistair, how did he get to be a detective so young? Granddad says it takes quite a while to be able to take the exam. He's only been on the force three years."

"You want the official response?" he asked.

I nodded.

"He did a good job on patrol."

"And the unofficial response?"

"A cruel trick," he said, shaking his head.

"Wonder who he knows," I said.

When his eyes met mine, I realized he also wondered.

"Thad Talon," he started and then added, "—the Scotsman—he seems like a straight up guy. Willing. Able. Doesn't mind asking an old veteran for help. Between you and me and the fence post, I'd like to keep him and ship Lipschitz off to Scotland."

"Poor Scotland," Solo put in.

"Poor Scotland," I repeated, and then I went on to tell Alistair about how Leland had been arrested, leaving out the part about our phone call and how Leland had temporarily blacked out. When I finished, he lifted the desk phone.

"He's a stable member of the community," he said, dialing. "Assuming no priors, he'll be released without bail." He spoke to someone on the other end and disconnected. "The good news is Leland has no priors."

"And the bad news?"

"Lipschitz wants to question him before he's released. Forensics found traces of blood on a plant near the kippah on Leland's hillside. Blood type matches Otto's."

"Then he was pushed off the balcony above," I said.

"That's the preliminary belief." He angled his head. "How did you figure that out?"

I liked his reaction. My plan was working. "A large rhododendron was crushed, like something heavy had fallen on it," I said. "And the balcony is a floor beneath the street level garage and only accessible through Leland's home office."

"Things are looking bad for Leland," Solo said.

"Now let's not be hasty," Alistair said. "So far the evidence is only circumstantial."

"But he doesn't have Bintliff on his side," Solo said.

"Shoeless Joe Bintliff?" Alistair asked, his brows up.

"Who?" I asked.

"Not exactly who, more what," he said. "It's the alias for an Internet gambling site."

"Is the person behind the Internet site named Bintliff?" I asked.

Alistair shrugged. "No one knows for sure. The operation moves around. They've become hard to pin down since Internet gambling became a Class C felony."

"Uh-oh," Solo mumbled.

I shot him a worried look, but he waved it off, so I filled Alistair in on the Bintliff note.

Alistair propped an elbow on his desk, rested his chin on a hand. "Can you think of any reason why a gambling operator would want to protect you?"

"Not a one. I don't gamble, even at the casinos on the Indian Reservations."

"What penalty does a Class C felony carry?" Solo asked, wringing his paw-ish hands.

"Five years in prison, a $10,000 fine. Or both for the site operators," Alistair said. "Are you a gambler, son?"

"No, sir." Solo said. "I've never gambled in my life."

"Good thing. The Gambling Commission is after these offenders. Mostly operators, but they've brought in several site users."

Solo swallowed hard, his Adam's apple bobbing.

The desk phone rang. Alistair answered it, said a few, "uh-huhs," and disconnected. "Leland's with Lipschitz. It's routine questioning for now. You two go see the mandala. After they're done, I'll give Leland a ride home if he doesn't already have one."

"Mandala?" I asked, then remembered the sand drawing. "Sounds good. One more thing, the Oleys, do you know anything about them? Their next of kin, maybe. I'd like to send my condolences," I added quickly when he raised another quizzical brow.

"Condolences, huh?" he said wryly as he opened the file on his desk, read. "It seems they're naturalized citizens since 1990. Semi-retired, living in a low-rent apartment in Seattle, near the wharf. One son, lives with them, works at Dragon."

"Driving for Dragon Fresh?" I asked.

"Main office. Why?"

I thought it would be melodramatic to say, "Someone wants me dead." Instead, I said, "It was a Dragon Fresh delivery truck that rear-ended me last night. The driver's name was Bill Loney. I left his license and insurance info in FoY's van."

"Bill Loney?" Solo repeated. "As in *baloney*?"

Everyone laughed but me. How had I missed such an obviously fake name?

"I'll get a copy of his ID from evidence," Alistair said, still chuckling.

"That'll be good," I said. "Does their son know about his parents?"

"I haven't reached him yet," he said. "Funny thing about the senior Oleys, they've received eleven citations for digging in Dumpsters."

"As in Dumpster diving?" Solo asked.

Alistair nodded. "It seems they're fond of the ones behind Pike Place Fish Market."

Cripes. Had Leland's first-rate Peruvian fish oil actually come from the Dumpsters?

Not risking a chance run-in with Lipschitz, Solo and I rushed through the rear lobby to the outside. As we strode through the parking lot to the station's street-side public entrance, I thought of the mounting evidence against Leland. The sweet guy I knew wouldn't hurt a soul, but I could not let feelings influence my investigation. We had to—at least for now—consider him a suspect. Nonetheless, for my money Booth was a better candidate. After all, he had the most to lose if Otto had made good on his promise to press charges for the theft of the watch lost in the poker game. So essentially, Booth was our blast-off into the investigative world.

We paused at the curb as several marathon runners sprinted by. Hordes of spectators milled here, there, and everywhere, watching the race, consuming foodstuff from the many street-side tents, or perusing the countless booths advertising wares or local businesses.

"It's sweltering." Solo wiped his sweaty brow with a beefy hand.

"Definitely a heat wave," I said.

"The sign at Shlomo's Deli says seventy-five degrees."

"That hot?" I said since in coldish Western Washington this was scorching for June. "And some say Global Warming is bogus. Hey, what was up with all those jitters back in

Alistair's office?"

"Man, I can't hide anything. That's why I like clown makeup. Look happy, be happy."

I gave his rotund mug a sidelong look. A tsunami of emotion could hide there. "You don't Internet gamble, do you?"

"Nope, but my uncle does. He lives with my mom. It would stink if he got arrested."

"It seems like they're more interested in operators than users."

"Hope so," he said. "Now the way I see it, we should check out the mandala, do our time at FoY's booth, then launch into—"

"Operation: Booth Jackson," I finished. "I think he's where we should start. That watch business sounds fishy."

"Agreed," Solo said, nodding.

"Do you know anything about poker?" I asked.

"Not much. A straight. A flush. Basic stuff. I'm more a Solitaire dude."

"Do you think you could ask your uncle a few gambling questions?"

"Sure." He reached into his vest pocket and grimaced. "No cell."

"Let's use the station's phone, but we'll have to be careful if Zach is within earshot."

"Roger," Solo said.

As we pushed through the glass doors to the public information and complaint desk, something wrapped around my ankles. I stumbled, but kept upright with a grab to Solo's arm.

"Zach didn't see that, did he?"

Solo ran his eyes around the room. "You're in luck. No one is here."

I sighed in relief. Not that Zach was unaware of my clumsiness, but why drive home the point? It might be that one day we'll discuss having kids; he'll hark back to my lack of grace and worry over a rogue Keyes gene. Might be a deal breaker.

I looked down, saw that Walter the Indiana Jones wannabe had lost his red whip. By all appearances, the stupid thing had taken a shine to my seamed stockings.

I freed my ankles and straightened. "Where is Zach? Where are the monks?"

"Spooky," Solo said. "It's like Rapture happened, and we've been left behind. The good news is Buddhists reincarnate. The monks should be popping back any time now."

"Zach," I called out. "Buddhist monks. Hello. Anyone."

Nothing.

"Maybe they went to the little boys' room," Solo suggested.

"As one big, happy group?"

"Yeah, too metrosexual."

I looked around again. The double doors to the rear police lobby were indeed under repair. Brown paper was over the glass with a sign that read: CAUTION BROKEN GLASS. USE REAR ENTRANCE. At the far end of the long main counter was a windowed door to what I vaguely remembered was a storage room. The door was closed. Inside looked dark. Hung all around the doorjamb were ceramic tiles, seemingly painted by children. The line above them read, *BE KINDER THAN NECESSARY, FOR EVERYONE YOU MEET IS FIGHTING SOME*

KIND OF BATTLE.

"This sort of freaks me out," Solo said.

"Me, too, but let's use the phone before they get back." I set aside the whip on the counter, swiveled the phone around, and handed the receiver to Solo. "Dial nine for an outside line." I relayed several questions for him to ask his uncle. While they talked, I wandered to the closet door, tried it. Locked. I moved to the plate-glass window to see if they were outside. Nope.

Solo hung up. "By the sound of it, Booth Jackson is a smalltime gambler."

"How come?" I asked, stepping back.

"My uncle said a pro would have asked for a signed statement that the watch was part of the bet and worth the agreed to value, or at least made sure someone else witnessed the wager."

"There goes that theory," I said.

"What made you think Booth was a professional gambler?" he asked.

"A twenty thousand dollar bet is a lot for a game in a small retirement home. Add to that the note to Lipschitz, which may or may not be from the gambler Shoeless Joe Bintliff, and professional gambler came to mind."

"I guess we've reached our first dead end."

I slung my arms across the counter and let it support me. "All right then, let's throw out more ideas and see what sticks. What about Bintliff? Has your uncle ever heard of him?"

"Yep," he said. "Bintliff is a real dude. Bad news owing him money, too. He has a gross way of dealing with folks who welch on bets."

I didn't like the pained look on his face. "Gross?"

"He chops off their feet, shoes and all, and keeps them as souvenirs. Then he dumps their dead bodies in Lake Union."

I closed my eyes, trying not to panic. No way did I want anything to do with a shoe stealing, foot-chopping maniac. Talon had to be behind the Bintliff note. *Had to be.* Though the truth is, I found that almost as upsetting. Talon terrified me. He reeked of heartbreak, yet each time he looked at me, I got a little wet. But that was just hormones. And the fact that I could not actually remember the last time I had had sex. Still, Talon had the most beautiful eyes—Omigod, what was wrong with me? Not even in a crazy alternate universe, one where Zach didn't exist, would I be interested in Thad Talon.

"Not interested," I repeated aloud then grinned sheepishly when Solo raised a quizzical brow. "I mean, no worries, I think Talon is behind the Bintliff note."

"Would you still feel that way if you knew both Bintliff Pier and Great Scott Café were owned by Shoeless Joe Bintliff?"

"I dunno—what's wrong?" I asked as his expression went from pained to grim.

"You'll never guess who lives in a houseboat on the next pier."

I admit it took me a minute for the worse possible name to surface. "Not Lipschitz. Nooooo, not him!"

"Yep," he said. "My uncle said Lipschitz is always coming into the café. He never makes any trouble, or even says he's a cop, but everyone knows he is. They mind their P's and Q's while he is there, though no gambling goes on. Rylie, this connects Lipschitz to Shoeless Joe Bintliff."

Crap, crap, crap. I was torn between hyperventilating and

peeing my pants. Hyperventilating won. It would be horrible to ruin this lovely marble floor.

"Uh-oh." Solo grabbed my arm. "You don't look so good."

"Yeah, protected by a shoe-stealing murderer never gets old."

"A karma boost." He pulled me across the room to the mandala. "That's what you need."

A stiff drink sounded better.

The mandala was a striking five-foot circle of vibrant sand, roughly ten distinct shades. The outside circle, geometric inside lines, and assorted figures were around an inch high. As though positioning a toy soldier, Solo placed me alongside the outer edge. Once he settled in beside me, he dropped his chin to stare down at the drawing.

I mimicked him. "Okay, now what?" I said, shooting him a sidelong glance.

His only reaction was when his eyes grew wide like a cat about to pounce.

"Hello. Tap, tap, tap," I said into a make-believe microphone. "Is this thing on?"

Still no response. Instead, he took my hand into his. We circled the drawing. When he let loose a big dopey grin, I suspected his karma was on the road to recovery. People like Solo believed in miracles. I wanted to believe in them, too.

Truth is, I wasn't sure what to believe about the giant unknown. Maybe there is something out there, in the cosmos. Don't get me wrong. I'm not a total disbeliever. If I were one, I wouldn't hope and pray to find my runaway parents someday. Then again, I feared I'd entered the dark side of disillusionment. Honestly, I didn't go there willingly.

However, I wasn't screaming at the door to come back, either.

"I need to find Zach." I started to step away.

He squeezed my hand. "Stay here."

I opened my mouth to say no, but Solo had a firm grip on me, tugging me along the outer edge for another time, chanting something soft as we circled.

"Do you feel it?" he asked. "That's the purifying power of wisdom."

Hard to say nope to such a hopeful face. "Maybe," I said, and then he asked me for details. "Is there going to be a test afterwards? I'm just curious."

He narrowed his eyes. "Are you making fun?"

"Yeah," I said, grinning. "I'm kind of an ass."

"You need a more open mind." He wheeled me around some more, only stopping to reverse directions.

I had to admit Solo was in his element. He looked calmer, had lost his furrowed brow. So I closed my eyes, trying to absorb this energy.

"Help me help Leland," I said under my breath. "Show me what to do, where to go. And should I ever bump into my parents, send up a flare or something. But, please, *please*, don't let me walk on by."

"Uh-oh," Solo said. "Your shoe just took out that deity's head."

I frowned at the colorful smear at my feet. "Oh, crud."

"This is bad." Solo bellied down on the floor. "I gotta fix this."

He had his index finger out and was doing a motion somewhere between a sweep and a push. The deity's head did look better after a few minutes. Well, sort of, if you squinted a bit. But then each time Solo got one line back into place, his massive forearm would wipe out another. Then two thirds of the way through the circle, he sneezed and blew the big white central yang away from its big black yin.

"I give up." He climbed to his feet. "Do you think the monks will notice?"

"Maybe only a little," I said.

"You think?"

"I do. I do," I said. "Man, I can't help having a bad feeling about this empty lobby."

"Think positive," he said. "They're probably across the street sucking down a Jamba Juice."

Through a nearby plate glass window, I scanned the crowd again. No Zach. No Buddhist monks.

"Hey," Solo said. "You do look better. Your hair is real shiny."

"No way."

"Way."

We inspected my hair in the window's reflection, paying little attention to anything behind us. The crack of a whip made us freeze. I realized right away that the sound had come from the wannabe's toy. *Snap, snap, snap.* We both wheeled around.

I saw his wild eyes first. Walter was behind the counter, doing grand sweeping motions with the whip. A frenzied mind had a keyed-up look, and seeing exactly that on his face, I froze like a fish stick in the freezer. He snapped the whip a few more times.

Solo stepped forward, but pulled up at a sharp, "Stop right there," from Walter.

"Okay, be cool. Be cool," Solo said.

Like a sword of battle, Walter brandished the whip in one hand, while the high counter hid two thirds of his body. Nearby, the storage room door was now ajar. Somehow, in spite of myself, I didn't shout out Zach's name. My gut said he was inside, perhaps bound, or hurt, and because of this, there was no room for error as I pondered what to do. I took a second to skim a look over the surveillance cameras. Blacked out with spray paint.

"The voices say you are evil," Walter said. "They say both of you are evil!"

Solo cast a rueful look at the ruined mandala. "Guilty as charged. We are a little evil."

"Evil infests you." Walter's eyes were pinpoints. "Evil spews from you. Evil!"

"Now wait a minute. Wait a doggone minute," Solo said. "At least we're honest about it, not like those deceptive fat-free labels. Under a gram of fat is still fat, you know?"

"That's right. Joke around. You wanna know what happens to evil? I smite it!" Walter barked comically. "I smite it with my whip."

Solo laughed. "Well, if that isn't a little overkill."

I jabbed my elbow into his side to shut him up.

"Well it is, Rylie. Bleach kills everything, even evil, I'm bettin'. And the guy has a whole bottle of it under his hat. Nice hat, by the way. Is it genuine fur felt?"

"Quiet!" Walter vibrated with anger through a couple beats of silence. Muttering something that was too low to hear, he raised his concealed right hand to level at us a scary-ass gun.

Air stuck in my chest.

The gun was sleek, black, and police issue. A dead ringer to Zach's.

I told myself not to jump to conclusions. No jumping. *No jumping!*

Solo shifted sideways, shielding me from Walter. Hands up in surrender, he glanced over his shoulder and told me to stay put. His fear was obvious, but it was not the lip-trembling horror I knew was plastered on my face. I was a coward whereas Solo was anxiously brave.

"Looky here, the big guy isn't so funny anymore," Walter said, snickering.

His sick laugh made me brace for gunfire, but instead he just stepped to the storage room door and pushed it open. "Join us, one and all. We've got ourselves a comedian."

I'd been expecting Zach, so when Walter—using the whip as a prod—forced five bald monks of various ages into the narrow space behind the counter, where they assembled shoulder-to-shoulder to face us, I eased out a relieved breath. I couldn't help it, even though we were still in harm's way.

Walter made a great circle in the air with the handgun. "Come on! Come on!" he said to an unseen person in the storage room. I thought—more like *hoped*—Zach would enter the lobby and say, "Just kidding, Rylie. It's all a joke."

Instead, I got, "Hold your horses," from FoY resident, retired Nazi hunter, and long-established germaphobe Gilad Kupper as he sauntered into view. He never looked at me, not once, just took his place beside the last monk in line. "I gotta hand it to you," he said to Walter. "You do crazy well."

I couldn't breathe, could barely stand. *Where was Zach?*

Gilad looked at me—finally. His intense brown eyes were cunning darts in a deeply lined, furious face. A hunter's face. The face he assumed when he talked of hunting down Nazis, of sometimes killing them if they resisted arrest.

"Genius plan, Rylie," he said, his voice sharp, and oddly harsh. "Asking Tita to pick up your forgotten items at the trestle is why we're here—at the mercy of this lunatic."

Everyone looked at me, even Walter. It was like being scolded in class. I knew my breath was coming out in pants. "I'm sorry," I said with a whimper. "Is Tita okay? Where is Zach? Please, please tell me they're all right."

"Have some respect." Gilad spat. "Stop begging."

I swallowed hard, feeling dazed and humiliated.

"Go ahead and talk." Walter pressed the gun to Gilad's shoulder. "Have fun with her, make her squirm."

"You'd like that, wouldn't you? Well, tough." Gilad slapped away the gun as though it were a dreaded germ rather than a lethal weapon. "Zach, get out here. You, too, Tita."

Zach stepped from the storage room, followed by Tita, who was still dressed in kitchen whites, her dyed blond hair sporting considerable brown roots. They took their place beside Gilad, wordlessly, sullenly.

I bit my lip. Blood streamed down Zach's cheek, the result of an angry gash at his temple. My eyes rounded, and I forced myself to focus on his chin to keep from fainting at the sight. Zach swayed a little, his legs buckling. Tita grabbed his arm to support him.

"Hey, you, Walter the Nutcase." Tita pressed my jacket to Zach's head wound. "This man needs a doctor. Let us go or else."

A shiver ran up my spine.

Walter swung around on Zach, talked low to his ear. "You won't press charges, will you, Officer O'Neil? Not when shaking that tree will bring forth the truth. And you don't want that, do you? Believe me, a cop who gives up his gun without a fight is bad news."

Zach finally met my gaze, and in his eyes, I saw the truth behind Walter's accusation. I stared at him over Solo's shoulder. There was no fight left on his face. He looked lost.

"Let me tell you, O'Neil," Walter went on. "Kids fight harder to keep their candy than you did your gun. Search me how you ever made it on the force."

Tita stared at me, her eyes weighty—signaling. My mind blanked on what she was trying to tell me, so I shrugged.

She rolled her eyes, shifted to Gilad, and nodded.

Gilad fell into a diatribe of hot-blooded Yiddish, followed by the five monks releasing a volley of what sounded like soft-spoken Tibetan.

"English, please!" Tita shouted.

"Oh, that's rich," Gilad said. "You illegals always refuse to learn English."

Walter watched them, fascination on his face, his eyes bouncing from one to the other.

It struck me, then. This argument was a diversion, so I could perhaps do something brave like launch over the counter and subdue Walter. However, my legs were pickets of ice.

"You must be senile," Tita told Gilad. "I speak English. I'm a citizen."

"Groyseh Macher," Gilad said, his tone insulting. "So you say."

"Don't get me started, old man," she said. "I'll make mincemeat with your liver."

Gilad bristled. "This is what happens when we don't fence off our borders. You're sucking dry our resources, exhausting my tax dollars."

"I told you, I'm a citizen!" Tita said. "And I pay a lot more taxes than you do, you social security bloodsucker. And my parents paid taxes before they retired. We are good citizens. We vote. We support our church."

"Pish posh," Gilad said. "Try being a Nazi hunter. Now that's a good citizen."

Waking from a nightmare would not have surprised me more than Walter looking at Gilad with eyes full of wonder. "You're really a Nazi hunter?"

"One of the best before retirement."

"Cool," Walter said. "I wanna be a Nazi hunter. Can you get me a job?"

Gilad eyed the gun in Walter's hand. "I might be able to arrange something."

"*You* a Nazi hunter," Tita said with a laugh. "You gotta be kidding. You are insane. They don't let insane people hunt Nazis."

Walter's nose flared.

"You wanna piece of me?" Tita egged him on. "Come on. Ditch the gun. I'll show you how big girls smite evil."

"For chrissake, Tita, shut up," Zach hissed.

Walter grinned. "Looky here, paging *Seattle Times*. Frozen with fear cop finally finds his voice. Cat got your gun." He laughed at his own joke.

"We aren't done with this yet," Zach said with gritted teeth.

"*Oooo*, I'm scared." Walter leveled the gun to Zach's temple.

My heart skipped a beat. Somehow, I broke my bond with fear and rushed forward. "Don't be a dope, Walter.

Assaulting a cop is a felony."

He rolled his neck my way; his eyes hard as he stalked around the counter, closed in. "It was you. You!" he shrieked in a sudden blind rage.

A chilled black silence engulfed me. When he pressed the gun to my nose, my knees buckled; I hit the floor. *Thump.*

"I'm gonna blow out your brains," he hissed.

I begged for my life, my hands up in surrender.

"Say the word dope, slower this time. Say it!" he screamed.

"Sweet Jesus," Zach said in the background.

I stared at him, bewildered. What did he know that I didn't? And what did the word dope have to do with it? Then it hit me. Sweet Jesus was right.

Before I could think, I babbled out a slew of panicked apologies. Never once did I consider my suicide training. How could I? My mind was empty. Gone was all knowledge of negotiation, of taking command of a tense situation.

"Walter," I began. "Please don't be mad." I was too scared to meet his eyes. "I never meant to hurt you. I didn't know it was a live call. I was only a trainee on the suicide hotline. Believe me, please. I'm begging you."

"You dumb bitch. I almost killed myself that night."

"I'm sorry," I said repeatedly, my eyes blurred by tears.

And then, out of the haze around me, Solo came up from behind, wrapped his arm around Walter's neck, and yanked. Walter wilted, tongue out. I was halfway into a sigh of relief when the gun slipped from his hand, bounced on the floor, and discharged. A female scream only vaguely penetrated. To clear my vision, I blinked several times. All eyes were on Zach. He had Tita pressed against the wall behind the desk, his forearm thrust against her throat. Angry color flooded his face.

"Zach, no!" I scrambled to my feet, swayed.

His eyes met mine, held. I got a vague feeling that what Zach feared most—a flashback—had happened. I couldn't move. I could only stare back at him, his tortured gray eyes, and his white-knuckled grip on the arm he had pressed to her throat.

"Let her go," I said softly. "This isn't the convenience store."

Slowly he released her, and slowly disbelief crept into his face as he stared at his open hands. "I heard the shot," he said. "She was—was firing on us. I had to stop her. Kill her."

I rushed to him on woozy legs, but he shook me off.

"Leave me alone. Just leave me alone."

Footsteps approached, thundering. The broken door flew open, glass shards scattering across the floor. A sea of officers rushed in, guns drawn. A lot of shouting arose, followed by a cacophony of explanations and thanksgiving in several languages.

Eventually two officers led a stirring Walter to the holding cell, while another carted off the gun to the evidence cage. Yancy tended to Zach's head wound. Solo and I stood by in silence, awaiting our turn to give statements.

I cast a sideways look at Tita, whose statement had followed Gilad's and appeared to be wrapping up. "Boy, no free rides around this place. He grilled me like I was still a *Las Chicanas*," she said in reference to her former gang affiliation. "Damp, cold, and barely fit for people, these cop hideouts are, you know?"

Gilad joined us from the front window where he'd stood for the last fifteen minutes. "I had no idea Otto was dead.

Why didn't somebody tell me?"

All three of our mouths stayed shut for several seconds, and then Solo described the accident, how Otto's body was found, concluding with, "It was no random act of violence."

"That's unfortunate," Gilad said. "Come on, you three. Do I have to spell everything out? We're all suspects."

The station chief strode in, looked around, and asked to speak to Zach in private. He rose, followed her through the broken doorway. He never looked back.

~Due to recent cutbacks, the light at the end of the tunnel has been turned off~

"I hope Zach is okay," Solo said for what was the tenth time in the last hour.

I put on a brave face. "He'll be fine."

We were mainlining Slurpees from 7-Eleven as we worked FoY's booth at the ongoing marathon. Actually, it was more a canopy with tenting overhead and no sides. Runners drifted past in patchy groups or as singles on the cordoned off street. Lots of spectators still milled about, but few stopped to pick up FoY brochures or ask questions. Most hurried past, eager to sample some hot wings from the Roaring Wing's booth next door, or juice from Jamba Juice across the street.

"You can't always be sure," Solo went on, frowning. "My mom's kid brother was never the same after he came back from the Iraq War. PTSD did a real number on him."

"Zach will be fine," I said again, a little desperately.

"Hope so. Tao just took off one night. We haven't seen him since."

Beneath my calm veneer, my nerves wheeled. But that wouldn't help Zach. I needed to be strong for him. He was a fighter. Fighters fight. Fighters win. I'd seen that on a bumper sticker once, it had to be right.

"Uh-oh, your hair is dull again," Solo said. "We should hit the mandala again."

"I'm okay." I tossed my empty cup into the trash. "My karma is in good shape."

"How do you know?"

"Walter didn't kill anyone," I said. "You were awesome, by the way."

I couldn't say more, couldn't call attention to my failure. Yet I could not ignore the truth, either. Even if I had remembered my negotiation training—stay calm, meet their eyes, no pleading, and no apologies—I doubt I would have used it, my fear had been so deep.

Solo rested a hand to my shoulder. "For a minute there, I thought we'd lost you."

"Thanks for saving my life." I said the words, but recognized their inadequacy.

"I think Walter will be okay," he said, looking shaken. "The paramedics thought he would. I sure hope he is. I'd hate to have hurt him for good, like brain damage or something."

I covered his hand with mine. "I know violence bothers you. I'm sorry."

For a minute neither of us spoke, just looked at each other, thankful to be alive.

"The good news is the monks weren't mad about the wrecked mandala." He held up a small silk bag. "They even gave me some sand."

"What for?"

"To scatter over water, spread the blessing of the mandala. Good timing, too. I need my karma squeaky clean by audition time."

"You got an audition?" I asked, surprised. "When? How come you didn't tell me?"

He looked playfully at me from under his bushy eyebrows. "It's sort of been a busy morning. I've only known a few hours. It was on my recorder when I stopped by the sailboat. It's in October, right before Halloween."

Though my heart sank, I made a triumphant gesture with my fist. "So many cities to perform in, so little time to be at home. I'm gonna miss you."

He blushed. "It's been awhile since someone missed me."

"Mama birds love to see their fledglings soar," I said, my cheeks burning now at my clumsy attempt to catchphrase like Alistair. "Point is, your mom will, too."

"Maybe," he said, looking doubtful. "But Cirque du Soleil isn't the NFL."

"I think we're going to need to bring in a referee on this one. Cirque du Soleil is *so* much more than the NFL."

"Thanks." His face pinched with concern. "Here comes Gilad and Tita."

"Why the frown?" I asked.

"Here we are putting all our energy into proving Booth guilty, but is it wise to focus on only one suspect? We can't exclude anyone from last night's fundraiser."

I considered a moment. "Looks like I've reached my first investigative low point," I said. "I should have known that. We need to get them apart, question them. I call dibs on Tita."

"Be careful," he said. "She may be a friend, but she has a dark past."

I was nodding now, certain we both had our work cut out for us. "No need to ask what strategy you'll use. Gilad responds best to flattery."

"Paved with good intentions of course."

"Of course," I said.

Tita and Gilad sauntered up to the brochure table. As usual, they were bickering.

"So it's official. I've run out of patience," Tita told him. "Just suck it up. A bit of fat won't kill you."

Gilad's eyes bugged. "When one asks for a fat-free blintz, one oughtta get a fat-free blintz."

Tita grabbed the blintz and pushed it into her mouth. "There. You've dodged a bullet."

"Astounding," he said. "You would clog your arteries for me."

"Don't get all mushy. To shut you up, I'd eat bacon fat."

"Now you're just embarrassing yourself," he said. "And here you're married to a Jew."

"Was married to a Goldberg, not anymore," she told him.

"Either way, you know we don't eat pork."

"Don't be silly. Otto did, and he was Orthodox." She looked to each of us before going on. "If you wanna know the truth, Otto slipped me something extra to bring him breakfast in bed. Coffee with milk, eggs, and bacon. It's no secret now because I already told the police. The *dinero* wasn't huge, but it fed my new car fund. I wanna buy a Subaru."

"I'd have never guessed," Gilad said, scratching his head.

"You saying I don't look like the outdoorsy type?" she asked him.

"What?—no," he said. "I just never knew an Orthodox who ate pork."

"That's it," I said, looking at Tita. "That's what you were hiding on the phone."

She nodded. "Yeah, I was afraid the cops would think I'd tried to shake down Otto for more *dinero,* maybe killed him by accident," she said in a voice riddled with worry. "No way was I gonna take that chance. I've got two kids. They need me, so I told them *pronto.* A Detective Talon took my statement over the phone. Hot accent," she said with a lusty whistle.

"Hot guy," I said, then felt my cheeks go pink again.

"About damn time," she said. "Face it, you and Zach are destined to remain friends."

"I think Talon is soft on Rylie," Solo said with a wink.

"Hey, I have an idea," Tita said. "Why don't you ask him out?

I gave a start. "Are you crazy? I couldn't do that."

"Why not?" she asked.

"I just couldn't, that's all."

Gilad cleared his throat. "On a more important note, those yentas at the deli said something interesting about Leland."

Solo and I exchanged an anxious glance.

"What?" I asked.

"The whole thing sticks in the head as idiotic," he said in lieu of an answer.

"What did they say?" I asked again.

"I can't believe Leland would be so stupid," Gilad said.

"And the streak continues," Solo said. "Just tell us what

they said about Leland."

"Well." Gilad leaned in. "Supposedly he has a skull tattoo."

"That's bad?" I asked. "Like bacon?"

"Worse. A skull tattoo was the insignia of a select SS group of concentration camp guards, and is *ech* to my family after the personal blow they delivered us. Most of the war criminals I brought in were from this SS-Totenkopfverbande Division. They called their insignia *Death's Head* and proudly tattooed it on their bodies. And even when they burned off the tattoo with cigarettes, claiming it was a bullet wound, we caught them. Their x-rays showed no bone damaged. We got 'em, all right. Those filthy bastards."

Nothing about this made sense. Leland revered his family, his religion, and paid homage to Holocaust victims by housing them at FoY for reduced rent, or in Otto's case, no rent at all due to his impoverished state. Then it hit me, Leland's disbelief earlier in Otto's excuse for not wearing his watch. It wasn't due to his psoriasis, but I suspect more because he feared he would lose his rent-free room if it got out that he owned an expensive piece of jewelry.

But that was that, and this was this. I could not wrap my head around Leland getting a Nazi tattoo, especially at seeing his near coronary at learning he had eaten taboo dog meat.

"—I'd have stopped him," Gilad was saying, "had I known. I would have reminded him of *my* mother, *his* great grandmother. How the Nazis arrested her and my older brother while they visited family in Poland, how one Nazi bastard robbed her of jewelry sewn into her clothes in exchange for my little brother's life."

My mouth dropped open in horror.

"You get where I'm going with this, don't you?" Gilad asked me.

I shook my head, not wanting to know.

"What counts here as unclear?" he asked. "My mother had only a few pieces of jewelry: a ruby necklace, an opal ring, a timepiece, a cameo broach, and pearl earrings. In spite of that, the bastard demanded more, so she gave him her body."

I gasped.

"Still he left her behind to be gassed," he said.

"And your big brother?" Solo asked. His eyes were moist.

"Dumped at a nearby farmhouse, he died of typhus a week later. The farmer kept his diary. He gave it to my father after the war. In it, my brother described the skull insignia, how Alric Mueller's hand was tattooed with it. How it terrified him. I dedicated my life to hunting down Mueller for what he did to my mother, my brother."

"Did you find him?" Solo asked.

He shook his head, sadly. "His trail went cold, but I did manage to capture others—many others from the SS-TV group. I got 'em, all right. The filthy bastards."

"Gilad, you look like a man in need of a blintz," Solo said. "Come on. My treat."

"It must be fat-free," Gilad said.

And as they strode toward the deli, Solo cast a *watch-yourself-with-Tita* look back at me just before the crowd swallowed them.

Several people dropped by the booth over the next ten minutes. Then it quieted down again. After another group of marathon runners rounded the corner, the street cleared as well.

"Hey, before I forget, here." Tita handed over my cell phone. "I had to toss your jacket, *chica*. No saving it. Bloodstains, Zach's blood." Ours eyes met, and I registered a war waging inside her. "I could have handled him, you know? Someone gets up in my shit, I take 'em out, but it was Zach, you know? He and I go way back. Catholic school, years of catechism with not much to show for it but stupid collages. I couldn't hurt him, you know. Couldn't."

I pretended to fiddle with my phone. I was pretty sure what I was about to say would anger her and gave myself a little time to prepare. "Tita, did you kill Otto?"

She said nothing for a moment, but eyed me shrewdly. "No."

"Do you know who killed him?"

She shook her head. "Straight talk, that's rare," she said. "I gotta a long sheet, you know? Been bounced out of jail more times than I care to think about. But something funny happens when you get kids, you go sort of soft, you know?" There came a pause where her face took on the look of someone eating something sweet. "But thanks for thinking I could kill Otto. I never wanna come off weak."

"You scare the hell out of me," I said.

She smiled as I opened the contact list on my phone. Tita was there, as was Leland and Gilad. Booth, too. All suspects were still on the table, but to my mind, Tita and Leland were at the bottom of the list.

On a sigh, I dialed Zach's number, but hit cancel. I waited a few beats and called again. I was looking at my feet when he answered.

"You gonna stand there staring at your feet, or are you

gonna say something?" he asked.

"How—how did you know?"

"You always stare at your feet when you're nervous. Rylie, I screwed up today." His voice held a note of desperation. "Looks like I'm a head case."

"Zach—" I tried to say *I think I love you* but stopped, not out of my usual cowardice, but more that it felt oddly insincere, wrong somehow. "You can fight this," I said. "Have faith."

A tense silence fell between us.

"What did you say?" he said finally.

"You can fight this," I said again.

"Not that."

I had to think. "Have faith."

"You always did know what to say. Pure and simple," he said and hung up.

"Zach, wait!"

Tita nudged me with a shoulder. Sympathy, girl gang style. "He'll beat this." She crossed to help a woman inquiring about accommodations at FoY.

I wandered the booth, straightening this, stacking that. I was relieved that Zach had opened up a little more. It was a positive step toward healing, and it helped relieve my fears that he would do something totally out of character, something desperate. My sense of panic had departed with the silly urge to complicate his life with my true feelings. I thought about those feelings, what my heart wanted. A strange flatness came over me, as when finding savory food flavorless. The best explanation was that feelings went into hiding during troubled times.

Then my cell phone rang. The number was unknown.

"Hello?"

"Judging by the sound of your voice, you fared well. I am relieved," a man said, his voice heavily accented and aggravatingly charming.

I was tempted to ask, "Who is this?" But of course, I knew it was Detective Talon. "Everybody, sooner or later, sits down to a banquet of consequences," I said.

"Robert Lewis Stevenson. One cannae go astray with a Scotsman's quote," he said. "But sounding well and being well are two different matters. Are you okay?"

"Not really, but I'll survive."

"I admire your honesty."

Now I was curious. "I said something insensitive on a hotline and hurt a man who was suffering, and it almost cost several people their lives. Do you still admire me?"

"Will you make that mistake again?" he asked.

I said no, meaning it.

"Well, then—" he began.

"Please don't say all's well that ends well," I said. "I have no desire to forgive myself."

"It's a pity, how much you suffer your failures. Your successes, are they felt as keenly?" he asked. "Don't judge each day by the harvest you reap, Rylie, but by the seeds you plant."

More Robert Lewis Stevenson. "Is there something else you want?" I asked.

"Aye, lass, but now is not the time," he said and disconnected.

Passing clouds covered the sun, blotted out the vivid glare, and muddied the air into something normally seen in the dead of winter. It hardly surprised me. The weather matched my mood, reflective, pensive, and if I could find the courage, hopeful. In a perfect world, Zach would conquer his PTSD, Walter would get mental help, I would earn my grandfather's approval, keep my job, and pay off our back taxes, and I would share my life with—I tried to picture Zach's face. Of course, I knew every inch of it, the curve of his jaw, the hollows of his cheeks, his wounded eyes; I couldn't picture it now, any of it. I looked around, confused, tired, and a little lost, but I had to let it go. Somehow, someway, I had to focus on finding a killer.

Up ahead, a cab arrived, its engine screeching as it pulled into the parking lot behind FoY's booth. It bumped over the cement divider and parked at the adjacent deli. I thought for a second that the Audi right behind it was also going to ignore the divider, but it parked in the first lot, the one just behind our booth. The Audi's male driver turned our way, his shaggy blond hair spilling over his forehead. His pasty coloring drew my eye, but he had focused his grim gaze on the cab. When a large group of teens wandered past, I lost sight of him.

"What a shitty tent," said a nearby male voice.

I turned my head.

"No side walls. What if it rains? I hate rain, see. My hip hurts in the rain." Booth Jackson crawled from the cab with a series of grunts and groans, rubbing his hip, cringing.

"Why aren't you cooking? Why are you here?" Tita asked.

"Don't start with me," he told her. "And just so you know, I didn't walk out on the job. Think back on how Otto clogged up his new low-flow toilet just the other day and not even twenty-four hours after it was put in. Well, to make a long story short, another damn senior did it again. Crap went everywhere, into the mudroom, the hallway. And now the water is off. So there is no cooking, Boss Lady. Delivery pizza is what's for lunch, and delivery pizza is what they'll eat."

My mouth watered. I was starving.

"So you've come to help us with the booth?" Tita asked, her tone skeptical.

"No getting out of it if I want a paycheck," he said, his wiggly brows bouncing. "But first things first, see. You are looking at a man in need of a new cell phone. And Roaring Wings is giving away an iPhone to whoever can eat the most Nitro Wings. Did you hear what I said? Banging hot Nitro Wings? Bring it on."

"If you croak, it's on your head," Tita said. "You've got that irregular heartbeat."

"Living dangerously." He scratched an angry rash on his left forearm. "I'm suffering a bit of a crisis, see. I need to break my grip with my two-cent phone. It's dulling my bling."

I had a sudden thought. "If you win, can I buy your old phone? Solo needs one."

"Sure, why not?" He wore a vague smile. "I guess I owe him. Ever since he came to work at FoY, Leland has stopped nagging me about exercising the seniors. If I've told him once, I've told him ten times, I've got a bad hip." He hauled out a small bottle of lotion and dabbed it on the rash. "The big boss ain't any good at listening."

My unspoken thought was he needed a bigger bottle. The rash had taken up residence on his arm. Then I thought of the stinging nettles growing near Otto's discarded kippah. Sure, it was a long shot as Washington was riddled with the bushy scourge, but I wanted to see his reaction. "That's some rash. What's it from?"

His brows shot up, twitching. "What's it to you?"

"You've got welts," I said. "Like maybe you tangled with some stinging nettles?"

"Don't know what that is," he said, expressionless.

"It's a flower, perennial. It causes a rash."

"Oh, is that all? For a minute, I thought you were saying I had a social disease."

"Huh?" I said. "That's sort of random."

He cast a wary look over each shoulder. "If there's gossip around FoY, you can bet your sweet bippy I'll hear it. And hear it I did this morning. Two seniors have herpes."

My mouth fell open. "Shut up."

"If I'm lying, I'm dying."

"Which seniors?" Tita asked.

"The Colonel won't say, but he'd know since he works in the clinic. Unreal, right? Can you imagine? Sex at their age," he said, shaking his head in apparent surprise.

I made the smart decision not to remind him that he was well over sixty, and if one believed his workplace boasting, sexually red-hot and active. A loudspeaker announced the wing eating competition would begin in twenty minutes.

"So do we have a deal?" I asked. "You'll sell me your phone."

"I'm open to the possibility. It's tight, though. Can't let it go cheap, see."

"But it cost only two cents. That's thievery."

"Sick world we live in, uh?" He limped toward Roaring Wings tent. Halfway there, a twenty-something black woman with an extraordinary body joined him, wrapping her arms through his. The limp abruptly disappeared. Interesting.

"Tita," I said. "Do you know how Booth hurt his hip?"

"Car crash, I think."

I looked back at Booth as he and his female friend waited outside Roaring Wings. The blond driver who had followed his cab into the parking lot approached Booth with an outstretched hand. The man gestured toward a nearby display table between the FoY and Roaring Wings booths, which up until now I hadn't noticed. A spangled banner stretched between two poles at each end of the table read: WHITE'S JEWELRY. A perfect name, as the man looked almost transparent. A sandwich sign beside the table read: FREE APPRAISALS AND CLEANING.

Booth turned his back on the man's obvious solicitation for business. The man scowled on his return to his display table. Booth and his female friend entered the tent, Booth immediately slouching into a chair at the contestant table. His friend whispered in his ear and stepped away to make a call. With his eyes fixed on her, Booth drew out a prescription bottle from his pocket and downed several pills without water. He placed the bottle on the table, left it there, and grabbed a glass of water from the nearby set-up table. But he didn't take a drink. He just held it in his hand, crossing to his friend.

I wondered about his pills. If they were for pain, and if once taken, could he climb Leland's steep hill, or if he was merely faking the pain to throw off suspicion. I had to get a look at those pills.

Sizzling oil smoked as a chef dropped chicken wings into a hot pot. I thought about how I could examine those pills, visualized several scenarios, and settled on one.

Tita stepped back, talking about the weather, happy as a fat rat in a cheese factory for the uncharacteristically hot weather. "Looks like our replacements have arrived," she said as a FoY senior and an office staffer entered the booth.

Greetings were said all around, and we departed the tent and walked to the sidewalk.

"So when do you pick up Elsa from church?" I asked her.

"On the twelfth of never, I hope. She called a little while ago, said she was getting a ride from church to the Ready Clinic. Gunk in her eye, or something. She will call, you know. When she's done."

Big grin. "So you have some time to kill?" I asked.

"Maybe. Why?"

Funny thing about Latino chefs. They love themselves some habanera peppers, and amazingly, they can eat tons of them without fanning their *sombreros*. So who better to eat a boatload of piping hot wings? Me, who cannot eat a red-hot candy without gasping for air? Or Tita Iglesias, FoY's resident fire breather.

"Yum," I said. "Smell that hot sauce? It's like the Mother Ship calling you home."

She eyed me suspiciously. "What are you up to?"

I filled her in on the investigation and how I had to—*had to*—get a look at Booth's pills and win Solo a new iPhone, as I didn't trust Booth to give me his old one. "So are you in?"

She looked over at Booth, then back to me "You really think he killed Otto?"

"That's the working theory."

"I'm in. I hate that bastard," she said. "But don't put all your eggs in Booth's basket. Gilad is right, everyone is a suspect, especially him."

"Why him especially?"

"I saw him slip away after the bonfire got going. Come to think of it, it was about the same time Booth left."

"Where did Gilad go?"

She shrugged. "I lost him in the dark. You know I knew a private investigator once. One day he just up and went. Mysterious disappearance some say, gang killing I say. The PI biz is like that, you know. They uncover secrets. People kill for that. How bad do you want this?"

"Real bad."

"Buckle up, *chica*, it's gonna get bumpy."

After signing a waiver—Tita rolled her eyes rather than show weakness by reading the cautionary document—the five contestants congregated behind the cafeteria-style focal table. A big crowd watched. Each competitor donned a plastic bib and latex gloves, then took his or her seat. Tita let loose an excited hoot.

"So you're ready to do this?" I stared at her across the table.

As if to say, "duh" she hooted again.

She sat between Booth and a man wearing a dingy muscle shirt. Fuzzy pale hair covered his body and his eyes were a piercing golden brown. He looked like a blond werewolf. The two college-age guys seated beside him looked preppy, rich, and buzzed. Frat boys, almost certainly.

Nearby, two chefs in heavy white aprons dumped heaps of wings into two bowls, poured on the sauce, and placed them under warming lights.

"As you can see, folks," the announcer said from the

podium as the awaiting crowd quieted. "We've only got one portable stove, so we're running behind. Five minutes, promise, till the competition begins."

As the chefs loaded up the hot oil with another batch of wings, the noise level resumed to a steady hum of conversation.

Another whiff of peppers made me blink, and my eyes started watering. "You sure you're okay doing this?" I asked Tita.

"Piece of cake. Easy as pie. Sweet as mother's milk," she said.

Booth regarded Tita. Big glower. Squirming brow pinched. An equal match to a bulldog: one lip corner up, showing some tooth, *a little plaque*. He was pissed. The good news? The pill bottle was still where he had left it.

Each contestant was allowed one friend for encouragement, so I circled the table and stood between Tita and Booth. I looked around. Booth's female friend stood in the back of the tent talking on her cell phone again. Booth had his back to me, watching her, his hands fisted and his knuckles white.

"Here goes." I crouched and took out my cell phone. I made a pretense of showing Tita some pictures on it, but in reality, I was snapping photos of the label on the prescription bottle, which read on closer inspection: OXYCODONE 5MG. TAKE TWO TABS EVERY 4 HOURS AS NEEDED FOR PAIN.

"You know taking painkillers isn't a crime?" Tita whispered.

"But taking them so you can climb a big hill and kill Otto is," I whispered.

Booth turned around. "What are you doing?"

"Er—nothing, I'm not doing anything, right, Tita?" I said. "Er—we're just discussing strategy. I have lots of ideas about how to eat the most wings."

Judging by the look on his face, he thought that hilarious. "My win is in the bag," he said.

The time was right to prod him for answers. "Funny the company Leland was keeping." I watched his eyes for a reaction. "On second thought, it's probably not that funny to you, Happy Hye being arrested. Leland, too. Curious mix. Does it make you jealous, maybe?"

Tita leaned in. "The boss was arrested?"

I gave her a sidelong look. "A couple hours ago."

"You're out of your damn mind if you think any of that bothers me," Booth said. "Common mistake, married folks messing in each other's enterprises. Happy Hye and I have a good thing going, see. It pays the bills."

I gaped at him in shock. "You two are married?"

"Five long years," he said. "Don't tell me you thought I was her pimp."

My mouth was still open.

"Pretty clear that's exactly what she thought," Tita said.

Booth's companion came up behind us. "What's going on?" she demanded.

I started, my elbow slipping from where it rested on the table, and knocking over the bottle of painkillers. When I scrambled to pick it up, the top popped off, and I got a whiff of a familiar, yet unidentifiable nasty smell. I started to ask about it when Booth bolted up.

"Who was on the phone?" he asked her.

"Don't start, not here," his female friend said. "Calm

down."

He grinned sickly. "Go on, then. Convince me, baby. Every second counts."

There came a pause as her face stiffened. Then she rose on her tippy-toes, and dutifully, slightly theatrically, she kissed his cheek.

"See, was that so hard?" he asked.

"Don't look so smug," she said, bristling.

"Like it or not, pleasing me is the key to everything, see."

She looked down and saw me watching. "Who are you?"

She laid on the tough girl act so thick I was tempted to say *Xena: Warrior Princess* but knew I couldn't pull it off with a straight face. "Rylie Keyes," I said. "I work with Booth."

"No kidding?" But after Booth whispered in her ear, she added with a suggestive shake of her ass, "I work with Booth, too, if you get my drift."

Booth grinned, his jowls aquiver. "She gets your meaning, Queenie. Don't you, Rylie?"

I wanted to gag in my hand, but decided this Queenie would likely slap me to high heaven. "Congratulations," I said instead.

She stared at me with a highly stubborn glare. I had the impression I had seen her before, not because of her face so much as her eyes. They were oval, angled, and hung for dear life from her perfectly bowed brows. French poets would call her *le beau ideal*. French painters' *création d'Art*. No matter the language, she was drop-dead gorgeous and by standing next to her, I was reduced to primordial pond scum.

"Congratulations," I said again, though I knew full well she had heard me the first time.

Her responding *humph* was almost a bark, as though her

mouth had farted, which I was pleased to note showed a flaw in my earlier assessment. Her beauty was only skin-deep. And no, I was not smiling. However, I was sidelong watching as she pulled Booth aside to say something close to his ear.

Booth hesitated, and then he said, "See, the thing is, she won't thank you."

"I'll break your face if you tell her," Queenie said through her teeth.

"Silence costs, baby," he said.

"Your price is too high."

Booth shrugged and moved back to take his seat. "But you'll pay it for her."

Queenie blew out a breath and joined him.

When the announcer tapped on the microphone and announced the competition was about to begin, I scrambled to my feet, crossed to the set-up table, and barreled back with a glass of water for Tita.

"My victory waits," Tita said, pounding her fists on the table.

"Whatz with the diarrhea mouth?" Queenie asked.

Tita grinned; it was not a nice grin. "Booth," she said, "how come you never told me that you had a dog?"

Queenie gasped. "You take that back!"

"Be afraid, geezer chaser." Tita wielded a threatening finger. "Be very afraid."

I wedged in between them, turned my back on Queenie, and placed the water in front of Tita. "Here you go," I said. "You might need it."

"Oh yeah, she's gonna need it," Queenie said. "Game on. Let's trounce this bitch."

Tita's nasty smiled widened.

When a waiter set down a bowl of wings on the table in front of her, I leaned in for a whiff. My nose went up in flames. "Omigod, that's hot."

"Stop worrying," Tita said.

The Roaring Wings announcer tapped on the microphone again. "Nothing but the hottest Trinidad Scorpion Moruga peppers, chocolate, red habaneras, and vinegar, folks. We at Roaring Wings want to wish everyone luck. Five seconds till start."

"Milk," Tita said in a hurry. "I need milk. Lots of it."

"How come?" I asked.

"I've never eaten Trinidad Scorpion Moruga peppers, but I've heard they're shitloads hotter than habaneras." She whimpered, froze in horror. "You didn't hear that. No whimper. Got it?"

I nodded.

"Get milk," she said. "Now!"

The crowd had closed in, stalling my progress.

Tita scowled. "Why are you just standing there? Hurry!"

"Ready. Set. Go!" the announcer shouted from the podium.

The contestants dove into their wings. I rushed into a wall of onlookers. No one budged. Beyond them was a sea of gawking and pushing people. I felt like a spawning salmon, swimming against the current, thrashing for speed, bouncing off rocks. Going nowhere fast.

When my knee bumped into something hard, I looked down to find a sleeping toddler in a stroller. The little girl wore a one-piece jumper embroidered with the name Dodo Baby. And—like manna from heaven—a discarded bottle of milk lay in her lap. I scanned the nearby crowd for the child's mother. No females, only men. All eyes focused on the competitors.

No way could I take Dodo Baby's bottle. *No way*.

Then a gut-wrenching howl split the air. It was Tita. I cut my eyes to the child again. This was wrong. *Really wrong*. But it was no time for principles. Fragile taste buds were at stake.

In a quirk of fate, Dodo Baby opened her eyes and smiled sweetly. I pointed to the bottle. "May I?" I asked, and she giggled. Necessity required flexibility, so I took that as a yes. "I'm coming, Tita!" I said on the run.

The frat boys were out of their chairs, bent over, and retching. Puke splattered everywhere. It was like running on oatmeal.

The werewolf was ringing his help bell. "Omigod!" *Gasp. Gasp. Gasp.* "I'm on fire!"

I squirted a weak stream of milk into his open mouth.

"More!" He clawed at me. "Give me more!"

Tita shoved him aside and, after clamping her hands over mine, she raised the bottle to her mouth, but still a meager bit of milk came out the nipple. I attempted to twist off the top while trying to wiggle free my other hand trapped beneath her death grip. The bottle tilted and the milk spilled on the floor.

On a cry of "No" the werewolf dropped to his belly and began to lap at anything white, which I'm sorry to say included some frat boy puke.

Tita gasped for air. I looked for water, spied a glass near Booth, and grabbed it.

"Give me that," Queenie insisted. "That Latina got hot sauce on my top. You give it to me, or I'll scratch your eyes out." She flexed ten digits with ten red talons. "Give it!"

"Don't—let—her—have—it—" Tita croaked.

Probably Queenie would gouge out my eyes if I didn't. Then I would be blind over a T-shirt emblazoned with skulls and snakes. So I loosened my grip, but the cup whipped back and drenched her face with water. *Oops-a-daisy*.

"Oh. No. You. Didn't." She came at me with those badass nails.

A hush fell over the crowd, and I swear I heard Booth chuckle.

Queenie narrowed her eyes. I narrowed mine. Her mouth lathered up. I started to apologize, but stopped. Funny how hard it was to say sorry to a frothy mouth.

"You are dead." She stabbed all ten nails into my shoulders, a ring of Jolly-Roger tattoos beneath her shirt collar exposed and straining from the effort.

"Oh, stop it, both of you." Tita body-checked Queenie off me.

Queenie's mouth made a sucker of an *O* as she flailed backward, her arms whirling, and squished—butt-first—into a huge bowl of hot wings.

Booth pushed aside his empty bowl, climbed to his feet. "Looks like I won. Maybe I'm full of bullshit, I don't know, but that was fun. Come on, baby. Let's get my iPhone. Here." He tossed me his old phone. "Don't say I never gave you anything."

"Thanks," I said, hoping against hope that he had left behind his SIM card for some evidence. "I owe you."

"Bet your sweet life you do." He strode away with only the barest of a limp.

Queenie followed him, her tiny butt even sexier thanks

to the two well-defined circles of hot sauce. Where was the justice?

Then from behind, a female voice yelled, "What asshole took Dodo Baby's bottle?"

Uh-oh.

~There is a fine line between fishing and just standing on the shore like an idiot~

I pleaded insanity to Dodo Baby's mother—strange, how easily she accepted my excuse—then I tickled Dodo Baby under her chin and left the tent. Tita managed to stay upright—more like bowed and humped. If she dragged a leg, she would be Quasimodo—as she walked beside me on the sidewalk. I knew she was a wild stallion to the core, but right now, she looked more ridden hard and put away wet.

"Sure you don't want any?" I held out one of four Roar Energy drinks she had received from Roaring Wings as a consolation prize.

She shook her head. "Keep 'em. I may not eat or drink ever again. Man, I was killing it until my throat closed. Two more wings. That's all that stood between me and that iPhone."

Physically, I was fading fast from lack of food or sleep, so I downed one of the energy drinks and pocketed the rest.

"It's all good, though. It may not be an iPhone, but I think Solo will be happy with Booth's cell. And you want to know the best part? I discovered Booth is on painkillers. So all I need is some real incriminating evidence, something not just circumstantial."

"He's no barrel of laughs." She righted from another stumble. "Watch yourself. He won't go down easily, you know?"

"Gotcha." I was anxious to get inside so I could look at Booth's phone without him seeing me as I knew he planned to work a shift at the FoY booth. I scanned the front of Shlomo's Deli, spied Solo and Gilad in a booth by the window, and waved. I grabbed Tita when she stumbled again and headed that way.

I was tickled pink about how my first dip into the investigative pool was shaping up. We pushed through the double doors. Solo and Gilad were bent over a table, combing through a cheese blintz with dueling toothpicks.

"Whatcha doing?" I asked.

"Looking for this varmint's cohort in crime." Solo pointed to a dead fly pasted to the plate in creamy cheese. The men resumed their hunt, trash talking the as of yet discovered second insect.

"Duck and cover, you germ spreader," Gilad said.

"Watch yourself, you low life. A new sheriff is in town," Solo added.

Tita's response was neither pretty nor printable.

The guys made room for us as I relayed the details of the hot wing competition. I slid the cell phone across the table to Solo. "It's Booth's," I said.

"Holy moly," he said.

We stared at each other then stared at the phone. In the background, Tita and Gilad were discussing the competition.

"SIM?" Solo asked me.

"It's there."

"Perfect, mawn."

I nodded toward Gilad. "Anything?"

He shook his head. "Tight as a tick."

I was still marveling at how Solo and I could communicate in few words when Gilad unleashed a raucous guffaw.

"Trinidad Scorpion Moruga peppers!" he cried out. "I swear, Tita, is there anything you won't put down your gullet?"

She shrugged. "Could have had an iPhone if Rylie had gotten me some more milk."

I was doubtful. Booth had been a hot wing-eating machine. "Fine. At least let the record show, I sort of took a bottle from a baby," I said and filled them in. "Come on. Come on. That's enough laughing. I gave it back."

"Empty," Tita reminded me.

"Tut, tut," Gilad said. "Guilt should be nonexistent when the crime is justified."

I looked at him. "You believe that?"

"Yes," he said straightforwardly.

I was reminded of his words to Elsa last night at the fundraiser. *Otto isn't here. He was too chicken shit to show up.* What did Otto have to fear? I wondered. A jealous boyfriend, perhaps? Now that I thought about it. Gilad and Elsa had been arguing a lot lately.

I looked at Gilad again, frowning, and saw him frowning back. "How's Elsa?" I asked. "Tita says she went to the ready clinic."

"You've come to the wrong place for that answer. Ask her," he said.

There was a sudden rocking of the table. Solo had shoulder bumped Tita. "You're off the chain, girl. Thanks for trying to get me an iPhone."

She managed a thin smile. "Rylie can be very persuasive," she said. "Seriously, *chica*, you oughta go back to sales rep'ing for Coca-Cola. You've missed your calling, you know?"

"Fat chance," Gilad said. "Hawthorne told me she got fired for drinking Pepsi while calling on Coke customers."

I sighed, more dismayed than surprised. Granddad had such a big mouth. Maybe it wasn't a good idea, having an honest relationship with a senior. It seemed with age came a sort of free rein to tell stories, even a granddaughter's humiliating blunder.

"In my defense," I said, "7-Eleven *was* out of Coke."

Tita rolled her eyes. "I mean, really, what choice did you have?"

"I can't look at this fly anymore." Gilad pushed away the plate. "It's nauseating, not to mention non-kosher. I think that yenta put it in my blintz on purpose."

"Well," Solo said in a clarifying sort of voice, "you did say something about her not knowing her ass from a hole in the ground."

"I was within my rights," Gilad shrieked, his bony face purpling. "I'm sick of being slighted. No one leaves what is mine alone. Hey, you!" he called to the counter girl. "There's a disgusting fly in my blintz."

"No charge for bugs," she said.

"Does that sound like innocence?" Gilad popped up and rushed to the counter. "Young lady, I demand a refund!"

"I better go referee." Tita rose. She was a salad bar of conflicting signals, tough talk, fragility, and protectiveness all assembled in one person for the choosing. "I need a drink anyway. What do you think the chances are of getting a margarita?"

If only. I handed her a ten from inside my bra.

She stared at the limp bill. "Ever thought about carrying a purse?"

I shrugged. "Go ahead, if you want, buy us both a chocolate blintz. Solo, want one?"

"Ya, mawn."

Tita grumbled something about being no one's damn maid and strode toward Gilad. "Hold up," she said to the counter girl. "Better watch out, he's a Nazi hunter, you know?"

The girl's eyes widened. "Holy smokes! Really? You must be a gazillionaire from all the rewards. I mean, it's totally cool getting rich by tracking down those murderers."

A radiant Gilad leaned a hip against the pastry case. "I did okay. Now had I captured Alric Mueller, I would have retired in style. A quarter of million would purchase a lot of Florida sunshine."

"I'm sorry about the fly." The girl then hollered to someone in the kitchen, "One *Oy Vey* special. We've got a Nazi hunter in the house."

Several people waiting in line to order food moved in to crowd around Gilad. He regaled them with graphic tales of midnight chases and violent gun battles, his voice loud and swollen with pride. The counter girl was bent over the glass, captivated, a hand to her mouth. And behind the throng, wearing a tired but protective expression, was Tita, even when Gilad finished one story and changed to another.

"There definitely is good money in hunting Nazis— probably why some do it—I've hunted down so many vile ones it's hard to keep count, so unlucky they were to be in my sights. I'm sure history will show the very mention of my name made many a men quiver," Gilad said.

I looked at Solo.

"Now?" he asked as if reading my mind.

I nodded.

He went to work on Booth's phone as something outside the window caught my eyes. The sun was still low-ish on the horizon, so I had to squint to see through the glare. I was about to pass it off as nothing, when I spied Leland, bondage outfit hidden by a baggy trench coat. He gazed around nervously as he hurried toward a plainclothes car parked at the rear police entrance. At the wheel was Alistair.

Leland had one leg inside the car when buxom Queenie crossed the parking lot to him. Huh? So Leland and Queenie knew each other. I didn't like it, not one bit. I thought it looked bad, Leland having another connection to Booth. Unfair guilt by association? Probably. All the same, it gave me a bad feeling.

My stomach squirmed as if filled with live snakes. I watched Queenie take Leland's hand in hers, twist his wrist, and draw a finger down his palm like a fortuneteller. This was crazy. "What is she doing?"

Solo looked up from the phone, blinked.

"Over there," I explained. "Leland is talking to Booth's girlfriend, though I think Booth has some competition for her heart."

Solo stared out the window, squinting. "Where? Oh,

there he is. I didn't know Booth had a girlfriend — Wow, she's his girlfriend. Sick!"

"I know, right?" I smiled at his slack jaw. "She's young enough to be his granddaughter."

"Yeah, that's what I meant." His cheeks were a vivid shade of scarlet.

Seeing them, I realized his remark hadn't been about their winter/spring pairing, but about Queenie's amazing beauty.

"It's shocking," he went on.

"Oh, stop it," I said. "So Queenie is a little pretty."

"A little pretty? Queenie is beau-ti-ful. Look, Leland is in the car now. They're driving off. Is that Alistair behind the wheel?" he asked, and I nodded. "Where did Queenie go? I don't see her. Get out of the way, everyone. Did you see where she went?"

Men.

"I got another shocker for ya," I said. "Booth is married to Happy Hye."

He mouthed, "Omigod."

I continued to search for Queenie in the crowd when something else grabbed my eye. It was Booth, and he was leaving the White's Jewelry table just outside Roaring Wings. Then he crossed the street, heading in our direction, appearing to fasten a wristwatch to his left arm. His smile was overblown. As he drew near, he spied us through the window and gestured for me to come outside.

He was standing on the sidewalk when I pushed out the door. There were still loads of marathon watchers milling about, yet I had the strangest impression of being on my own in the lair of a monster.

"Have you lost your damn mind? A Jewish deli?" Booth said. "Kosher foods? All those stupid rules. It's bad enough we have to eat that way at FoY."

"Leland only has you making a couple kosher dishes," I reminded him. "Plus, Shlomo's serves a chocolate blintz."

"I'm allergic to chocolate."

"Omigod, Booth. Help. Help. Not chocolate."

His expression soured. "Is there a grown-up around I can talk to?"

I dropped my gaze to the medical alert bracelet he wore alongside a half dozen other gold bracelets on his right wrist. "Is that why you wear that, because you're allergic to chocolate?"

"I'm not decrepit, see. I have a few allergies, so what? I'm gonna need my phone back. What's with the long face? I just need the SIM card. Yo, Queenie," he yelled as she walked to a nearby parked Ford Explorer. "Come back in an hour. I should be done, then."

She nodded, angled into the SUV, and turned the key. Though the windshield, we locked eyes, snarling at each other like pirates.

"What's Queenie and Leland's deal?" I asked Booth as the SUV pulled away. "Friends?"

His eyes thinned beneath his restless brows. "Here's a nugget of wisdom. Don't pry into things that don't concern you."

"But it does concern me. Leland is my friend."

"Meaning?" He dug a finger under the wristwatch to get at his rash.

"Seems kind of obvious, doesn't it? You set up Leland with Happy Hye for—for—"

"Just say it, Rylie. He wanted to practice S&M. So what? I'm a generous man."

And he pecked me like a chicken. "Are you generous with Queenie, too?"

His face went hard. "No."

"Never?"

"I want my SIM card."

I glanced over to the deli. Solo was no longer in the booth. "Unless you mean later, we've hit a road bump. Solo has it."

"Oh, yeah, we've hit a bump. I want it now."

Just then, Gilad in the company of a stylishly dressed older woman left the deli. Gilad paused to hold the door open for a man in a wheelchair.

Gilad's female companion waited a few feet away from us. She was dressed in navy tapered pants and a red double-breasted short blazer. A designer striped scarf (bragging label visible) swathed her halo of black hair. She held a miniature poodle, its dyed pink hair shaped in a pompom. It looked like a cotton candy cloudburst.

"A woman in Denver got fined for dying a dog's hair," Booth said to her. "Get a thousand bucks ready should PETA see that mutt."

She scowled at him, then at his rash. "I hope that's a flesh eating fungus."

"It's a social disease," he said with a heated snort. "Want to see if it's catchy?"

She glanced over to Gilad, who was fast approaching. "The only thing I'm interested in catching is a Nazi hunter."

"Don't get your hopes up," Booth said. "Even the best razors dull."

Gilad rushed forward. "I am not dull!"

Or modest. Or discreet. Or faithful to Elsa.

"Listen, I'd love to hear another round of your amazing Nazi stories." Booth continued to scratch the rash on his wrist. "But I have business with Rylie."

Gilad cut his eyes to the rash and paled. There came an awkward moment where he appeared to assess its infectiousness, the sight creeping him out.

When Booth barked his name, Gilad looked up, his eyes narrow. "You should see a doctor about that urticaria—that rash," he said. "Leland's party is tonight, so I assume you'll be working it."

"You assume right. Why?" Booth asked.

"Nothing important, but when you see Leland, will you give him my apologies for not attending? Sunny and I have plans for the evening."

"All night," Sunny said with a creepy wink.

"Easy there, tiger," Booth told him. "You don't want to pop a gasket, see. Penis arteries get brittle with age."

"Bleh!" Gilad said. "You cannot be serious. Sunny is new to Bellevue, she doesn't know about me. Tell her, Rylie, you tell her how big the hill is from your lake house to FoY. How I trudge those three miles at least twice a day, up and down, back and forth. You tell her, Rylie, tell her what fine shape I'm in. Go on."

"He is fit," I managed.

"There is just no denying that, sugar," Sunny said. "You're a Nazi hunter, after all. Oh, look. There is my rabbi. Hello, Rabbi Cohen. Got a minute?" she called and trotted away.

"Gilad," I said. "What about Elsa? Don't do this, please."

There was no mistaking his disgust: cavernous frown,

eyes pointed. "Elsa has herpes," he said. "She's dead to me."

Was I speechless? *Oh yeah.*

Booth chuckled as he stepped aside briefly for a passerby with a Golden Retriever. "In case you haven't noticed, Rylie." He pointed to his round visage. "This is my *I told you so* face. Score one for the rumor mill."

Totally. Yet had not that same mill said two seniors had herpes, which led me to wonder if Gilad had it, too. Or had Elsa got it from another man? If so, which one?

Sunny's voice rose to chastise teasingly the rabbi for his modesty. "Oh, you must know how very clever you are, you really must."

"You're very kind," the rabbi told her as the Golden Retriever doubled back to sniff at his pant leg. "Few people know that my father was a comedian."

"Was he famous? Would I know him? Had he been on Johnny Carson?" Sunny asked. Her poodle eyed the retriever as its owner tugged on its leash.

Somehow, the poodle wiggled free, released some yaps, and dashed for the retriever.

Sunny shrieked. "Duchess, no!"

But Duchess kept running, a tiny pink blur in hot pursuit of a rapidly disappearing retriever. People scattered to make way. Sunny grabbed Gilad's hand, pleading with him to save her precious Duchess.

Gilad wrenched free, wiped his hand on his pants. "I don't know. I heard the former French president was mauled by a clinically depressed poodle."

"Well, then," Sunny said. "Sex tonight is off the table."

Gilad held his ground, his face a riot of revolving emotion. I burst out laughing. I couldn't help it. He looked so conflicted.

"Oh, for Christ's sake." Booth thrust his angry rash under Gilad's nose. "Catchy, catchy."

Going. Going. Gone was Gilad as he took off after Duchess, with Sunny at his heels, leaving us alone.

"I want my SIM card," Booth said to me.

"Solo has it," I said again.

"Is he here?"

"He was." I pointed to the empty booth inside the deli. "But he's gone now. I don't know where. We're both working the party tonight. I'll see that he gives it to you then."

"No can do," he said. "I need it now. It's got my contacts."

I needed to distract him, so I blurted out, "You got that rash from the stinging nettles on Leland's hillside, didn't you?"

His eyes widened. "This curiosity with my rash wouldn't have anything to do with a detective needing to talk to me?"

"Sounds like they know you introduced Leland to the seniors who ran me off the road."

It was difficult to see guilt behind his cool facade, but I managed.

"Detective Lipschitz brought them up when he called earlier. I hear they're dead. No matter, see, as I didn't know them. I got their names off a bulletin board and gave it to Leland. So like it or lump it, I gotta now go see some Detective Talon and straighten this out."

"Then tell me this—" I began.

"This is where you witness my pissed off face. I know all about your silly PI fantasy. But listen, and listen good, I don't talk to amateurs, even when I got nothing to hide, see."

His eyes were challenging, and I knew he expected me to back down. I wouldn't give him the satisfaction.

"How about Otto's watch?" I said.

His look of irritation turned to joy. "Meaning this?" He raised his wrist to show off with some fanfare the apparent object of my interest. Only problem, I hadn't known his watch had been Otto's. Nothing about it appeared special. Not with its plain, wide burgundy leather band, white face, blue hands, and two crisscrossed flags below the twelfth hour.

"That's Otto's watch?"

"Yessiree, Bob. This is my first time putting it on. Not bad, huh?"

Hard to believe it was so expensive. "May I see it?" I asked. "Off your wrist."

"Why?"

Good question, for which I had no answer. "I just want to."

"Then you'll need to pry it off my cold, dead body," he said.

"You like it that much?"

"Hell, I'm filthy rich because of it."

"Twenty thousand hardly makes you filthy rich." *But I'd take it.*

"What would you say to fifty grand?"

I mouthed my best holy mackerel pie hole.

"Yep, just like Otto this watch is ancient, yet unlike Otto, it's a collector's item." He held it up for me. "See, it's a pocket watch. The weird band holds it in place."

It was indeed a pocket watch, and an unremarkable one at that.

"I think it's the shit." Translation: cool. "Otto told me not to wear it, said it didn't go with my swag, like he was a fashionista."

"Why would Otto wager such a pricey watch?" I asked. "Did he know its value?"

"Don't know. Don't care. But he brought it on himself, see. He'd been losing hand-over-fist all night, was down to his last dollar. The dumbass could have said all in, but instead he bet the watch."

"All in?" I asked.

"Never mind, what's important here is that he lost the watch to me fair and square."

"Leland says it's worth twenty grand, you say fifty. Who's right?"

He gave me a steely smile. "You're looking at one lucky son of a bitch, see. My jeweler friend offered me twenty. That's where Leland got that number. But that bloodless bastard over there." He pointed to White's Jewelry table. "He just offered me fifty."

I thought that was a good description of the man, bloodless. "Wow, why the difference?"

"Can't say," he said.

A hunch about the bet surfaced. "Otto meant the watch to be just collateral, didn't he?"

"It's called a marker," he said, giving nothing away.

"I suspect you were to give it back once he paid up. It seems to me a deal like that would need to be in writing, especially since we both know Otto trusted no one."

"Are you going somewhere with this shark tale?"

I refrained from remarking on the aptness of the word *shark*. "A note like that could prove you didn't steal the watch. Pretty important note, maybe important enough to cut off Otto's air until he is unconscious so you could search him. Maybe he fought back and died."

"See, if that was true—and I'm not saying it is. I would want a note like that destroyed? With it, see, I'd have no legal claim to the watch, speaking hypothetically of course."

"Of course," I said, thankful for the safety of a busy street. "Booth, it was premeditative, wasn't it? You meant to kill him, destroy the marker."

"One flaw," he said with a radiant smile. "My bad hip won't let me climb that hill, let alone climb from your driveway to Leland's garage. And Leland's tram is busted."

He slipped up! "I never mentioned that Otto fell from Leland's garage balcony."

"Too bad it's all over the local news."

"Oh," I said, deflated.

"Better luck next time, greenhorn."

I absorbed the smug look on his face as he left, and I absorbed his remark: *greenhorn.* I couldn't move. I went on standing there for some time, my hands crossed in front of me, my eyes on my feet. I turned, my doubt about solving this case rising. I walked into Detective Talon.

I stumbled back, apologizing as he reached out, steadying me with a gentle hand.

"Thank you," I said awkwardly, shocked by the comfort I found in his touch.

There came a lengthening silence as he stared down at me. His handsome face folded in, brooding, deep into a frown.

I looked at him in bewilderment. "Is something wrong?"

"It's the way Lipschitz talks of you. It isn't right and proper," he said. "You do know he was once in love with you. And dammit, he quite possibly still is."

Such concern, he must have written the Bintliff note.

"There was never anything between us—why dammit?"

"A detective on a power trip, a vulnerable suspect, and an axe to grind—never ye mind, I suspect it's better if I say no more," he said, his voice steady but worried.

His assertion intrigued me on many levels. Though loosely exercised, it was a breach of the age-old police code of silence. Even when guilty of wrongdoing, cops don't talk bad about other cops.

"I never encouraged Lipschitz," I said. "He was too busy calling me *bastard baby* to realize that at the time. You should know something else. I had nothing to do with Otto's death."

"No mind, I already knew you weren't involved," he said. "Though it makes no sense to me, you trying to persuade your grandfather by solving Otto's murder."

I raised my brows, figuring he had learned this from Leland. "I need his blessing."

"Answer me this: does the grape ask the yeast what type of wine it should be?"

Puzzled by this man, by how he talked in riddles, I stepped back, clumsily turning on an ankle. He didn't steady me this time, didn't touch me. It shamed me how much I had wanted him to. "I find you so confusing," I said self-conscious, a bit shy.

"I cannae fault you for that. I'm up to my neck in confusion. There is no rhyme or reason in why I'm willing to break a dozen department rules to discuss this case with you."

"Don't risk your career for me," I said too hastily, too coolly, as one does when skeptical, for police officers carried another burden, the binding pressure of their code of conduct.

He picked up on my doubt and gave me a half-amused smile. "My career will survive, though my ego may not be as blessed."

I forced myself to say, "Ego complicates things."

"Aye, while laughing last and loudest. Petulant thing, ego."

He continued to look at me with his dramatic eyes. I saw the soulfulness in them and thought back to his anger over Lipschitz's contempt for me. I wondered why it bothered him, why he felt the need to write the anonymous Bintliff note. Surely, he had more to worry about than me. He was a man of contrasts; I could see that now. The dangerous detective with a discerning stare, concerned stranger abhorring the ways of a hateful partner. I smiled, oddly becoming more at ease with him. But there was something baffling, even staggering about the suddenness of this change. I was entering dangerous grounds, I knew I was, but still I said, "Maybe yours just got out of bed on the wrong side."

"Innuendo?"

"No," I said, but it had been, and I turned cold all over at my boldness. I was acting harebrained. It had to stop. "Talon, why are you doing this? I'm more often the friend than lover."

He raised his brows faintly as though to question why. "Perchance it's the men," he said.

I had the impression he left off the words *that you choose*.

"Rylie, I'd like to know you."

Not get to know me, but the more intimate *know me,* which meant he was purposefully being lovey-dovey for grins, or for a reaction, or worse, to poke fun at me. But I did not want jokes from him, or kidding. Not now, not when it strangely hurt more than amused. I had a ridiculous desire to cry, but instead I took back the power with a faux smile, a tilted smirk. "How can I be of service to you, my good sir?" I asked with an equally mocking salute at his inappropriate jesting.

He didn't answer right away. "I won't press," he said at last, very softly, very kindly.

And it shocked me when I grasped in that quiet moment, in those quiet words, his sincerity.

"Promise me this," he said. "Give my words a chance to breathe. That's all I ask."

I pictured it, how stupid my constant confusion over him must appear. "No, I'd rather not."

Standing there, in that awkward moment, feeling a pang of regret when he smiled again and nodded, I studied him. He was too beautiful a man for a girl like me to hold onto for a month, or even a week, let alone a lifetime. "I'm sorry," I said, and he surprised me with an even deeper smile.

"Everything has beauty, Rylie," he said as if my thoughts were open, "but not everyone sees it."

"More Robert Lewis Stevenson?"

"Confucius." He stepped back as Solo rounded the corner. "I'll leave you to your friend."

I stood there for several minutes watching him navigate the crowd toward the station. He was so perplexing, so enigmatic. I found it all too much to take in, especially on an empty stomach.

˜I have the answer in my head. I just haven't found it yet˜

I caught Solo up to speed on my chat with Booth. He hadn't said a word as I relayed the sad news of Elsa's STD and Gilad's infidelity with Sunny, but he did a lot of head shaking.

"Just the tip of the iceberg." Solo leaned on a light pole outside the deli. "Color me surprised. I didn't peg Gilad as a slime ball."

"Yeah, but if Elsa didn't get herpes from him, then she got it from another man. That makes them both slime balls."

"But who is the other man?" he asked.

I reminded him of what Gilad had said at the start of the bonfire, of his anger at Otto.

"*Nooooo*," he said. "You cannot think—Otto and Elsa. Gross."

Otto and anyone was gross. "Exposing a germaphobe to herpes just might be enough to make him crack. Add in jealousy, and he might murder. We know Gilad is capable of killing, but we don't know for sure another man exists. We need to look at FoY's medical records to—"

"Find out what other senior has herpes," Solo finished. "But that's against the rules."

I grinned. "What fun are rules?"

It was fifteen minutes later, and we were standing at the curb waving good-bye to Tita as she drove away in her ancient Pinto Wagon to collect Elsa at the Ready Clinic. I decided not to mention Elsa's STD, as I feared she would have the tiniest bit of fun with the news. My Latina comrade deemed misfortune a lucky reason to poke fun.

"Do you think Booth suspects we're onto him?" Solo asked me.

"What Booth thinks is anyone's guess." I took a bit of the cinnamon bun he'd saved for me from the *Oy Vey* special. "He is just spinning a web of vague comebacks."

"He killed Otto to keep the watch, I just know it," he said. "Fifty grand or even twenty grand is a lot of money. Premeditative murder, the big kahuna, murder one is what he did."

I was more open-minded. "I wish I knew if Otto had known the watch's value."

"I don't think he did," Solo said. "Otherwise, he would have sold it. He always complained of being broke."

"It might have been his safety net, to use in an emergency, for a health crisis perhaps."

Solo shrugged. "One thing is for sure, without a witness to the game, it's gonna be hard to find out if he bet the watch or used it as a marker."

I chewed on that and the cinnamon bun, staring at the police station. "Solo," I said. "Talon implied—well, more than implied—he sort of came right out and said it. It's all so odd, but he is willing to discuss this case with me. Why do you think that is? Solo?" I turned when he didn't answer. "What's that grin for?"

"It isn't a question of why, but a question of why not. He likes you."

I let out a steadying breath. "But it's against the rules. I'm a suspect."

"What fun are rules?" he asked with another grin.

"Well, as far as I'm concerned the issue is closed. I will not jeopardize his career, which means we must get cracking if we're to do this on our own. It's already one thirty. So, what did you find in Booth's call history and don't tell me again to wait and see. I wanna know now."

"All right. All right. Check your cell phone."

I hit the power button and scanned my messages. "Are these last three texts Booth's?"

He nodded. "Copied, pasted, and sent to your phone."

"Omigod, you're brilliant. What would I do without you?"

"It's so nice to be needed." His massive arms crushed me into a hug.

I struggled to breathe. "Solo—you are—you're killing me." I gasped, gasped again. "Seriously—you're killing me."

"Oh," he said, jumping back. "I got sort of carried away."

I sucked in a deep breath and laughed. "I'm sure glad you're on my side."

His eyes twinkled. "So what do you think? Too cool, huh?"

I read the messages again, slower this time, finding it hard to see a reason for his excitement in these three short messages from only initialed senders. To wit:

1) CALL ME FROM Q.

2) I'M HERE FROM J.S.

3) ANSWER YOUR DAMN PHONE FROM H.H.

"HH has to be Happy Hye," he said.

"It sounds like her. And Q is probably Queenie, but who is JS?"

"Him."

I lifted my gaze to see Solo pointing a finger at a car rounding the corner. I looked back, confused. "A taxi?"

"Listen," he said.

Then I heard it. The sound of an engine squealing as the cab pulled to the curb in front of us. "This is the cab Booth took this morning. The squeal is the same."

"Ya, mawn," he said. "I heard it when I called the number. That's why I asked him to pick us up. Come on, we have some investigating to do."

I remembered giving Tita all my cash. "I don't—"

"Before you say no," he said, misinterpreting my hesitation. "Look at the time of the cabby's text. Nine forty-five last night, which means he picked up Booth from the fundraiser. Maybe he saw something, like Booth and Otto arguing?"

Solo bent as the cabbie rolled down the passenger window. "We need a ride to Fountain of Youth Retirement Home on Northeast 156th, between Northeast 24th and Northup," he told the bearded driver. The man wore a navy vest over white pants and tunic along with a bright orange turban.

"How much to you charge per mile?" I asked the cabbie.

"Two-fifty drop off. Two dollars per mile. Get in, please." His voice lilted with a strong East Indian accent. "You are my last fare. Hurry now. I wish to go to temple and pray."

"Do you take credit cards?" I asked.

He shook his head. "Cash only. Oh, look at that, a bird made a mess on my back window." He climbed out of the cab and went to work on the splatter with a wad of napkins.

I turned to Solo. "I gave Tita all my cash. How much do you have?"

"I used my last five on Gilad's blintz." But he waved a ten. "Tita returned yours since the *Oy vey* special was on the house."

Awesome. "Let's go, then."

We climbed into the backseat, finding it tattered and torn. I twisted, gazing around. Gray duct tape held together the headliner, while the driver sat on a worn out beaded seat cover. Draped across the front seatback was a banner saying: I AM NOT MUSLIM.

Solo caught my interest. "He's Sikh, a religion born out of Hinduism, without the idols and caste system. It's the fifth largest religion in the world."

"How do you know that?"

"PBS," he said simply.

I scooted forward and peered over the seatback, looking at the many colorful beads hanging from the rearview mirror, and spied the driver's name on the dashboard. Jaspal Singh.

"You go to Northeast 156th?" Jaspal Singh said as he clambered in behind the wheel. "That is most funny. I live very near there, across from Crossroads Park."

As we drove away, Solo told him about the dogs that had

escaped from the shelter.

He slammed on the brakes, whipped around, a loose end of his turban flopping. "Stray dogs are loose in my neighborhood, no! That old woman with pitchfork got crazy when that happened last time."

"Pitchfork?" I said.

"Yes. Evil woman, Ma Hye."

"Do you mean Happy Hye?" Solo asked.

"No, no, Ma Hye. Happy Hye is her daughter. We are neighbors. Their house is on the corner of Northeast 8th, very pretty garden, crazy people," he said. "Praise God if all the dogs are captured now. My daughter works at the shelter. Many dogs are stolen."

Solo and I looked at each other, both knowing why. Dog soup.

"Mr. Singh," I began. "Will ten dollars take us to where we're going?"

"Very nearly." He hit the gas, detouring due to the marathon before he stopped for a red light. "I saw you two this morning with the police."

"I had an accident," I said. "About the fare you had then. Where was he going?"

"Home."

This confused me. "Didn't you say Happy Hye was your neighbor, in the Crossroads Park area? Isn't she his wife?"

"Hope for his soul," Mr. Singh said. "Booth has new place. He visits there only sometimes. He has big plans."

"What sort of plans?"

Mr. Singh frowned. "I drive Booth a lot, but I want nothing to do with such plans, understand me? Why you ask?"

I shrugged. "Just curious."

He glared at me in the rearview mirror. "Maybe I tell Booth about you, maybe I find out what is up your leg."

My mind blanked on an excuse. "I think—"

"She thinks he's hot," Solo said in a rush.

What! I gaped at him.

"Rylie really loves her some Booth," Solo continued. "She thinks he's USDA prime beef, bacon-wrapped tenderloin, porterhouse terrific, sexual chocolate, don't you, Rylie?"

I didn't answer.

"And now with him leaving Happy Hye. That's what you mean by big plans, I assume," Solo said. "Did you hear that, Rylie? Booth will soon be free."

If only murder was legal. "Terrific," I said, my voice half-hearted.

Mr. Singh spat sideways. "That is you throwing yourself down a rat hole. Astounding. You American girls" —*Spit. Spit*— "you are most gullible. Booth is bad. He is most wicked."

"Has this wickedness something to do with his big plans?" I asked.

Mr. Singh braked when another light turned red. "My wife says it is not my business. I will not say any more."

"Will you tell us where Booth went last night? Please."

Brief pause. "Most strange." He appeared calmer with the change of subject. "I no pick him up at his work like usual, but at the lake. But God prevailed, he gave me another fare to the area. Grumpy man he was, refusing at first to get into my cab, waiting and waiting by a fountain until nine thirty-six exactly. Fine, I meditated, charging him for the wait."

"Sabbath," Solo said. "Nine thirty-six would be about the

time it ended. Strict Jews won't ride in a car until it's over."

I grinned. "Mr. Singh, was your fare a small man with a long white beard and a Jewish hat? Did you pick him up at a retirement home?"

"But how do you know these things? Yes, yes, that was him."

"So you drove this man to Leland's?" I said.

"I know nothing of this Leland." He maneuvered the cab off one road and onto another. "But if you mean the house with giant numbers on a sign by the garage, then you are most correct."

"One hundred and fifty-five?" I asked.

He nodded.

"That's Leland's!" Solo exclaimed.

"Did you wait for Booth after dropping off your fare?"

He shook his head. "Life is full of roadblocks. I tried to wait, but there was no parking on the parkway. And then a nasty woman with a garden trowel ran me off her private street. So I drove to 7-Eleven, came back a little after ten with a winning Lotto ticket. God is good. Forty American dollars I won. Booth was not angry about my lateness. He was not on time either."

So Booth had been late. "Your fare, did you see him talk to anyone?"

He shook his head. "He just pressed buttons on that machine for going up and down."

"Leland's broken tram," I said.

"Then he went into the garage." He pulled the cab to the curb. "We are here now."

I looked around. "But Fountain of Youth is several blocks away," I said.

"Ten dollars brings you this far. Pay me, please, and get out. I must go to temple."

I grabbed the door handle. "Thank you, Mr. Singh. You've been very helpful."

"About Booth? Let him go," he warned. "Stay away."

I said nothing as my heart had just tripped.

Zach, driving his old Porsche, had stopped at a nearby red light. He was not alone. His focus was away from us, but I saw a woman's fall of chestnut hair as she bent forward in the passenger seat. He was caressing a loving hand across her back, pausing only to run his fingers through her hair. When she curved into him, he kissed the top of her head, left his lips against her hair. It was Mackenzie Desmont.

They moved on swiftly, leaving only empty pavement, where so much affection had been obvious. I turned away and sat there, staring out the windshield. I waited to breathe again and for the thaw that would follow. But it didn't come. I didn't move.

Little by little, I felt Solo's hand around mine on the seat, and when I heard Mr. Singh speak again, looking at me and frowning, I managed, "Excuse me."

"I said do not wait until it is too late," Mr. Singh said.

I knew he was referring to Booth, but I wasn't when I said, "It's already too late," and climbed from the cab.

Solo and I were silent as we walked to FoY, our friendship enough to fill the open space. A bald eagle was shrieking overhead in the trees, and I could see a crow defending its nest with its beak that was inferior and yet victorious at the same time. It was an ugly and spiteful thought, but Mackenzie was that crow and her spoiled brat attitude that beak. That was how the heart, my wounded heart soothed me.

I had lost Zach to a lesser woman.

But from the murky water that was my mind splashed a sudden awareness where a minute before there had been only sorrow and jealousy. I had some trouble with this awareness, a kind of reluctance, denying it as absurd at first, considering it again, denying, but when all was said and done, I came away knowing I had never loved Zach as more than a friend. He was a safe friend, one I could trust not to hurt me in the same way my father must have hurt my mother: heartbreak so greedy, so devouring her only recourse had been to abandon me. Oddly enough, I found this realization—with its air of tragedy—calming, somewhat heartening. I may never have Zach as a lover, but always, *always* he would be my friend.

I looked at Solo, who walked close by, frowning and looking down at the sidewalk. He glanced over at me, his dark eyes heavy and discerning.

"Why didn't you tell me I only loved Zach as a friend?"

"Some things need to be seen for what they are, not heard," he said. "It's a good thing."

"A good thing," I repeated, meaning it.

"Plus, the timing is right. Life is all about timing."

I attempted to look shocked, though I wasn't. I knew what—who—he meant. "No, absolutely not. I'm putting one foot forward, not jumping off the cliff with a man like Talon."

"Go on, Rylie, spread you wings a little. You may turn a fall into a flight."

"Or I might crash and burn."

I was about to ask to change the subject when he stopped

me with a hand. "We never found out where Booth went last night."

"You know, you're right." I took out my phone and hit redial. When Mr. Singh answered, I first assured him I was not actually interested in Booth. "It's complicated," I said. "But I really need to know where you dropped him off last night."

He hemmed and hawed. "Pikes Place Fish Market," he said finally and hung up.

I pocketed my phone, pondering this further link to the fish market, and mentioned it to Solo when my cell rang. I fished it out again and scanned the screen. Alistair Barclay.

"Hi," I said.

He sighed. "Rylie—"

"You aren't calling with good news." I prepared to hear that Leland and I would soon be arrested by taking a deep breath.

"I've got interesting news. We located the Dragon Fresh driver. He won't be crashing into you again. We found him dead in the apartment. No word on a cause of death and no outward signs of foul play. Now to the interesting part, he was the Oleys' son. He was also a software developer at Dragon. And it appears he stole the Dragon Fresh truck from a storage lot. We found it abandoned. His fingerprints were on the gas cap."

I sat down on the curb before my legs gave out. "Wow."

"Medical records show he had a history of seizures."

"Do you think a seizure killed him?"

"We'll know more after the ME does his magic. Could be his breakfast did him in."

"How so?"

"We found bits of a poppy-seed muffin in his mouth. He could have had a seizure and choked. No matter the findings, it appears the Oleys had it out for you."

"Great."

Alistair passed on a warning to be careful and disconnected. Solo sat on the curb beside me. I relayed the news.

He draped an arm over my shoulders. "You're safe now." He looked anything but relieved. "It's weird, all three Oleys working together to kill you, but for whom?"

I had no answers.

Overhead, the gigantic sun frenzied the sky with glare and heat. Swollen, sporadic clouds shuffled from south to north, looking to link with other opaque vapors and drop rain. It was fifteen minutes later and, hot and sweaty, Solo and I finally reached FoY.

"Man, it's hot," I said.

As we rounded the circular drive, Solo crossed to the fountain Leland had installed to honor his great grandmother. I followed him, catching my heel on something, and grabbing the memorial plaque on a granite pedestal for support.

Solo looked up, his face dripping with water. "Have you thought about this? Maybe the murderer isn't anyone at FoY. Maybe it was someone else, or just a random mugging."

"My gut says it isn't random." My hand slipped from the pedestal, scratching my arm on something rough. I looked down. Someone had etched an intricate Darth Vader face across the brass memorial plaque.

Solo bent for a closer look. "Pretty cool. But why here?"

"Someone scratched over the Kupper family crest."

"What's the crest look like?"

I shrugged. "The plaque took longer than expected to make. It was put in just last weekend. This is my first time to see it, but I know the crest was there." I gasped and grabbed Solo's arm. "Mr. Singh said Otto waited by the fountain for Sabbath to end?"

"Why would Otto ruin this?"

"Out of spite. Remember how he was mad at Leland for putting it here. Complaining about how it brought back horrible memories of Auschwitz," I said, thinking ahead.

"Is that a glimmer of doubt on your face?" Solo asked.

"Yeah, I'm just having a tough time believing Otto could etch something this good."

"That makes two of us. This looks like the work of a real artist."

I gnawed on that a moment, and sucked in a breath. "I knew this guy in high school," I said finally. "His name was Brian Oliver Problem, but everyone called him B.O. Problem."

"Didn't that piss him off?"

I shook my head. "He liked it. He was eccentric," I said. "He was hauled into the principal's office at least a dozen times for defacing school property. He even etched a picture of our chemistry teacher smoking a reefer on the flagpole. His defense was always the same: the objects were already scratched and ruined."

"You think he did this?

"I don't know why I should, but it couldn't hurt to ask," I said. "I heard somewhere that he opened a gallery here in Bellevue, but I'm not sure where."

"We could Google his name. Something is bound to come up."

"Good idea," I said.

We crossed the grass to FoY's entrance.

Colonel Jeffrey Abbott pushed open the door. "Welcome to the Ritz Hotel," he said. "Have you any luggage?"

I smiled, as his mild craziness was harmless. "We're traveling light today, Colonel."

"Very good, miss. The front desk will assist you with your key." He swept an Air Force uniformed and decorated arm toward reception.

I adored the Colonel. I even adored when he occasionally assumed his late wife's personality. Nutty, yes, but the simple fact was he missed Ruthie. Here was a man who after fifty years of marriage found a way to go on without the love of his life. And here was a man who touched my heart by doing it.

"We're having some excitement today," the Colonel said. "Several residents are participating in a sit-in. They're demanding pie."

"No pie?" Solo asked. "Why no pie?"

It was FoY tradition to commemorate the life of a recently departed resident with pie, in great variety and abundance.

"So everyone knows about Otto," I said with the somberness the moment required.

"The police told me," the Colonel said.

"That reminds me. You shouldn't have told Booth about Elsa's STD," I said.

"It wasn't me. Ruthie must have blabbed," he said, blaming it on his late wife.

I raised my brows. "Ruthie shouldn't have done that. Health records are private."

"So Elsa's got the clap, uh?" The Colonel grinned. "Can I tell Gilad?"

I froze, feeling a flicker of guilt over perhaps revealing a secret. No, I decided, there must be some informational exchange between both personalities, the Colonel must have already known, or would have soon.

"Gilad already knows," I said. "But let's keep it to ourselves. Leave it to them to sort it out. Elsa and Gilad love each other."

He tsked. "I like that Scottish detective," he said, his voice lifting a few octaves that meant he had switched over to Ruthie mode.

"Thad Talon?" I asked.

"Is there another Scottish beefcake?" Colonel/Ruthie asked.

"I guess not," I said cautiously.

"It isn't an idle thing, attraction. There is energy about it, like a separate life," the Colonel/Ruthie said. "Men on the hunt commonly ask a lot of questions about their loves and even more commonly call attention to their lover's habits or follies, behavior so outrageous that one cannot help but grow to be love-struck."

Huh? "Colonel—Ruthie—are you sure we're talking about Thad Talon?"

"Of course I'm sure," sputtered out an indignant response. "The detective seemed fixated on knowing what kind of flowers you liked. He had his notebook out and insisted on an answer. I told him daisies, and he wrote it down like it was too important to forget. I knew you liked those from our walks at the park. I noticed how you always stop to pick them."

My heart sank. In truth, I had believed Talon was on my side, but now it appeared he had played me for information. But why my favorite flower? And what did it have to do with the case? I wrenched out my cell phone, readied to meet him head-on and find out.

"Those weren't daisies," I told Colonel/Ruthie. "They were weeds. I picked them so Gilad wouldn't sneeze."

"One man's weeds are another man's flowers." The Colonel stepped to the door to greet the fast approaching postman.

As I looked through my call record for Talon's number, Solo said something about checking on the rioting seniors and strode away. I was heavy into a scowl when Talon answered. He was chuckling.

"Ah, Rylie, just the girl I was thinking *aboot*."

I had intended to express my anger calmly, rationally, but my mouth had a mind of its own. "Do you really think I killed Otto? Smothered him?"

"He didn't die by asphyxiation."

So the fall had killed him. "For the record my favorite flowers are foxgloves."

More chuckling. "Good to know. No foxgloves at the crime scene."

"Listen up, buddy!" I was outraged even more by his casual disregard for my fury.

"Are you being cheeky with me?" he asked.

"I called to tell you that I think you're a jerk. You offered to help me, but in reality, you still consider me a suspect. Look, I didn't throw Otto off the balcony. I didn't kill him, or try to dispose of his body. Take a page out of Lipschitz's book and be honest about your suspicions. If you think I killed Otto, just say so." I uttered one of Gilad's Yiddish curses.

"Does your mother know you swear in Yiddish?"

"I don't have a mother. If you were any good at your job, you would know that."

"You've a fearful temper, Rylie Tabitha Keyes, not that I mind. I like a touch of fire."

"That's all you have to say for yourself?"

He sighed. "When I drove down your driveway earlier, I ran over some foxgloves at the tight bend. I wanted to replace them with your favorite flowers as an apology."

"Oh—" I wanted to say more, say sorry, but feared my shame would make me blubber like an idiot. "Well, then, there's another reason for my call."

"Aye?"

"Do you ever wear a kilt?" I asked.

"Do you want me to?"

~Even if it kills me, I'm gonna smile~

I was familiar with misconception, more so than a young woman should be. Missteps and blunders spoiled all my job performances. Even at FoY, I was trapped in a cycle of making do, of my own doing of course. I carried out work obligations with a somewhat empty heart and to all watching eyes that made me a flake. This was a mistaken belief, of course, as had been my rash condemnation of Talon.

With my feet cement blocks, I shuffled across the lobby. Get me near a large body of water, I would be shark bait. I stopped at the front desk, leaned a hip on the corner. Ivy Valentine, FoY's receptionist, was on the phone. Ivy looked like Dolly Parton, only with bigger boobs. Actually, I wasn't sure her breasts counted as boobs, more like weather balloons. She was saving for a reduction. I tossed in a few bucks each paycheck. It was only fair, as I figured she had somehow ended up with my allotment, too.

As I sifted through a stack of junk mail, a foul odor made

my nose wrinkle. I spied the source, bacon flavored mints Ivy habitually kept on her desk. I started to push them away, but paused at the familiarity of the scent. Then it hit me. Booth's painkillers had smelled the same.

I looked up when she ended the call. "Does Booth like these mints?"

"If there was a stronger word than crazed, I would use it," Ivy said. "No joke. He loads up a pill bottle with them daily. That's funny. Your eye just twitched. That can't be good."

"Fatigue," I said. "I've been up for almost twenty-four hours."

"You know there are over forty known nervous disorders?" She popped a mint into her mouth and chomped on it. "A tic can be the first symptom. Most of the forty are fatal."

Great. "Why does Booth mix painkillers with mints? Couldn't that cause an overdose?"

"Not a chance. He's allergic to painkillers. That prescription bottle once held the very pills that almost killed him. He carries it now as a lucky charm. Weird, huh?"

"He can't take *any* painkillers?" I clung to hope that my investigation wasn't circling the drain.

"Nope, totally lethal each and every kind, especially ones like Vicodin, Codeine, and Morphine."

I sighed, reluctantly demoting Booth to the bottom of my suspect list.

"Why? What's up?" Ivy asked. "Is this about Otto's murder? Reporters have been calling all day. Hey, should I put on war paint? Are you caught up in this?"

I cut her an annoyed look.

"Rylie kill Otto? *Oh, pleeeezzze*, I told Lipschitz. The asshole."

Ivy used to date Lipschitz. Then he cheated on her. Everyone has her periods of insanity. "Not that I don't get wet when I see him," she said. "He's so yummy."

Paging Dr. Freud.

The desk phone rang; she rolled her eyes and mouthed, "Reporter."

"No comment," Ivy said and disconnected. "It's a cliché, but one for a reason. That Scottish detective is hot." She waited for my response.

"Hot," I repeated mechanically.

"Technically, he's 98.6, but figuratively he's smokin'. And you know what? He is interested in you, sister. I saw it on his face, especially when Lipschitz insisted you were involved in Otto's murder. Omigod, just imagine those glorious baby blues looking at you across the pillow."

She fanned herself.

I shrugged.

"Sister, you need a hormone shot. Oh, guess what? Elsa caught Farley going through Otto's room last weekend." She was referring to Farley McCray, a local high school sophomore and community service volunteer at FoY. "Elsa told Leland about it, and he ordered her to forget what she saw. What do you make of that? Weird, huh? I didn't tell Lipschitz. I mean, it sort of looks bad for Leland. Maybe I should have said something. I mean, he is the law and all."

It was the *"and all"* that still had me worried. Something about Lipschitz becoming a detective so young and a timely sister-city exchange program to partner him to another young detective did not ring true. But I had no time to give it more thought as it was a quarter past three and my investigation was a fast-moving, ticking clock.

"Is Farley working today?" A quiet word with him was in order.

"He was helping the plumber earlier, but I haven't seen him for awhile."

"How about Leland?" I asked. "Is he here?"

"He was earlier, but for only a few minutes. Then he left." She hauled up from beneath her desk a carton of a dozen or so bottles of liquid vitamins. "Deliver the rest of these to the staff and seniors, will ya? I can't leave the phone."

"Sure." I hefted the box on my hip and took off toward the resident hall.

"And watch out for the wing over the kitchen," she called after me. "Some areas are still a real mess. And Tita rented a van for you to drive the seniors to Leland's party tonight. Aero Rentals is dropping it off later. Party blast off is at eight sharp. Crazy day, huh?"

She had no idea.

Even though I'd downed half of another Roar Energy drink, I dragged my feet down the second floor hallway, placing outside each appropriate door a vitamin bottle wrapped in a clear plastic bag and a tag bearing the recipient's name. I needed this type of mindless task. I was in a tailspin over Booth's allergy to painkillers, unsure of where to take the investigation from here. Gilad Kupper was my only thought.

I dropped back a step when I heard Elsa Utterback grumble something from inside her apartment. I looked through the partly open door. The news was on the TV.

Elsa came forward, relying heavily on an unadorned cane. She looked a century older than her sixty-five years, her face drawn, and her salt and pepper hair wilted. Her blue dress was a shirtwaist and plain. She wore a dark patch over her right eye and an anxious look in the other.

"Where is Gilad?" she asked me. "Tita said you were the last to see him."

I hesitated and another senior stepped into view from behind the door.

"Elsa, stop acting desperate," Jane Gettelfinger said at her shoulder.

"Be quiet," Elsa told her. "Haven't you meddled enough?"

Jane bristled, her ruby earrings flashing. She was a decade older than Elsa. She'd gone the same route as Joan Rivers by having her creases of olive skin clipped and tucked somewhere higher than her forehead. Her amazingly toned body, swathed in gym sweats, raised mental images of what Arnold Schwarzenegger's mother might look like at seventy-five.

"Meddled!" Jane railed. "You hit the jackpot when I introduced you to Hank. No doubt the finest night of your life."

I squashed a smile. One of FoY's most excellent rumors was how Jane kept a dildo named Humongous Hank under her pillow. Not only was Hank supposedly gigantic, but he multitasked with heat and vibration.

"That's a lie," Elsa said. "I never used that horrible thing. Not once."

"Then you're a damn fool." Jane Gettelfinger was rumored to be pretty well fixed, not Leona Helmsley rich, but well off. She had come to live at FoY several years back when her Lake Washington estate was being treated for black mold. She never left; I suspect out of loneliness.

"Excuse me, ladies," I said. "I need to deliver these vitamins. Only six to go."

Elsa white-knuckled her cane. "But that was Gilad's job. Leland asked him to do it last night. He gave him the box while we waited in the van. Gilad is with another woman, isn't he?"

I didn't know what to say.

"I knew it!" she went on. "He's always with another woman."

"Stop it, Elsa! Leave the poor girl alone," Jane wailed then shifted to me. "In honor of today's passing of one of our own, I must ask. Rylie, have you ever thought about what sex with an eighty-nine-year-old man would be like? Young lady, you're beginning to frustrate me. Do you ever stop grimacing?"

I should mention Jane is a nymphomaniac.

"So," Jane continued. "The news is some of the best-looking men have unimposing doo-hickeys. Nevertheless, just last weekend the vilest man rang my bell with his remarkable steed."

I was thinking of the tendency to use horse references when speaking of the male sex organ. Wishful thinking by both genders, perhaps.

Jane blinked twice when she noticed my attention return to her. "And land sakes alive," she said, "did he ever rock my world. Once I removed his kippah and rubbed his bald spot of course. But what are ya going to do? Turn-ons, everybody has theirs. Okay, pop quiz, girlie. Who was my mystery hunk?"

I muttered Otto Weiner's name and tasted bile.

She nodded, glanced at her jeweled watch. "Remember it all comes down to the doo-hickey. The rest is just window dressing," she said and breezed away.

I stared after her until she turned the corner.

"I'm sorry about your eye," I said to Elsa. "Is it serious?"

"Nothing that won't pass," she said, fingering the eye patch.

Due to an A in health class, I suspected the cause was herpes, but kept it to myself. "What was Farley doing in Otto's room?"

"Rummaging through his things," she said.

"Otto owned very little. Everyone knew that," I said. "Don't you find that strange?"

"Of course, especially since Jane leaves a fortune in jewels lying around, yet finds her adjacent room untouched." She shrugged. "All I can think is that he was looking for prescription drugs, at least that's what I told Leland."

"And he said to forget what you saw. Why?"

"He didn't say."

"Why do you think?"

She looked stumped. That made two of us. Then sudden tears filled her blue eyes—eye. Only one visible due to the patch.

"Are you all right?" I asked.

"It's Gilad. We're at each other's throats."

"Is that what happened at the bonfire?" I had to get her talking about last night. "You fought and he left."

"Heavens, no. We'd had a huge fight earlier. We were barely speaking by then. No, he took off to look for some stupid bats nest."

"The one near my house?" I asked.

Her brow rose.

"My grandfather suspects one is under our deck. Maybe he mentioned it to Gilad."

"Gilad romping in the filth beneath a house," she said. "Like I believe that."

"What do you believe?"

"It's no big deal," she said

I thought to her that it was *a big deal*.

"Gilad has his ways, and I have mine," she went on. "Everybody does, you know?"

"What ways?"

"To get even."

"It's strange," I said. "I've heard Gilad complain about the bats around the lake. He says they're vile creatures, full of germs. Why would he look for a nest of germ carriers? Could he have been doing something else?"

"I have no idea what you mean." She reached for the doorknob.

"You two will find a way to work it out." I hoped to keep the conversation alive.

She smiled weakly. "Yes, what crazy things we women do for our men. I shouldn't say, but I'd win an Emmy for the lies I've said to stroke Gilad's ego."

A sudden image of Otto Weiner on the television drew our attention. The photograph was of Otto in younger days. The caption—man found murdered in Bellevue—was an obvious lure for the viewer to stay tuned through the commercial.

I knew what I had to do next. Since the presumption of Gilad's guilt rested on his rage over Elsa not only having an affair with Otto but also contracting herpes, I needed confirmation of the pairing.

"My condolences for your loss. I know how close, how intimate Otto and you were." I said it sympathetically, watching her reaction for shock or sadness.

But her face broke out in what I could only call revulsion. "Otto and me? Are you out of your ever-loving mind?"

Her profound look of horror struck me as wholly genuine. I absorbed this switcheroo, wondering what to make of it. Then I remembered a lecture from my high school Health-Ed teacher. "Remember, students, always sterilize you sex toys."

Time to stop pussyfooting around. "Elsa, did you get herpes from Humongous Hank?"

The horror on her face deepened. "What a horrible thing to say. What is wrong with you? Herpes, I don't have any such thing!"

She slammed the door in my face.

Five minutes later, I was down to two bottles of vitamins, Booth's and mine. I was mentally betting dollars to donuts that Elsa was lying, but I needed to get a look at FoY's medical records to prove it. I also had a sneaky suspicion she lied to Gilad about how she contracted herpes.

But then, I wondered why she would tell him in the first place if her plan had been to lie all along. I gave that some momentous thought as I walked down the stairs toward the administration area. One possibility was she figured Gilad would find out on his own as he did clerical work for Leland. Also, there was, as she had mentioned, the very human desire to get even for his repeated infidelity.

I can hear Elsa now: "Forgive me, Gilad, please. I satisfied my jealous rage with Otto."

It was possible she believed that of all things to shrivel (pun intended) Gilad's fragile ego, the news that his longtime ladylove twisted the sheets with the grimiest SOB on the planet would do the trick.

Outside Leland's office, I used the key he kept under a potted fern to open the door and slipped inside. With the window shades drawn, it was dim but not dark. I sat in his threadbare chair and fired up the computer. While I waited, I gazed over his desk. Not much was on it, aside from what looked like bills. I shuffled through them without picking them up. I learned FoY's carbon footprint was huge: gas bill enormous, electric off the charts. Might be time for solar panels. The next statement was on amber paper with scrolled writing. With a glance at the computer to see if it was done yet, I picked it up and read:

POISON INK
TATTOOS BY QUEENIE, SPECIALIZING IN SKULLS AND SNAKES

The receipt had a close up of the Jolly Roger I had spied tattooed around Queenie's neck during our tussle at the wing competition. Beneath that photo was a description of services rendered; a temporary skull tattoo—scrolled in gold ink, and the time—7:15—scribbled in black. So Leland's connection to Queenie was his temporary tattoo. But I was still lost on his reason for getting one. Yet I knew the importance of not forcing an answer during an investigation, to let it surface organically from later developments, so I made myself file it away and move on.

I managed to sign into Leland's computer after only two tries. I thought his wife's name as a password was too easy for a genius, but I supposed a brilliant mind wants what a brilliant mind wants. Problem was, once in, I found no medical records in his folders, which meant I would have to search the paper records filed in the clinic. Since I was already online, I decided to do a search on BO Problem. He came up on page one linked to Absurd Reality, an art gallery near FoY. Interesting coincidence. I was skeptical.

My first call was to Solo, by way of Booth's cell number. He didn't answer. I knew he was probably trying to sort out why Tita wasn't making her enormously popular bereavement pies for the rioting seniors.

My second call was to Absurd Reality. A woman with a southern accent answered, and I said my name and asked to speak to Brian Oliver Problem. There came some loud throat clearing. Then he came on the line.

"Dude, call me BO or dumbshit, but never Brian," he said in a voice that was both laidback and stern.

I laughed, but it was a sad laugh. Lipschitz had called him dumbshit in high school. "Good to see we've both put Lipschitz's bullying behind us," I said. "How have you been, BO?"

"Fair to middling, you?"

"The same. So you own an art gallery now?"

"Prepare to be amazed, dude. I'm barely making my rent."

"I'm sorry. I hope you don't have to lay off staff."

"There is nobody to fire. You're talking to Absurd Reality's sole employee."

"Oh, I thought the woman who answered the phone—"

Maybe she was a friend or girlfriend.

"Dude, she was me. Bill collectors are such nags. Lucky you, you get to talk to the BO-ster, everybody else gets I.D. Claire. Get it? I declare!"

"Hilarious." I figured he would appreciate honesty, so I asked straight-out about the etched Darth Vader on the plaque.

Silence. "Oh God, dude, don't tell anyone. Look, I'm sorry, please."

"No, no, I won't," I assured him.

"Old habits, you know? It was already scratched up, promise."

"Did you see who scratched it?"

"Dude, he was bizarre, totally. A tiny geezer with a long white beard and skull cap."

Bingo. Otto Weiner. I thanked him. "I only wish there was something I could do for you."

"Dude, you can," he said. "Send any artists you know my way. It's not customers I lack, but art. No way can I keep up with demand. People are cray-cray for absurd stuff."

"Will do," I said and started to hang up.

"Sounds wicked, I know," he said.

"What?" I asked.

"The little dude," he said. "He kept mumbling 'work brings freedom' as he ruined the plaque. Totally wicked, huh?"

"Why?"

"Dude, I'm surprised you don't know. I mean, we were in history class together. Work brings freedom is a sketchy translation of what the Nazis hung on the gates of Auschwitz."

"Jeez," I said. "Otto was imprisoned there."

"Wow," he said. "Must be some sort of Stockholm syndrome. That's grisly, being so brutalized that you gotta mentally align with your jailers to get through it."

"Grisly," I agreed.

We disconnected.

The clinic was adjacent to Leland's office and accessible through a connecting door. It was locked, but after a quick rummage through his top desk drawer, I found the key. The clinic's medical records were well organized with a folder for each senior, so the hunt was easy.

I spied evidence of Gilad's stellar health, blood pressure amazing, and cholesterol low enough to rival a mild fever, yet I found no folder for Otto. Perhaps he skipped doctors altogether, maybe out of fear. Strangely enough, there were no folders for Elsa or Jane either. I thought of examining all the medical records to prove by a process of elimination that Elsa and Jane were the two seniors with herpes, but that would be inconclusive. And I worried I would be caught in the clinic if I hung around too long.

I turned and did a quick search. No haphazardly strewn folders. I closed and locked the door as I returned to Leland's office and readied to give his computer files another look-see. Then I saw it. Gilad's favorite woolen sweater hung over a chair in the corner. The chair faced the wall at an inconspicuous desk. A bottle of hand sanitizer and a stainless steel *Broad Exposure Germ-Eliminating Wand* convinced me this was where Gilad did his clerical work for Leland.

I found some folders in the tray labeled FINISHED &READY TO FILE. I lifted the stack and found Otto's on top. Hands shaking in anticipation, I opened his folder, scanned his cardiology report. Lilith Desmont had been right; he was on beta-blockers for heart issues. His endocrinology report: oral med for Type 2 diabetes. Urology summary: benign enlarged prostate. I read further and smiled.

"No herpes." I stomped my feet in glee. "No STDs at all."

Then I thought of a problem, scanned the date on the urology report, and found it current, dated only last month. One down, two more to go. Beneath three other folders, I found Elsa's file. Two knee replacements, inner ear issues, and—herpes. I let fly a quiet, "Woot, woot!"

Jane's folder was at the bottom. Finger to the tab, I hesitated, knowing without a positive diagnosis my Humongous Hank theory would be all wet. I flipped it open and gasped. Jane was the second herpes victim.

I did a little snoopy dancing. Though a sad diagnosis for both women, I couldn't help my excitement at having figured it out. Then I heard it—*oh God*—someone was opening the office door. I whipped around in time to see young Farley McCray running away.

I dropped the files back into the tray, grabbed the box of vitamins, and took off after him. I found the hallway empty, so I quickly closed the door and headed down the hallway. Just as I reached the turn to the kitchen area, someone shouted, "Hurry up." Then some frenzied goading arose. And a thunderous, "No!"

After that: gunfire.

~The first rule of holes: if you're in one, stop digging~

I raced toward the kitchen. A clash of shouting bellowed from around the corner. Then I heard Solo yell over the din, "That's dirty pool. You guys cheated. And someone untied my lava-lava. Now it's drafty."

"Stab him. Stab him," the crowd shouted.

"Give me a break!" Solo said. "It's not my fault Tita said no."

The crowd shrieked and another gunshot. *Boom.* I rounded the corner and skidded to a stop behind a throng of seniors.

"All right, coming through," I said, wading in.

Solo was up ahead and blindfolded. Behind him was a portrait of Leland's great grandfather. As I found Moshe Rosenberg's beadle black eyes scary, I only gave it a quick look, but it was long enough to see the many push pins speckling his arm and hand, and from one pin suspended

Leland's toupee. I set aside the vitamins and untied Solo's blindfold.

"Did I win?" he asked. "Did I pin the toupee on Mr. Rosenberg's head?"

"Not even close." I turned to the crowd. "Shame on you. You scared the daylights out of me. And you promised I'd be the last staffer you'd make pay like this." Long story, don't ask. "All of you should be ashamed."

"Lighten up," the Colonel said. "One of us has met his maker and still no pie."

"But I heard gunfire," I said.

The Colonel shrugged. "Wally tripped over his hemorrhoid donut. It popped."

I cut my eyes to the rubber donut at his feet. *Pancake flat.* "But there were two pops."

Solo tapped my shoulder. "One was me. I got nervous."

"And you almost gave me a heart attack." I plucked the toupee off the portrait. "All right, who took Leland's toupee?" No one confessed, so I waved it around. "Fess up, I'll see about pie."

This brought Wally forward.

"You better return it to his office." Then I remembered how I had forgotten to turn off Leland's computer, so I said I would do it. "So what kind of pie does everyone want?"

Bedlam. Everybody shouted a different flavor. Some wanted fruit, some wanted creams. Someone yelled mincemeat and the crowd gagged. Wally lobbed his flattened donut at the troublemaker.

While they continued to argue, I grabbed the box of vitamins, dropped the toupee inside, and Solo and I hurried away. As we navigated back to Leland's office, I kept an eye out for Farley and filled Solo in on all I'd learned over the last hour. It was a boatload of information and his head was spinning when I finished.

"Why do you think Farley ran?" he asked.

I shut off Leland's computer. "Dunno. But keep an eye out. I want to know why he was in Otto's room."

Tita stood on top of the prep counter when we pushed our way through the still grumbling seniors and entered the kitchen. She had a covered tray in her hands and a pissed off expression on her face.

"Lock the door," she screamed.

Not necessary. Gripe the seniors might, but none wanted to take on Tita face-to-face.

"They want pie," I said.

"No shit," she said. "But I'm glad you're here. You two can help me escape." She pointed to the open awning-type window at her shoulder. "The stepladder is in the mudroom and it's off limits 'cause of the crap dripping from the floor above. Any no way am I carrying all this food out through that dinosaur mob, so out the window it goes."

"Why not just rustle up some pies?" I moved aside a box of baked goodies to set down the vitamins on the pastry workstation. "I'll help."

"Sure. No worries," she said. Then. "Are you out of your fricken mind? I'm supposed to be at the Desmonts' in less than a half hour to prep for Leland's party. By the way, I rented you a van to drive the seniors tonight."

"I heard. Thanks," I said.

"No problem. I was already at Aero."

"Why, did the Pinto break down?" Solo wanted to know.

She shook her head. "Only the good die young. I needed a refrigerated van to transport the food for tonight. You know that Lilith Desmont has called me five times today. The crazy spigot is wide open on that chick."

An impatient *hellloooo* sounded from outside and a man's face rose up in the open window. "Remember me?"

"Crap!" Tita handed him the tray in her hands. "He's helping me load the van."

The man grinned. "Do you know what I make as a plumber?" he asked Tita, and she shook her head. "Probably a good thing since I'm now getting double time."

Tita whirled around, slapping her hands in *chop-chop*. Before long, we had all the boxed and assembled food passed through the window. Tita followed the last box out and disappeared.

"Can you give us a ride to my house?" I called after her.

"No room," she said. "Take the Pinto."

"What do I tell the seniors about pie?"

Her face rose up in the window. "How can I put this? It's pie, Rylie, not caviar. Go to the store and buy some. Use petty cash. And go easy on the gas or the Pinto will stall." She tossed me the keys and left.

"Let's go," I told Solo, striding over to the pastry workstation. "We're burning daylight." I paused, looked around. "That's funny. I could have sworn I put it here."

"What?" Solo asked.

"A box of liquid vitamins—and Leland's toupee," I added at realizing I had forgotten to return it to his office.

"Uh-oh, I handed that box to the plumber. I guess it's in the van now."

I shook it off. "I'll get them later tonight."

We breezed into the hallway and told the seniors we would soon be serving store-bought pies. They booed us. *Tough crowd.*

We strode through the building, heading to the reception area to get the petty cash. Feeling happy, we discussed how to tell Lipschitz and Talon the identity of Otto Weiner's killer.

"You should call Talon," Solo said. "Ask him to meet you for a bite this afternoon then drop it on him over—I dunno, Chinese food, or Mexican."

I liked the idea of telling Talon without Lipschitz, and eating something made my empty stomach growl, but I wasn't sure I was ready to call him. "We'll see," I said.

"Better to fail fast than go on wondering," he said.

I socked him in the arm. "All right, Cupid, aim that arrow elsewhere."

As we passed the employees bulletin board, we saw the flyer for the Oleys.

"This must be where Booth got their names," Solo said.

"Gilad, too," I said, absorbing the gravity of someone I knew wanting me dead. Though not close, we were friends. Then there was the fact that Leland was Gilad's nephew. Had he meant for Leland to take the rap for Otto's death, or had it just happened that way? There were still so many unanswered questions.

"You wanna drive?" I asked Solo.

"Oh, sure," he said.

"I'll get the money and meet you at the Pinto."

"Roger," he said and strode out the side exit.

Ivy was at her desk when I approached. "How'd it go?" she asked. "Seniors still mad?"

I nodded and asked for the petty cash. "I'm buying pies from the grocery store."

She opened a drawer, hauled out a metal box, and opened it with the combination. Only the box was empty, apart from a sticky note and an Abazaba candy bar. The note was an IOU from Leland. The candy bar was a peace offering for taking the last of the cash.

"Isn't he something?" Ivy said. "He feels guilty for taking his own money. Nava is sure lucky, not that she realizes it. The witch," she whispered the last two words.

I thought a moment, struck on an alternate plan. "I have a friend who might give us credit."

Solo had the engine running when I climbed into the Pinto. He gave me a pained look. His head was wedged against the roof, his butt and arms spilled over the seat, and his knees high to heaven. "Looks like my '*oh, sure*' to drive turned into '*oh, shit* ' I'm driving," he said.

I laughed. "There's been a change of plans." I explained about the petty cash. "Tally ho, we're off to Trader Joe's."

"Ya, mawn." He eased his foot on the gas pedal.

We had only two blocks to travel, but when he punched the gas too hard while making the turn into the parking lot, the Pinto stalled. *Los muertos.*

"You know I never swore until I started driving," Solo said.

As he tried to restart the engine, a Hummer screeched to a stop at our bumper, blinked its brights twice, then the driver leaned on the horn. When Solo threw up his arms and clambered his huge body from the car, the Hummer squealed in reverse and pealed rubber down another parking lot aisle.

I looked back to the next car waiting. I stared at the man behind the wheel. *Talon.* He waved, albeit unenthusiastically. I waved back with matching zeal.

My insides quivered as I pondered his reasons for following us, considering but rejecting the notion that he was in fact investigating me. It wasn't easy of course, as I had no other theory to put in its place, which made me wonder if I was being naïve to trust him. But for all his good looks, there was something quiet, unassuming, and honest about him. I suppose time would reveal all, and make me either sensible or foolish.

Someone was saying my name. It was Solo, bent and staring at me. "Talon must think you're still in danger."

My eye twitched again. I hadn't thought of that. "But that would be a good joke if it made sense. The killer has nothing to gain by killing me now. It's too late. Don't you agree?"

He shrugged. Then he wedged back behind the wheel. "It's a good day for Mexican food," he said, kibitzing, as Gilad would say. Steamrolling was more like it. "He did write the Bintliff note, so you sort of owe him."

I don't know what made me do it. I wasn't even aware of coming to a decision, but the next thing I knew I was out of the Pinto and heading toward Talon. He climbed out of the car. I put on a smile, but I knew it was cautious and woefully ordinary.

"Are you lost?" I asked him. "Bellevue can be confusing. Granddad says a drunken sailor laid out the streets."

"I know exactly where I am," he said.

My knees weakened at the raw heat in his voice.

He leaned back inside his car and came up with some

potted flowers. "For you."

Foxgloves, I realized with a sigh. "They're lovely, but you shouldn't have—"

His finger pressed softly to my lips. "I wanted to."

The sunlight glimmered off the hood of the car, and there was a gentle breeze through the cherry trees where song sparrows crooned to charm a mate. He moved his hand to toy with a lock of my hair, and I bit my lip, lost in the bottomless azure of his eyes.

"Foxgloves grow wild in the glens at home." He moved a little closer. "They drop their seeds far and wide."

"I—I know. I collect them, on roadsides." Nerves skipped down my back. "What you said before about understanding why I was looking into Otto's murder, did you mean it?"

"I spoke the truth."

I relaxed enough to smile, felt better for it. "Would you like to meet for an early dinner? Of course I understand if you're busy—" I caught myself, censured my silly, nervous voice. "Have dinner with me, please."

His beautiful face brightened, charming me. "Aye."

"I can get away from work in about an hour. My treat."

Slowly, inch-by-inch, he leaned closer. He had the scent of a man who loved the natural world, and for a wild heartbeat, I imagined us as one in the forest, stealing kisses under the noble cedars, lying under the canopy of leaves where the lichen clung.

And now his breath was warm against my neck, his lips against my skin. "My treat."

I thought of Talon as I had seen him watching me as he drove away, and the hint of smile on his gently tanned face, and I worried I was embarking on something I wasn't woman enough to handle. He was out of my league. He was the guy beautiful girls dated. I could go out with him, but I could never keep him.

"I've done it now," I said as we crossed the parking lot to Trader Joe's.

"You've done it now," Solo echoed.

"You're partly to blame."

He shrugged. "I think you'll have a nice time, and that's what matters."

"I suppose," I said, doubtful, but brushing it aside. In less than an hour, for no more than an hour, he—no, that would never be—rather his time was mine.

Trader Joe's was full of activity. My friend Kevin Shapiro was standing behind the storefront employee counter. He had mink-colored hair and his eyes were amber.

He shifted in our direction as we approached. "It's about time. Two months, and not a peep from you. Where have you been, Rylie, busy breaking hearts?"

"Be nice." Solo appeared to take him seriously.

Kevin gasped in horror. "Wanna fight?"

Solo's gaze stayed level.

"Solo, he's kidding," I said and made introductions. "How's your wife, Kevin, the kids?"

"Doing fine, everyone is fine," he said. "Hey, here's a story for you: a blind man strolls into a store with his Seeing Eye dog. Suddenly, he yanks the leash and whirls the small dog over his head. The manager shouts, 'what are you doing?'

The blind man replies, 'Just looking around.'"

Kevin burst out laughing. I joined in. Solo was not amused.

"Mawn, that's mean to dogs," he said, "and blind people."

"Cut me some slack." Kevin lifted a white cane from behind the counter. "I know a little something about blindness."

Solo gaped. "You're blind?"

"Totally."

"Then how did you know it was Rylie? She hadn't said anything."

"Lavender and honey, shampoo and conditioner, I forget which goes with which," he said. "Rylie smells great, I'd know her anywhere."

"Kevin is Leland's brother-in-law," I told Solo. "So, Kevin, how've you been?"

"All right. I guess with Leland and Nava separated, you don't see much of my big sister. Shocker. I don't either," he said with a small sigh.

"Then nothing has changed between you two?" I asked.

"Nope," he said. "So what can I do you for?"

I told him about the pies, and each time I paused, Solo said, "And no mincemeat." Kevin agreed to bill FoY, so all we had to do was bring our purchases to his office, which he pointed to with his cane as he strode off.

Several dozen pies chosen, I pushed the shopping cart toward his office while Solo walked alongside. We entered after a quick knock. Kevin wasn't there.

"What?" Solo said over my shoulder.

I looked around and saw what was what. In the corner stood a huge stack of orange and black boxes, floor to ceiling, all in various sizes with a Hermes logo on the lids. Thunderstruck, I looked up and down, up and down.

"This is bad, Solo, really bad," I said.

"It sure is crazy, but why bad?"

"Kevin was a kleptomaniac as a teen. Klepto, they called him. And he stole only empty Hermes boxes." Sick at heart, I sighed. "He's been straight for over ten years."

"Maybe these boxes were from before," Solo said.

I shook my head. "His therapist made him cut all ties to past behavior. He gave back or tossed everything he'd stolen."

"You're right, then. This is bad," Solo said.

I nodded thoughtfully. "What should I do?" I asked him.

He brooded a moment. "Be honest, I guess. Tell him what's bothering you."

"Okay." I groaned.

Whistling, Kevin strode into the office, rounded his desk, and took a seat with the ease of a sighted person. "I know you're there," he said after a minute of silence. "Hello, hello."

"We have pies," I said, stupidly lost for a way to bring up the Hermes boxes.

"Awesome," he said and pulled closer the Braille calculator on his desk. "Fire away."

I looked at Solo, and he shrugged.

Then came the sound of glass breaking in the hallway. A clerk opened the office door and popped his head inside. "It's just a jar of pickles. I'll get it cleaned up in a jiffy. By the way, boss, there wasn't a single Hermes box in the Dumpsters this morning," he said and closed the door behind him.

The surprise of that, and the sight of Kevin's face unruffled and free of guilt, had me shaking my head. I bit my lip, willing myself not to blurt out cruelly, "Kevin, are you stealing again?"

Instead came a muttering from Solo. "So you hide the boxes in the Dumpsters?"

Kevin grinned at him, then at me. "Now I get it, the long silence. Guys, I am not stealing again. I'm clean, I promise. No more stealing to silence the noises. Believe me, all these boxes didn't come from me," he said. "I've got the staff collecting them from the Dumpsters out back each morning. It's sort of a game now. A sick game, but they've no idea the significance of Hermes, or my history."

I finally found my voice. "How long has it been going on?"

"Two months, shortly after I took over this store as manager."

"Now you're freaking me out," Solo said. "Someone is out to get you by putting them close by so you'll be blamed."

"Exactly," he whispered, the anguish in his tone roaring in the murmured word. "Their goal, I suspect, is to destroy my career."

"You're taking this pretty lightly," I said.

He shrugged. "I don't have a choice."

"We always have choices," I contradicted him. "Who's doing this to you?"

He stared blindly ahead, but said nothing.

"Kevin," I urged. "Who wants it to look like you're stealing again?"

"Ya, mawn, tell us," Solo said. "Maybe we can help."

Kevin remained silent until at last I went to him and crouched beside his chair. "Rylie," he said, a heartbreaking gleam in his sightless eyes. "I can't."

"But why?"

"There's a weapon for every fight, and sometimes that weapon is silence," was all he said.

The pies looked delicious. If I wasn't so nervous about meeting Talon in a little while and worried for Kevin, I would have had a piece or two, maybe three. The seniors kept coming back for more. They munched as happily on the fruit varieties as they did the creams. In fact, it was only now with most on their second serving that I could get ahead of demand.

I had three plates of pecan awaiting pick up when Solo handed me a cherry pie from the box. With no one currently in line, I took my time cutting wedges and transferring them to plates. Though when I turned to place these beside the others, the three pecans where gone.

I scanned the vacant dining hall, hailed Solo, and asked if he'd seen who had taken them.

"Nope," Solo said, and when I still looked stumped, he added, "All the seniors are outside on the patio. That Kevin sure was a nice guy, and he sounded sincere about not stealing again," Solo said. "Wonder who's trying to sabotage him. I think he knows, though. What kind of low life would want to kill his career?"

I was arranging the plates of cherry pie on the linen tablecloth. "A sibling low life," I said. "I bet it's Nava. She's been jealous of Kevin forever. She thinks he gets more of their parents' attention because he's blind."

"Unbelievable."

I gasped. "Unbelievable is right. I just remembered something. I saw orange and black boxes in the Oleys' van this morning."

"So you're saying they're putting them in the Dumpster for Nava?"

I took a moment to puzzle it out. "No, I think it's more likely that they're taking them out. You know, I bet that's why Leland paid them extra money. He's trying to save Kevin's career. Even though he loves Nava, he knows what she's like, and he's very fond of Kevin."

"Aw, so nice," Solo said.

"I know, right?"

With the seniors eating pie outside, we relaxed a little, our backs to the serving table, congratulating each other for our stroke of luck at putting together another piece to the puzzle.

Solo's eyes went huge.

"It's okay," I said. "I'll tell Talon, explain about the extra cash. It'll be one less black mark against Leland."

Eyes frozen wide, Solo pointed a finger over his shoulder.

I turned my neck, my eyes narrowing as a skinny hand crept up from beneath the linen skirted cloth, fingered a plate of cherry pie, and dragged it beneath the table.

We both bent and lifted the skirted cloth. Teenager and FoY volunteer Farley McCray was beneath the table and beside him were three empty plates. The missing pecans.

"Taste good?" I grabbed another plate of cherry. "Let's make a deal. All the pie you want in exchange for why you were in Otto's room."

He shook his head, his spectacles slipping down his slender nose.

"Probably should have asked him before he ate three pieces," Solo said.

"You and Leland are close," I said to the boy. "Good buds."

Farley smiled a little, nodding his fine-haired head. Truth was I knew Leland saw a lot of himself in Farley as both were smart and bullied for it.

"I want to explain about being in Leland's office," I told him. "I know how it must have looked, no lights, looking through files. But sometimes being straightforward and investigating a murder don't always mix —"

"Leland didn't kill Otto," he said.

"I know," I said. "And I'm glad you know it, too. We're trying to clear his name."

Short silence. "I've been hiding from the police. Two were here before. The blond one seemed sort of mean."

Lipschitz. "The truth has to come out," I said.

His bespectacled eyes narrowed.

"I'll tell you what," I said. "Tell us what happened, I'll see what I can do."

He thought for a moment. Then he nodded.

However, first we had to serve more pie to a group of fast approaching seniors, while Farley ate another two slices. Anthelme Brillat-Savarin decreed, "Tell me what you eat, I'll tell you who you are." Farley was pie.

Suddenly Jane Gettelfinger pushed through the line of seniors and bore down on Elsa. "Where is it?" she demanded. "Where is Hank? What have you done with him?"

From the prep table, I looked to Solo, and he looked over at me. We both smiled. It was not a rumor of Hollywood proportion, but just as juicy, the seniors broke out in murmurs and chuckles.

"Tell me," Jane said, almost in tears. "Where is he?"

Elsa shrugged. "Then tell me the truth."

"Bitch," Jane spat and stomped from the room.

Solo strode over. "Why would Elsa steal Hank?"

"To get even, I think, for her, you know, herpes," I whispered.

A puzzled look came to his face. "Where was it again you found the medical files?"

"On the desk Gilad uses in Leland's office. They were in his finished tray."

"Finished as in worked on, information dealt with, stuff looked at?" He sounded worried.

"That's my guess since the tray was labeled FINISHED & READY TO FILE."

"Rylie." His face was now grim. "Wouldn't that mean Gilad knew Elsa had lied about the affair with Otto and the way she got herpes? Gilad would have seen Otto's chart, Jane's too."

Omigod. "Gilad has no motive. He has no motive."

"It's all right. It's okay. This isn't as bad as it looks." He skimmed a hand through his thick hair. "This is only a minor setback. We just need to move on to the next suspect."

Needing something to take the taste of failure from my mouth, I licked pie off my fingers. "What other suspect? We've proved everybody innocent but Leland."

"Then the best way to prove Leland innocent is to prove him guilty." He flashed a smile too cute to be insincere. "So far it's worked like a charm."

I let myself lean against him. Let it soothe me. "Do you ever feel like you're going backward?"

He tipped up my chin. "Not when the train is still on the track."

It took another ten minutes, but finally the seniors had their fill of pie. Solo and I were anxious to talk to Farley, hoping his information would help exonerate Leland. For example, Leland might have found out about Otto breaking Jewish law by eating pork and sent Farley into his room to confiscate his morning bacon.

The moment had arrived; we were alone in the dining hall again. All three of us at a corner table, Farley still eating pie—peach—and Solo and I sitting across from him.

"Trust me, I didn't go into Otto's room to steal," Farley said in between bites.

I slumped a little. "Not even bacon."

"Huh?" he asked over his fork.

"Never mind. Go on," I said.

Farley bent. "Otto hid something. I saw it when I mopped up after his toilet overflowed."

"Damn low-flow toilets," Solo put in.

Farley nodded and shoveled in another forkful. "I watched until Otto left and went back into his room. I wanted to show Mr. Leland, but it was gone. That's when Miss Elsa saw me."

"What did Otto hide?" I asked.

"When I hit the wall with the mop, a tile popped off. And there it was," he said.

"What was it?" Solo asked.

"A stupid looking watch. I told Mr. Leland what I saw."

"I saw that watch," I said. "It's the one Otto lost to Booth in the poker game."

"Expensive watch," Solo said.

"Totally," Farley agreed. "The next day I listen in while Mr. Leland—" He grimaced, looked down. "I hide sometimes under Gilad's desk, to read his medical journals. I would have asked, but you know how he is with, you know, germs. He's got lots of journals. I like the ones on bacteria, rashes, and plagues best. They're so creepy, especially the pictures."

"Go on. Tell us what you overheard Leland say," Solo said.

He scooped up a fork of pie; let it drop to the plate. "He called some jeweler about the watch. He said he was a collector of Holocaust memorabilia, especially stuff for a Nazi group called Death something—

"Death Heads," I suggested after a moment.

"That's it," he said. "Mr. Leland told the jeweler he ran a secret Neo-Nazi museum."

"That would explain the temporary skull tattoo," Solo said. "I mean, if he wanted to pass himself off as a Neo-Nazi. He could pull it off, too, with his blond hair and blue eyes. And of course, he's white."

That popped a name into my head. "Was it White's Jewelry?" I asked Farley.

He shrugged. "Leland never said the name, but he did tell this jeweler that he'd pay seventy thousand dollars if they could locate the watch mentioned in a boy's diary. Then he described it, Otto's watch."

My eyes met Solo's, and I could tell we were of one mind: Leland's great uncle's diary, the one who had died of typhus as a boy after escaping from Auschwitz.

"That so weird," Solo said, "Otto having an heirloom from Leland and Gilad's family."

The wheels inside my head spun, but I didn't like the direction. "Farley, what was it about the watch that made you think to tell Leland?"

"Moshe Rosenberg's ring," he said as though obvious,

"the one on the painting in the hall outside the kitchen. It has the same crisscrossed flags. Leland says it's the Kupper family crest, I say it's creepy."

"Creepy," I agreed, realizing my aversion to the picture was why I had missed it.

"Then those same crossed flags must have been on the fountain's plaque before Otto ruined it." As I settled on an outrageous thought, I turned to Solo. "What if Otto Weiner was actually Alric Mueller? Is that too crazy to even consider?"

Solo bit his bottom lip, giving it some thought.

"Do you mean the Nazi?" Farley asked.

"You know about Alric Mueller?" I asked.

"Only that Leland made another call about him to a friend, I think. Patrick something."

"Patrick Allen?" I asked.

He shrugged. "All I heard was Patrick, but it sounded like he worked for a newspaper."

"Patrick Allen works for the Bellevue Journal. He's Leland's buddy."

"He must be a good buddy because Leland asked him to print up a fake newspaper with a bogus headline, saying a Nazi war criminal was hiding in a Bellevue retirement home. He said to mention the name Alric Mueller, and to say the hunt for him is ongoing. Leland said he'd pick up the paper the next morning."

"What morning would that have been?" I asked.

He thought a moment. "Wednesday."

"And the poker game was Wednesday night," I said.

"Let me see if I have this straight," Solo said. "Leland masqueraded as a Neo-Nazi to flush Otto—or rather Alric

Mueller—out of hiding."

"Looks like it." I pursed my lips. "This is so complicated, but it fits. Otto Weiner was a Nazi in hiding."

"Fits like a proverbial glove," Solo said. "Now what?"

I glanced at my watch and gasped. "Oh God, I'm late for dinner with Talon. But—"

Solo took one look at the conflict I knew was on my face. "Go on. Go. We'll figure out the rest of the mystery later. Go."

I released a moaning laugh. "I'll be back in an hour. Thanks for all your help, Farley," I said and left.

˜Behind every damsel in distress is a fire-breathing dragon˜

Drivers stared at me as I ran down the sidewalk to the nearby Mexican restaurant where Talon and I had arranged to meet. Not a surprise as I was not only running in heels, straightening my hair and suit as I went, but also absorbing the sudden upturn in my investigation. More than ever, I was convinced Otto Weiner had been Alric Mueller, and with this development, new life was breathed into Gilad's motive for murder. Welcome back, Operation: Gilad Kupper.

A fire engine passed and stopped at the signal up ahead, and I recognized the firefighter in the passenger seat. There, for the third time today, was my first crush in junior high, Curtis Hobbs, now all grown up with meaty muscles and oodles of chestnut waves. Weird, how I hadn't laid eyes on this guy in years, but in the course of one day, since his arrival at the accident scene and fire this morning, I'd bumped into him all over the place.

A strange look came to his face as he leaned out the open window to watch me, an indefinable worry that reminded me of my own over Talon. I wondered if Curtis thought me pursued by an unseen attacker. I waved and smiled, doing my best to appear all right.

I had to say something as I came nearer. I couldn't just run past, smiling and waving like an idiot. "Guess what?" I said to Curtis, slowing. "My mouth *has* gotten wider."

He waited a few seconds. "Cool," he said just like that, seemingly unfazed by my long-overdue comeback to his criticism during our kiss in middle school, though his eyes were still serious, a little pensive.

I had the feeling he wanted to ask me something. Maybe why I was running or why I allowed ancient history to bother me.

"Did the Bintliff note work?" he asked out of the blue. "Did Lipschitz go easy on you?"

In a leap that I would later find both shocking and amazing, we were face to face, with my hands clutching the fire engine's window frame and my feet teetering on the huge front wheel. "What did you say?" I asked him once, then asked him again, more insistent, demanding.

Curtis grinned, and turning, he slapped the firefighter behind the wheel on the shoulder. "Didn't I tell you she was something? Did you see that move? Like a gazelle."

The guy nodded, lifting his fingers off the wheel to give me a tiny wave. I didn't wave back for fear of losing my tenuous hold and falling on my ass like a bonehead.

"What gives?" I asked Curtis. "What do you know about the Bintliff note?"

Curtis smiled. "Only that I sent it to Lipschitz."

I stared at him, my mouth open.

Then he bent and gave me a quick peck on the lips. "You can thank me later," he said. "We have six buckets of extra crispy getting cold. I'll call you. I've got your number."

How I managed to climb down, I didn't know. I stood on the sidewalk as they drove off. I took a step backward then another. Then something hard at my shoulder made me turn.

"Hello," Talon said, his tone impassive, but his eyes easy to read, displeased.

I returned his greeting, and then we walked in silence to the restaurant. I kept in step with him, wondering how long until Curtis called me. My fingers itched to call him now, and I knew a couple people who would have his number. Considering, I slanted a look at Talon, only to see his lingering displeasure. I decided to call Curtis later.

The restaurant was dim, like a north-facing cave. As the hostess led us to our booth, I got the jitters. It was at the rear, and very private, but it was cool under the air conditioner and the leather seats soft as velvet. I ordered tacos, handed the waitress my menu, and sipping my ice tea, I studied Talon's profile as he asked about the today's special: red & green enchiladas.

"I'm sorry I was late," I said after the waitress left.

"I should have picked you up. Next time I'll insist." His frown deepened. "I don't like being angry. It's out of character for me."

"Don't be mad," I said. "I'm usually on time—well, more often than not."

He smiled slowly, leaving me to feel I had missed something. "The man—that is, the firefighter you were talking to." His voice was pleasant, but there was a hard edge to his azure eyes. "Who is he?"

I took another sip of ice tea, watching him over the rim of my glass, baffled by the contrast of voice and expression. "Curtis Hobbs," I said. "We went to junior high together."

"Aye," he said, after a moment's hesitation. "I had no right to ask."

"Yet you did."

"Yes, I did. I had some fool idea you two were involved. It's not an excuse, an explanation. Now you've every right to be angry with me."

I shook my head. "Do you believe in love at first sight?"

"Indeed, the heart knows before we do."

"I don't think so," I said, shrugging. "The heart needs love, so it makes mistakes."

"That must be upsetting."

"Upsetting," I said. "I loved Curtis Hobbs once, with a twelve-year-old heart. It made a mistake. And with Zach—" I turned toward Talon, but when our eyes met and I saw the sharpness return, I switched subjects. "Tell me about the sister city exchange program."

He studied his water glass. "I'm here to learn your investigative ways, show you ours."

"What Scottish city is it?"

He blinked, blinked again. "You wouldn't know it. It's barely more than a village."

There was something there, something evasive and wary mixed in with his gentle dismissal. "Are you—are you hiding something?"

"I don't think I like where this is going, Rylie."

"Me, either," I said, shaking my head. "I was just hoping you were a spy."

A smile crept across his face. "Who do you wish me to spy on?"

I didn't have to think. "Lipschitz," I said through my bubbling laugher. "People who hate butterflies should always be on someone's watch list."

"Beautiful creatures, butterflies," he said, not laughing. Then he leaned over and touched his lips to mine. "As are you. You're truly lovely."

Flustered, flattered, I blurted out, "Gilad Kupper killed Otto Weiner."

"Did he now? You better fill me in," he said.

I told him everything while we ate our meal, how Otto Weiner was a Nazi, how Gilad must have tried to subdue him with the plastic bag, only to have him fall over the rail to his death. I explained Leland's deception in order to flush out Otto, going over things he already knew like the poker game and how Booth won the watch.

His arm rested on the seatback, his fingers playing with the tips of my hair. He listened, treating me like a colleague, nodding, asking for more details, clarifications. And in his eyes, those exquisite eyes, I saw validation, something I had not realized until now I badly needed.

"The way I see it," I went on, "White's Jewelry must be part of some kind of underground network that helps Nazi war criminals find safe havens. And Otto was using the Kupper family's twenty thousand dollar watch to finance his escape."

"'Tis possible, if not likely," he said. "The owner of White's Jewelry has been suspected of sympathizing with Neo-Nazis for awhile, but we have nothing certain. The man is also law abiding, with a family, and a dog."

"Let me guess, a white dog," I said.

He nodded.

"Otto wanted Booth to take the watch to them," I went on, "but instead he took it to his jeweler friend."

"Ah, that'll be the reason for the theft charges Otto threatened to file against Booth."

"He wanted the watch back," I said. "Maybe that's why he came to the bonfire, to try to convince Booth to hand it over. But why didn't he just take the watch to White's himself?"

"It's unlikely they wanted any link to him in the event of his capture. Though a touch roundabout, and as Otto learned, uncertain, Booth selling the watch to White's created distance."

A thought struck me. "Could you ask the coroner to x-ray Otto's hand?"

"What exactly are you looking for?"

"Bone damage," I said. "Otto said his scar was from a bullet wound."

"But you don't think so?"

"I think that's where a Death Head skull tattoo had been—until he burned it off."

"You're quite good at this, Rylie, quite natural."

Then he smiled, easy and warm in itself, but the respect it held meant so much. Rendered speechless, I managed to smile back, a simple smile that I knew could never match the happiness inside me.

We were still grinning at each other when the waitress cleared our plates, and the moment was lost. I couldn't look over at him again, not just yet, not when the depth of those blue eyes made me question what I'd always wanted from a man: stability, faithfulness. And above all, a vow of permanence.

But I could gaze at his hands, his lean fingers on his water glass that drove me to wonder the feel of them against my skin. I reminded myself that that pleasure would be temporary and took another sip of ice tea. "You know I originally thought Gilad had killed Otto over Elsa Utterback."

"What changed?" he asked.

"I found out he knew Elsa and Otto hadn't had an affair." And then I told him about Gilad's anger with her at the marathon, about his two-timing tryst with Sunny, and Booth goading him with the rash.

"What was that, the name Gilad call Booth's rash?" he asked.

"Urtic something."

"Urticaria?" he asked.

I nodded. "Gilad was afraid it was contagious. He lost all color at seeing it."

Talon ran his finger around the rim of his glass. "Rylie, if Gilad knew enough to call urticaria by name, I suspect he also knew it wasn't contagious. Where was this rash again?"

I didn't know what to make of this shift. "On his forearm and wrist, the left one."

"And Booth wore Otto's watch on which arm, left or right?"

"Left." I almost gaped at him in horror. "You think Gilad's shock was over the watch, over realizing he'd been living with the man he'd hunted all this life?"

Talon didn't say anything. He sat beside me, his eyes narrowed, staring ahead.

"And since it looks like at the time of Otto's murder, Gilad didn't know he was Nazi," I said. "Gilad had no motive to kill him."

"It would seem."

"It would seem," I repeated, and then at a sudden confirming thought. "I also missed when Farley mentioned Gilad had medical journals, one on rashes in particular. I missed both clues, dammit."

"Farley McCray? The laddie who told Leland about Otto's hidden watch?" he said, still not looking at me. "I should think the quarter million dollar reward for Alric Mueller would buy a bit of time for a chemist bent on putting right an anti frailty drug."

"Oh God, everything I do makes Leland look guiltier." I balled my hands on my thighs.

He covered my hand with his, held it—securely, resolutely—as though he feared without him, I would fall apart. "I'm sorry, Rylie."

For all the comfort his touch gave me, I realized it also made me weak. I doubted I could ever stop my heart searching for someone to take care of me if I didn't somehow find the strength to do it myself.

I tugged free, hesitating only as our fingertips slipped apart. "I'll be fine." But since my hand felt suddenly cold, I grasped the other in my lap. "I'll be okay."

Still, he didn't face me.

"Talon, I refuse to give up," I said.

"You mustn't," he said. "All the same, perhaps stop rushing so much."

"Until I have my grandfather's blessing, I have no choice but to rush." I slid across the seat and stood. "I will solve

Otto's murder, and I will do it before noon tomorrow."

He didn't get up to say good-bye, only lifted his chin to look at me—*finally*. "It will go easier for Leland if he turns himself in."

I swallowed an oath. "You're going to arrest him?"

"I must. The evidence—I have to."

I looked down at my feet. "Check, please," I said to the passing waitress, handing her my credit card. "Poor Leland."

Talon shifted his gaze. "He needs you."

I took that to mean Leland, but there was an odd tension around his mouth. It moved up to his eyes.

"Don't worry about Leland. I'll find him," I said. "I'll tell him to turn himself in."

"First rule in investigating: never assume." He rose from the booth, turned me toward the door. There, a man stood, squinting against the dim light and looking around. It was Zach.

I hurried to him. "What's wrong? Are you okay?"

"Solo told me where to find you." He led me outside, where he took what sounded like a careful breath. "I have to tell you something. And I have to tell you now before I change my mind. I've finally realized a way to make the guilt go away. I only wish I'd realized sooner. I've found who makes everything better. I've found where I'm needed."

"Mackenzie needs you. You need her. That's the way it's supposed to be." I grabbed his hand. "I wish you happiness, both of you."

His laugh was quick and easy. "There's nothing serious between Mackenzie and me."

It made no difference, I decided. He was my best friend. He would be for life. "But I thought—" I began. "It's just that I saw you together, earlier, on Northeast 24th near FoY."

"I was driving her home, and she was upset about something her mother had said. I was comforting her," he said. "Rylie, I'm entering the seminary."

I hesitated a moment. Then: "As in becoming a—"

"Priest," he finished, his gray eyes twinkling.

This announcement was so unexpected, so abrupt that I was taken aback, and more than a little bewildered. How could I respond? What could I say? I knew nothing of religion, nothing of its power, of its push or pull on people. But I could imagine, despite my shock and ignorance, how positive this change would be for him. The budding joy in his eyes told me so. Gone was the hurt, the anguish, but still the guilt lingered on the fringe. Guilt was like grief, I suspected, something we never get over, just get on.

I found him watching me, and I hesitated again before saying, "I'm happy for you, Zach."

I had paled, I supposed, and he saw it. "I know it's sudden, but it's the right thing to do. It's the right thing for me," he said. "But first I'm going to get help for my PTSD."

"That's a good decision." I was still too stunned to say more.

"Both are good decisions." Glancing over my shoulder, his eyes narrowed. "Talon."

"Zach," Talon said, coming up behind me.

He stood so close I could feel him at my back.

"You're here. We're here." Talon brushed a tender hand down my arm. "Any problem?"

There it was again, in his eyes: displeasure.

"Thank you for dinner, Talon." I wanted to give him an

easy exit, but he stayed where he was, warm against me, and a possessive hand to my wrist, where he pushed a credit card into my hand.

"To thank me for dinner, you first must let me pay." He brushed his lips against mine. "Take heart, lass, as learning which bridge to cross and which to burn is what makes life interesting. I'll be in touch."

But as he moved to leave, Zach stopped him with a hand to his arm. And when I saw the worry and warning in Zach's eyes, I covered his hand with mine. "I don't need protection. I'm a grown woman."

After a brief war of emotion in his eyes, Zach dropped his hand. Talon said nothing and left, leaving us alone on the sidewalk.

"You know he's probably not the forever kind of guy," Zach said.

I watched Talon drive away. "Maybe," I said, wondering. "But I'll drive him crazy long before that."

He smiled, and the smiled bubbled into a laugh. "God help him."

I looked up, saw hope on his face, and smiled, too. "I'm going to miss you."

He dragged his late father's crucifix over his head. "For when I'm not here to keep you safe," he said, handing me the cross.

The worry on his face was so him, so Zach, so I took it, closing my hand around it. "You're going to be a great priest," I said.

He only nodded.

"Over there, look."

"Where?"

"GPS says it's the house on the corner." I pointed out the driver's side window as Solo pulled the Pinto to the curb across the street. "Maybe we should park one house up so we can watch without being spotted."

"Roger that," he said, nodding.

Fifteen minutes earlier, Zach had driven me back to FoY—with the promise of meeting up later—and then Solo and I rushed off in the Pinto to the address listed on the Poison Ink receipt. I caught Solo up to speed while we drove.

He switched off the ignition. "Just think about it for a minute. Father Zach O'Neil. Crazy, mawn," he said. "And how are you about it? Cool?"

I knew, somehow, it was for the best. "I'm not a martyr but God help me I'd have found a way to accept him and Mackenzie," I said. "What matters is Zach learns to forgive himself for killing that man at the robbery. If being a priest gives him that, I'm behind him."

"Isn't that what friends do?"

"Precisely."

Solo shot a glance over his shoulder, out the rear window to the corner house. "So why do we think Leland will be coming here?"

I checked my watch. "The receipt from Queenie was written in gold ink, but seven fifteen—five minutes from now—was scribbled in black. And it looked like Leland's handwriting."

"Makes sense he'd want to get rid of the tattoo before tonight's party," he said. "Especially with Otto dead and his plan spoiled. Queenie must work out of her house."

I nodded. "It was a leap, but one I need to make to find Leland before Lipschitz or Talon. That's some tall fence."

"It's scary, walled off like that. Looks like a fortress. Nice flowers near the garage, though. Foxgloves?" He grinned, and nodded several times toward the backseat where the foxgloves Talon had given me were. "Dinner good?"

"Very nice."

"And the company?"

I sighed. "Dangerously tempting."

"It's funny to think how much has changed in one day," he said seriously despite the smile. "And we've still hours to go. What do you think the night will hold?"

I hesitated, and when tamer words to describe the shamefully intimate image of Talon and me in my head didn't come, I shrugged. "The name of Otto's murderer would be nice."

"I really liked Operation: Gilad Kupper."

"Yeah." I laughed half-heartedly. "Now all we have is Operation: No Name."

"Something will turn up," he said. "The blessings of the mandala won't let us down."

"Hope so."

"First we tell Leland to turn himself in," he said in a slow, matter-of-fact way. "Then we regroup our investigation."

"Roger that, mawn," I said in a silly imitation of him as I looked around.

The eastside of Bellevue was a gridlock of homes more modest—*much more modest*—than Westside homes. The houses were unassuming, wood-sided ramblers. The yards were simple, and the views of Lake Sammamish and the Cascades Mountains mostly peak-a-boo.

Solo rolled down the window. "There's that smell again."

I took a whiff. "Gives me chills to think it's dog soup. Which house is it coming from?"

He shrugged. "Crossroads Animal Shelter backs up to this street."

"Didn't Mr. Singh say Happy Hye lived in this neighborhood?"

"On the corner of Northeast 8th," he said.

I looked through the back window to the nearby cross street. "That's Northeast 8th," I said.

"Yeah, but it has lots of cross streets. Chances are Happy Hye lives on one of those," he said. "I wish Curtis Hobbs would call. I'm dying to know what he has on Lipschitz."

Bothered by how easily I had stopped thinking about that mystery, I dialed the number of a mutual friend, but got no answer. But after a call to another friend, I had Curtis's number.

"If the mountain will not come to Mohammed, Mohammed will go to the mountain," I said as I dialed.

Anticipation was spinning toward annoyance as it kept ringing and ringing, only to finally switch to voicemail. I left a polite but brief message to call me.

When an SUV just like Queenie owned pulled into the driveway of the house on the corner, I gazed out the back window, while Solo watched via the side mirror. Queenie climbed from behind the wheel, and Leland—looking spiffy in black trousers and a silky shirt—jumped down from the passenger seat. Together they strode through a side gate and appeared to enter the house by way of a side door just beyond.

"Your hunch paid off," Solo said.

"Pure dumb luck." I grabbed the door handle. "Let's go."

I had a foot to the curb when Queenie's garage door rolled up and an ancient Asian woman with a wrinkled face strode to the mailbox. She carried a pitchfork.

"Uh-oh," I said, sighing. "More dumb luck."

"Are you kidding me? That can't be Happy Hye's mother."

I did a quick white pages search on my phone. "It's her," I said, wondering at the connection to Queenie.

"It's settled, then," Solo said. "We'll wait here until Leland's done. Then talk to him."

"Good plan." I eyed the woman's pitchfork as she dug up some herbs—cilantro, maybe—and trudged back toward the house.

A miniature dachshund bolted past her from the garage, but with only three legs, it went *splat*. She scooped it up with a hawk-like swoop, and when it struggled and barked, she silenced it with a hand clamped over its tiny snout. She entered the garage, only to leave seconds later with something fisted in one hand—*not the dog*—and the pitchfork in the other, before she disappeared through the tall gate to the front yard.

"Poor little doggie," Solo said.

"It matches the description of the dog Leland said Happy Hye was kicking."

"What should we do?" he asked.

I didn't think long. "Rescue it."

We climbed from the Pinto, crept down the sidewalk, and crouched behind Queenie's Explorer. I figured no one inside could see us, not with the windows barely visible due to the high fence around the entire house that left only the garage accessible from the street.

As we neared the garage, the smell of soup intensified. In the corner, a steaming kettle on a self-standing camp stove simmered over a low flame. We looked around for the dog but saw only half-empty garage-type storage shelves, well-used yard equipment, a refrigerator, a box of Fourth of July firecrackers, and the cilantro discarded on a wooden chopping block.

When a huge *bang* sounded from the vicinity of the front yard, I started. Some high-pitched wicked witch crackling followed the explosion.

"Artillery shells," Solo whispered, pointing to the box of fireworks. "Sounds like the old woman is setting them off in the front yard."

The door from garage to house inched open, and we froze, watching a fine-boned milky chocolate hand snake around to press a button along the doorjamb. The garage door sprang into action, rolling down and shutting us inside. The hand disappeared, but left the door ajar.

"Sorry about that," said Queenie's voice. "Looks like Ma Hye is back at it again."

"What's she doing?" Leland asked.

"Blowing up moles and shit. Just be happy I closed the garage door. Now let me have a look at that hand. I'll have that tattoo gone soon enough."

Solo stepped forward, but I grabbed his arm and pulled him into an open space near the slightly open door. "Why?" he mouthed.

"Shush," I whispered with a finger to my lips.

Moments later, there came the sound of dragging chairs and Queenie and Leland taking a seat somewhere inside.

Although Solo and I were now crouched between two storage shelves, their voices rang out loud and clear.

"Thanks for fitting me in. You're a lifesaver," Leland said.

"Hate to rain on your parade, bay-bay, but I ain't my mama. I'm charging you extra for working a Sunday," she said.

More fireworks exploded outside.

"Speaking of your mother, where is Happy Hye?" Leland said.

And what intrigued me even more was how I had missed Happy Hye being Queenie's mother as the resemblance, I thought now, was so strong through the eyes.

"She's with a client," she shot back. "A regular, some rich jerk who is always saying how she knows her stuff. Mama eats up that flattery shit."

"She does great stuff—" Leland began. "I mean—sorry."

"What? You think I'm embarrassed that she's a hooker? No way am I ashamed. Did you hear me? I'm not! But I can say I'm not thrilled with my stepfather. How he lets her sleep with other men, I dunno. But Mom is crazy ass in love with him regardless. It would kill her if he left her."

Solo whispered, "Omigod!" as it appeared both of us had neglected to realize that with Happy Hye as her mother it meant Booth was her stepfather.

"Is Booth thinking of doing that—leaving?" Leland asked.

Silence. "I won't let that happen. I will not," she said finally.

"What can you do?" he asked her.

"Never you mind," she said. "Come on. Hold still. I'm almost done. You know just this morning Booth said his broke ass life would soon be over. What do you make of that?"

"What exactly did he say?" Leland sounded troubled.

"Just that major cash flow was on its way. Said he found himself a cash cow."

"Cash cow?" Leland's voice was explosive as the firecrackers outside. "Who?"

She blew out a breath. "You think the bastard confides in me? Not a chance, even after all I done for him this morning, making me play up like he was my main squeeze to some girls he works with. And, shit, look at all you've done for him. You fixed him, or leastways your specialist friend did. Spinal cord stimulation to deaden pain. Incredible," she said.

At this next stunner of a revelation, I did not look at Solo, only crouched there smiling, and bumping Booth back up to suspect number one.

"The wonder of science," Leland said after a moment.

"Shit, it's like Star Trek," she said. "Look. Am I fabulous or what? Your tattoo is gone."

"Fabulous," Leland said. "Could you drop me off at my car? It's at Crossroads Park, near where Happy Hye parks her trailer. She's got a pretty good set-up, a pop out."

"Sure thing, bay-bay. Anything for a satisfied customer."

The sound of retreating footsteps came next, followed by a door closing. The side gate opened then slammed shut. They walked alongside the garage to Queenie's car, opened what sounded like two doors. I relaxed.

"Personally, I'd have told Booth he could keep the watch," Queenie said.

Solo and I hurried to listen through the closed garage door.

Queenie went on, "Just to see his face when you took it

back."

"You hate him that much?" Leland asked.

"Naw, I'm just mad about this morning. And Victor hasn't called all day. I'm always in a mood when Big Vic doesn't call."

"Is he your boyfriend?" Leland asked.

"Love of my life," she said. "If Booth doesn't chase him off like the rest. Well, we had better hurry. Isn't your birthday party soon?"

Leland nodded. "No rush. My place is just five minute down the road."

There was the sound of two doors closing, the SUV starting, and then they drove off.

Solo leaned closer. "Can I get a *woot* for the rebirth of Operation: Booth Jackson?"

"Woot!" I said.

There came a barely audible bark from behind, and I whirled. "The dog!"

We jumped into gear to find it. I looked around again, my eyes returning to one thing. The refrigerator. I rushed forward, yanked open the door, and the dog tumbled out like a sack of flour. I caught it just in time and brought it to my chest. It was shivering.

"You poor thing," I said, nestling it inside my jacket.

"Let's get out of here before Ma Hye finds us," Solo said.

I was searching for the best way to leave when the garage door opened.

I looked over my shoulder at the open/close button Queenie had pressed earlier, but no one was there. Then Solo grabbed my hand and pulled me forward. But when Ma Hye stepped out in front of us, we skidded to a stop.

She took her hand off an outside keyless entry and raised her pitchfork, prodding Solo in the chest with it. "Who the hell are you? You here to rip me off?"

"No, no," I said in a rush. "We have nothing that belongs to you."

"Especially the dachshund in her coat," Solo said and slapped a hand to his mouth.

"Thieves! Give me dog!" When she jabbed me in the chest with the pitchfork, the dachshund leaped to the ground and nipped at her. She kicked at it, but relentless, it kept barking and biting her shins.

"Stop it! Stop it!" She ran from it, around and around, insanely jabbing the pitchfork pell-mell. "Make it stop!" Then she got a good kick in and sent the dog skidding away, dazed. She bore down on it, the pitchfork aimed and ready.

I stepped between her and the dog. "Don't," I said. "Don't you dare."

She laughed, that insanely wicked witch laugh. "You get lost." She tried to prod me aside with the pitchfork.

I held firm, refusing to move.

"Then you bleed," she said.

When she reared back to aim the fork at my chest, Solo lunged forward to try to grab it but missed and went spread eagle on the cement floor. Ma Hye turned on him, and he rolled and rolled and rolled, eluding her. "Get the dog," he screamed with each turn.

I dove forward in a low, sliding lunge. Problem was as I got a hold of the dog I kept on going, knocking Ma Hye onto her butt. *Whump*.

She scrambled to her feet with amazing speed for a woman her age. "You die now," she told me.

I wrapped my arms closer around the dog.

Solo launched to his feet and grabbed the pitchfork. They grappled with it for several seconds before Ma Hye's grip gave out, the force of which sent Solo into the metal shelves. I didn't notice what else flew into the air, but I did see the box of firecrackers go flying, with several landing on the camp stove's open flame.

Bang! Bang! Bang!

Ma Hye roared. Solo pulled me to my feet, lifted me by the waist, and started running. Tightening my hold on the dog, I looked over my shoulder to see if she was following. All clear. Once at the Pinto, we dove in and locked the doors. Still no Ma Hye.

"That was close," Solo said, turning on the ignition.

"Too close," I said, settling the dachshund in my lap.

But after a quick U-turn, we were a car length from Northeast 8th Street when Ma Hye, looking pissed off and no worse for wear, ran from the smoking garage and hurried after us, her pitchfork zeroed in. Solo blew through the stop, turned right, and headed west. We lost her after another turn.

Solo looked over. "You gonna report her?" he asked.

"Yep," I said and pulled out my cell.

I had just located the number for Animal Control when my phone rang. It was Ivy Valentine from FoY. "We're on our way," I told her. "Five minutes, tops."

She was rambling, incoherently, crazily, but I managed to work out "Leland's Party" And "Driving the seniors" And—

"What?" I said, and she repeated it. I turned to Solo, my phone slipping from my hand. "Booth is dead," I managed. "They're saying Leland killed him."

"That's crazy," Solo said. "He was just with Queenie."

I shrugged. "But we don't know when the murder happened."

~There Are Some Days Even My Lucky Underpants Can't Help~

My head was spinning, my breathing difficult to get under control.

Since we were passing Crossroads Park, Solo drove into the lot and maneuvered into an end slot. I heard raised voices as I rolled down my window for air. Trying not to panic over the news about Booth, and Leland's possible involvement in his death, I looked toward the voices, which belonged to demonstrators in front of the Crossroads Fire Station. Their protest signs were hard to read, but I managed to pick out REINSTATE and UNFAIR FIRING. I sympathized. I also needed my job to keep Granddad in our home, but now with Leland facing double murder charges that was looking doubtful.

Moments later, Engine #16 pulled out of the stall, blasted its siren twice to clear the protestors, and turned left onto Northeast 8th Street toward Lake Sammamish. Curtis Hobbs was again at shotgun, leaning forward and looking at me as they passed. I took out my phone and called him again, getting his voicemail for a second time. I was upset enough to demand he tell me about the Bintliff note immediately. I didn't, of course. Maybe my voice was a little strained as I asked him to return my call when convenient. He was just busy, just putting out fires and buying extra crispy chicken. Then my cell phone rang again. It was Tita.

"We just heard about Booth," I said. "Are you at the Desmonts'?"

"You mean the madhouse. *Si*," she said. "I'm actually at the top of your driveway. The coroner is here. You should stay away. Lipschitz is also here, he's said your name three times."

"Who's he talking to?"

"Right now he's with Leland," she said.

"Why do they suspect him?"

"He and Booth were arguing, but I have no idea about what. All I know is Booth was eating when Leland arrived and immediately asked to see him privately. They walked into the Desmonts' garage. But Leland never touched him. Booth just grabbed his heart and keeled over."

"What, are you blind?" A woman's muffled voice said through the line. "I saw Leland poke Booth in the chest, which begs the question. Did he have something in his hand, a knife or syringe, maybe? Writers wonder about these things."

"Is that Lilith?" I asked Tita.

"Yeah, hold on. Look, Mrs. Desmont, let's dial back on the *loco*. Leland said he brushed a seed off Booth's lapel," she said. "Rylie, Leland is not doing so *bueno*. Gilad is with him now."

"Gilad's there?"

"With that pink-poodle *chica*. She is so obnoxious. Nazi hunter this, Nazi hunter that. If Booth hadn't eaten the last muffin, I'd have wacked her with it."

Lots of muffins in this deadly adventure. "What kind of muffin?" I asked.

"Dunno," she said.

I had an idea.

"Elsa," Tita said away from the phone. "Don't just stand there watching Gilad. Get in the van."

"Elsa is there, too?" I asked.

"She came by taxi, said she wanted to help, but helping she is not. I found her looking for something under your house."

"Bats." I remembered what Elsa had said about Gilad leaving the bonfire. "She was looking for a bat's nest."

Tita blew out a breath. "Why would she care about that? Elsa, were you looking for a bat's nest? Huh? She just told me to take a hike," Tita said with a half irritated, half impressed titter. "I must be losing my touch."

"Tita, I need you to think," I said "Do you remember what other senior or staff left the bonfire last night? Beside Booth and Gilad."

"Leland—"

"Yeah, yeah," I grumbled. "Anyone else?"

Brief silence. "Jane Gettelfinger, I think. Hey, Elsa, was Jane at the bonfire last night? Huh? Elsa said yes and flipped me off. Rylie, are you sure I don't come off as soft?"

"No, I'm serious. You really do scare the hell out of me. Okay, I gotta go—"

"Wait—Lipschitz has given me the go ahead to leave.

But I have a van full of excellent Tita Iglesias cuisine, and with the power now off at FoY, I have nowhere to store it. And the seniors are hungry, you know."

"I'll be right there," I said.

"No!" she said. "Ivy is bringing the seniors in the rental. We'll feed them at the park."

"How do you know I'm at Crossroads Park?"

"Talon told me," she said and hung up.

I figured Talon had tracked me via GPS, but I wanted to hear from him why, so I called, but got his voicemail. "A *wee* bird told me you're tracking my phone." I disconnected.

My curiosity over this came and went as I thought about Leland. I refused to believe he had anything to do with Booth's death. I decided a muffin similar to the poppy-seed variety found in both the Oleys' van and in the mouth of their deceased son was the guilty party. When I mentioned my hypothesis to Solo, he agreed, yet we were both lost for a perpetrator or motive. Nevertheless, I thought the information warranted further exploration, so I dialed Alistair.

"Problem?" he asked.

For better reception, I handed Solo the dachshund and climbed from the Pinto. "Well—"

"Rylie, like our forty-third president I don't like bad news, so break it to me quickly."

"Okay, but it flies in the face of those health food ads. Muffins aren't so wholesome today."

"Muffins? How so?"

"We've had another deadly sighting."

"No kidding?"

I scanned the darkening sky as mist fell around me.

"Scout's honor."

"Hawthorne said you quit Girl Scouts."

I rolled my eyes and told him about Booth.

He sighed. "I can't go into too much detail, but it was muffins that killed the Oley's. They were poisoned."

My mouth fell open. "Was Cokey Bill poisoned, too?"

"Looks that way," he said. "Now get out of the rain."

"How do you know I'm in the rain?"

"Rylie, its Western Washington. Everyone is in the rain." He disconnected.

The news of the poisoning hadn't surprised Solo. In truth, it hadn't surprised me either. But what to make of it I had no idea—yet. But I'd find out.

"Gilad showing up early for tonight's party bothers me," Solo said. "Didn't you say he wasn't planning on making it at all?"

"Yep, and he brought his new girlfriend. I'm sure to flaunt her to Elsa." *The rat.*

"I guess Booth dying clears him of Otto's murder, which leaves only Leland," Solo said.

"Not necessarily," I argued. "Jane Gettelfinger also left the bonfire."

"Ahhh." He did a seated happy dance. "Thank you, blessed mandala."

At the sudden activity, the sleeping dachshund woke up. She—for closer inspection had revealed she was indeed a she—vigorously wagged her tiny tail. Yet truthfully, she looked bedraggled, as though she had been living on the streets: ribs showing, dull coat, stinky smell.

"Come on, lil' girl," Solo said. "Time for a potty break."

We climbed from the Pinto and headed for the grass.

"Don't run away." He put her down. "Baxter, that's what I'm calling her."

"A boy's name?"

He shrugged. "I have a girl's name and it hasn't hurt me any." He referred to how his mother had desperately wanted a girl by the time he came along, so she named him as one. "Baxter was sure something else with Ma Hye, wasn't she?"

I nodded, wondering what motive Jane Gettelfinger would have to murder Otto.

"Don't worry. We'll clear Leland," he said, misinterpreting my silence.

"First we need to find a motive for Jane. You know she was intimate with Otto."

"Plaeezzze, I just ate pie." He looked over my shoulder. "Do you think that's Happy Hye's?"

I turned to see an elaborate motor coach parked in the corner of the lot, red tassels hanging from an awning, several frilly fans around the side door, a flag hanging over the windshield. "Is that the Korean flag?"

"Think so," he said.

Something Queenie had said surfaced in my mind. "Do you think Leland is Booth's cash cow? I mean, it sounds like Booth. Set up a guy with a prostitute, and then blackmail him. Leland sounded angry when Queenie mentioned it."

"Wouldn't Booth know Leland was broke?"

"I didn't," I said. "Did you?"

"Nope," he said. "But Jane's loaded. She'd make a good cash cow."

I raised my eyebrows. "Best cash cow *ever*. Maybe Booth saw her kill Otto and planned to blackmail her."

The dachshund ran after some crows poking in a trashcan

under a nearby covered shelter. We followed, doing high fives at this promising new development. The shelter was a recent city addition, so it was a minute before I noticed the intricate mosaic on the floor. It was a map of the world with gold stars inlaid to represent Bellevue's sister cities: Hualien, Taiwan, Kladno, Czech Republic, Liepaja, Latvia, and Yao, Japan.

"Solo." I stared down at it in shock. "There is no sister city in Scotland. There isn't one in the entire country, nothing nearby, either. The entire UK is blank."

He bent. "Let's have a look. Uh-oh," he said, after a moment.

"Talon isn't who he says he is. There, I've said it." I sighed. "Omigod, I knew something was wrong. Who the hell is this man?"

"Let's not jump to conclusions. It could be an oversight."

I rolled my eyes. "I am so done with men."

"Plaeezzze, you haven't even gotten started yet."

"Stop it." I was swamped by the sudden urge to cry, kick something, or do both. I was overreacting, of course. I barely knew Talon. But he had lied, *damn it,* right to my face.

"But—"

"I'm sorry, Solo. I just don't want to talk about it."

Behind me came the sound of crows clashing. I turned to see a slew of them attacking the trashcan. The dachshund dashed toward them, but when they took flight into the parking lot, the dog followed, stumbling once on her three legs before she ran into the path of an oncoming car.

I wheeled after her.

Solo was at my heels. But as where I stopped at the curb to call her back, he kept going, jumping into the path of the approaching car, forcing the driver to come to a squealing stop, its bumper inches from his legs.

The dachshund yapped at his feet, oblivious.

I rushed to get her, but she bolted. I was too busy chasing her around the car to notice anything else, but once I finally had her, I turned right into the driver as he climbed from his car.

"Oh." I hardly recognized Paul Desmont without his sunglasses. "Sorry we made you stop so suddenly."

Kindly Paul Desmont's lips were oddly pursed. "I could have killed you, Solo. And what about my car?" He rushed to check the older Volkswagen Beetle's hood. "These classics are expensive to fix. Hope you didn't ding it."

I thought Paul was overreacting. Solo clearly had not dented his car, yet Paul was opening and closing the hood as if a dent would miraculously appear.

"You understand how much it costs to work on these older cars," Paul said as a bright beam of sunlight speared through the twisty clouds. "A king's ransom."

"I never touched it," Solo said. "Sweet ride, though. Are you giving the Ferrari a day off?"

"Sold it. I'm in the market for something else." He tapped a tissue to his sun sensitive eyes. "I seem to have left my sunglasses at—" He looked around. "At—"

"The golf course," Solo said helpfully. "Did you just play a round?"

"Yes—yes, I did. I must have left them in the clubhouse."

I found it surprising that Paul Desmont golfed at a public course, as Lilith often claimed he played only the finest courses. "You played here at Crossroads?" I asked.

His uneasy look lasted only a second, but I saw it. "It's

a wonderful par three," he said, his eyes following mine as they traveled from the empty trunk to the empty backseat.

"No golf clubs today?" I said, recalling the empty racks in his garage.

"I'm renting, while I look into better equipment," he said. "I sold my collection as I'm sure you noticed this morning."

I nodded. "I also noticed Lilith's hands were bruised. She should wear punching gloves."

"She's thin-skinned about her books. Try as I might, I cannot convince her to ignore the critics. Gloves would be good, though. Luckily, she gets liquid codeine from Canada for the pain. She keeps several bottles on hand. Which reminds me, Mackenzie just called. Terrible news about your co-worker. Heart attack?"

I shrugged.

"Well, I'm sorry for your loss. And before I leave, I want to apologize for last night. Lilith tells me I was a little drunk."

"You were fine," I said honestly.

He smiled sweetly and climbed in behind the wheel. "At least I slept like the dead. I can't even remember my head hitting the pillow."

I tried to look as though I did not find this revelation interesting. "You missed a nice bonfire," I said.

"No argument there, but at least we snagged two of your wonderful s'mores before Lilith insisted we leave." He put the key in the ignition.

"That's right," I said. "She planned to write last night."

"I wish," he said. "It's not like I hound her word count, but I am watchful. Lilith has not written in weeks. I checked just this morning." He gripped the steering wheel in a move that seemed more frustrated than concerned. "Rylie, do you think you could talk to her?"

I stared into his watery eyes, an intense green identical to mine, and was utterly humbled by his faith that I could give anyone career advice. "Sure," I said. "I'll do what I can."

He pulled closed the car door, met my gaze through the open window. "It runs in your family, kindness. You, your grandfather. I'm happy to know you, Rylie Tabitha Keyes."

It wasn't the matching eye color so much as the paternal look in his gaze that had me sucking in a deep breath. "Did you know my mother?" I said, mortified by my own boldness and gnawing on my bottom lip. "I mean, I know you didn't live next door in the '80's, but you were just down the lake in Redmond."

He kept his vibrant eyes on mine. "No, I'm sorry. I never had the pleasure to meet her."

I felt even more embarrassed. He looked at me as if I were the hatchling in that famous book for children, but instead of mother, I was asking everyone, *"Are you my father?"*

It wasn't until Solo stepped closer that his eyes left mine. "No hard feelings," Solo said to Paul. "We just didn't want you to hit the dog."

All eyes but mine shifted to the sleeping dachshund in my arms. My gaze was fixed on the employment application for Crossroads Golf Course on the Beetle's passenger seat.

Paul noticed my interest. "I guess I'm hardwired to believe Mackenzie will always be looking for work. I pick up applications everywhere I go."

"That's nice," I said.

"More necessary than nice. I love my daughter. I would do anything for her."

I waved as he drove off. No matter how much I wanted to

believe the farfetched notion of him as my father, I couldn't get beyond the reasoning voice in my head. If Paul had had another child, even a bastard baby like me, he would never have abandoned it. "My loss," I said as the Beetle disappeared around the corner.

"I have a bad feeling," Solo said at my side.

I blinked back silly tears. "About the Desmonts' being broke."

"Roger, that," he said, nodding.

"And by the way Lilith throws around money, she doesn't know," I said. "And more to the point, with Paul asleep, perhaps even drugged—"

"Hang on," he said. "Drugged by who, by what?"

"By Lilith with codeine," I said. "Think about it. Paul was her alibi. With him asleep, she has none. And with their money issues a secret, Booth might have considered her a cash cow."

"Not just Lilith," Solo said, "but Mackenzie, too."

"And Paul." Though I found it unlikely. "We've got only his word that he fell asleep."

"But what reason would any of them have to kill Otto?" he asked.

"I dunno," Solo said, watching Tita drive the rented van into the parking lot. "But I always think better after food. Let's eat."

With Baxter happily trotting at our heels, we unloaded the food from the van to the picnic area. Once we finished, I asked Tita why the police had allowed any of it to leave the crime scene.

"I never made it down your driveway. Some tow-truck stalled in front of your house, blocking the whole driveway as it tried to tow away Mrs. Desmont's Mercedes. Repossessed," she whispered with a hand to her mouth, but added when I didn't act surprised, "You knew?"

"No," I said, shaking my head. "But I suspected that they had money problems."

"Please tell me Mrs. Desmont's check isn't going to bounce?"

I shrugged, told her I hoped not. "Where did Booth get the muffin?"

She paused, balancing a box of iced-packed chicken on her hip. "I dunno, maybe Lilith Desmont. I went in search of a dolly in their garage to carry the food downhill. I saw a Starbucks bag on the hood of her car, and beside it was the muffin."

"You never saw Booth eat it?"

She thought a minute, then shook her head. "I guess I just assumed since a little later it was gone, but he was nearby chewing. So you think the muffin had something to do with his death? Like he was poisoned?"

"Let me break this down," I said and explained the multiple muffin sightings.

"You know, when I was with my gang, we laughed about poison being a *chica's* murder weapon of choice. Whoa. Chill. When your face goes pale like that, your freckles are super scary," she said and strode away to serve the chicken.

I stared ahead, thinking how Mackenzie had worked up until today at Starbucks. Problem was, though nasty enough to poison someone, I couldn't see a reason why she would be involved.

Tita stepped back. "Look on the bright side," she said. "That Lipschitz guy might have it out for you, but Talon is on your side. I heard him say he liked your freckles."

"No one likes freckles," I said, absently serving sliced fruit to the seniors.

The rain had ushered away most of the earlier park-goers. Yet those who defied the wet were wandering the walkways or huddled under the covered cabanas, watching their children play, and gathered in conversation.

A few minutes later, Gilad and Sunny drove up and climbed out of a black Jaguar. They strode toward the group. Gilad greeted everyone with a lazy wave before helping himself to food. He made a point of warning Sunny about the high fat content in Tita's fried chicken, but promised her they would burn off the calories later. Sunny's high-pitched titter earned Gilad a piercing glare from Elsa.

Solo came up beside me. "You're not going to believe this, but Gilad is wearing the Kupper family watch. I saw it on his wrist. Just as Farley described."

"Nooooo." Just as I started to look over at Gilad, my cell rang. I blinked twice at the Caller ID: Leland Rosenberg.

"Rylie, you there?" Leland's voice was hushed.

I hit speaker so Solo could hear. "Leland, why are you whispering?"

"Shhh," he said.

"I'm not exactly yelling. What's wrong?"

"You're on speaker. I don't want to be seen on a cell phone."

"Thanks for clearing that up," I said, rolling my eyes.

"What part of speak softly don't you get?" he said.

"All right. All right," I whispered. "Why are you calling?"

"Are you still at Crossroads Park? Is Uncle Gilad there with you?"

"Yes to both, and he's wearing the watch Alric Mueller stole from your great grandmother." My eyes popped wide as he said a string of muffled words. "Okay, once again in English."

"Uncle Gilad is wearing the watch?" he said. "Is he out of his freaking mind?"

"How come you're not surprised I know about the watch?" I asked.

"Talon told me," he said.

Sheesh, what a Chatty Cathy. "Leland, what do you want me to do—?"

"Us to do," Solo put in. "I'm here, too, boss."

"Good, that's good. I want you both to do anything and everything," he said, "But get that watch here right away before Detective Talon leaves."

"He's still there?" I asked.

"Rylie, all of Bellevue is stuck in your driveway. Hurry. My freedom depends on it!" he cried and disconnected.

After a quick discussion, we decided I would talk to Gilad. Solo grabbed Baxter as she sniffed a passing dog and rushed to get the Pinto, while I explained the situation to Tita.

"Don't worry. We can handle it here. *Vamanos*," she said.

I looked around, finding Gilad alone near the restrooms.

"Get going—" Tita began. "Crap!"

I whirled to see Elsa shove Jane, to see Jane push her back, and then turn away.

"Not so fast, sister." Elsa's lips thinned. "You can't say that and just leave."

Jane reeled, the mega rubies at her neck dazzling. "What's your problem?"

"For Christ's sake." Elsa's fury almost choked her. "You slept with Gilad last night."

"Who slept?" she said with frosty sarcasm. "You're just mad because I said he's impotent. Imagine the great Gilad Kupper out performed by a feeble old man who turns into a tiger when you rub his bald spot."

Elsa gulped, tears slipping down her cheeks. "I'll never forgive you."

Jane's smug smile wobbled before she lifted her chin and marched away.

I stepped forward, but Tita waved me off.

"I'll look after her," she said and lead Elsa away.

Wally—hemorrhoid donut in hand—rocked on his heels. "Doesn't that just beat all? Not once have I ever thought to ask a gal to rub my bald spot. And here I've dropped a wad on Viagra, too," he said. "Funny thing, the news said Otto was found without his kippah."

"Lost me, Wally," the Colonel said over a brownie. Then his brows shot up. "You don't mean Otto had sex with Jane before he died last night?"

Wally smacked him with his donut. "Haven't you been listening? Jane was boinking Gilad," he said. "I always wondered why Otto carried toupee glue. Sure was full of himself, expecting to get lucky all the time."

Good God, had Otto been with a woman last night?

"So Otto glued on his kippah?" The Colonel downed the last bite of brownie.

Wally nodded. "Seemed he had a slippery bald spot. Time was, I wore a toupee."

"Is that right," the Colonel said. "What changed?"

"Damn glue. It stays sticky. Gets on everything," he said.

I ran toward Gilad with a puzzling question in my mind: What was it that I'd seen today? What was it that had been sticky? I simply couldn't remember. Of importance *non*. Frustrating *oui*.

Gilad's face was blank as he watched Elsa and Tita round the footpath in the distance.

"Elsa loves you," I told him. "She went looking for the bats nest under my house earlier. She wanted to believe you found it, to prove you didn't—" To clear him of all suspicion in Otto's death I needed verification he was with Jane. "Jane told Elsa about last night."

"Elsa knows I was with Jane?" Pause. "What does it matter? Elsa and I are through."

I had my answer, sadly. "You can argue that it's yours, but that isn't the point now. I need you to give me the watch."

"I'd rather pull my stomach out through my nose," he said.

"Leland's in trouble," I said softly. "Stealing the watch has only made things worse. I don't know the details. You need to think of Leland now. He needs you."

"Why did he not tell me Otto was that bastard Alric Mueller? Why did I have to find out by seeing the watch on Booth?" At a door slamming inside the restroom, he glanced over his shoulder. His eyes were a dark, stormy blue when he turned back. "Leland betrayed me."

"He was wrong," I agreed.

His shoulders slumped. "Have you any idea how humiliating it is to live alongside the one man you've hunted for nearly fifty years and not have the slightest inkling it was him?"

I touched his arm, understanding. "Leland needs you. Nothing changes that. Not hurt pride, not ego. Family comes first." My cell phone was ringing again. I clicked speaker. "Leland," I said. "I'm coming."

"This is bad, really bad," he whimpered. "Happy Hye just called. She has some crazy idea that Uncle Gilad killed Booth for the watch. He wasn't even here when Booth collapsed. Oh, God, Rylie, what have I done? If she hurts him…" He broke down, sobbing.

Gilad's gasp was soft, yet poignant. He unclasped the watch and pushed it into my hand.

"I'm on my way," I told Leland and hung up. "Come with me."

Gilad shook his head, staring at Elsa as she walked with Tita. "I've been a fool. Help Leland. Help my nephew."

Just then, Sunny breezed from the restroom. "There you are my big, bad Nazi hunter."

"I prefer the name Gilad," he said and strode toward Elsa.

~Did I eat a bowl of smarts for lunch?~

I yanked on the Pinto's door handle, but it didn't budge. I pocketed the watch, tried again, and snapped a nail low on the bed. I raised my finger to my mouth to avoid seeing any possible blood just as Happy Hye bolted from a row of shrubs, exploding this way.

I stood my ground. "Gilad Kupper did not kill Booth."

She fart laughed, not unlike Queenie's snort this morning. "Like I believe you. Which one is he?" She thrust a finger at the distant group of FoY seniors. "Which one?"

I shrugged. "I'm not saying."

"You dumb bitch. He killed my Booth. Tell me now," she said, her hands up, and her one-inch nails locked and loaded. "Maybe I won't scratch out your eyes."

Solo climbed from the Pinto, came around the car. Happy Hye seemed too busy preparing to claw me to notice. He caught her from behind in a bear hug and lifted her off her feet. She launched into a screaming fit, legs flailing about, thrashing as a plainclothes squad car skidded to a stop next to us. Alistair Barclay jumped out from behind the wheel.

"I'll take over from here," he said. "Go ahead and put her down."

Solo obeyed, but held her arms locked to her sides. Alistair linked a plastic tie around her wrists, reciting Miranda rights.

"I'm not pressing charges," I said to Alistair.

He frowned. "You sure?"

"I'm sure." I shifted to Happy Hye. "I'm sorry about Booth."

Her gaze sharpened, but there were tears in her eyes. "What you want from me?"

"Nothing," I said.

"Why you doing this—this no charge thing?" she asked, eyes suspicious.

"You're grieving," I said. "And not thinking straight."

She looked away. Another tear fell. "He was my Booth."

Alistair lowered her into the squad car. "I'll take her downtown, to cool off."

"How did you know we were in trouble?" I expected to hear, "Talon told me."

He straightened, his lips curved. "I've had you in my sights all day. I promised your grandfather."

So that's how he knew I was standing in the rain. "All day as in *all* day?"

He laughed, a rich, throaty chuckle. "I've alerted Animal Control as to what's going on at the Hye household," he said with a frown, then switched to a grin. "But entertaining doesn't begin to describe you two. What a hoot."

"What? That pitchfork was really sharp," Solo said.

Alistair climbed into the squad car. He was still laughing as he drove away.

Ten minutes later, we drove up to my driveway, but didn't turn in. Talon was at the top. I stared at him, my anger over the missing sister-city star bubbling back as he gestured for us to park in the private lane across the street. He crossed over, opened my door, and helped me out of the car.

"Big fat liar." I shook him off. I was being childish, of course. But it was how I shut out the hurt, the hunger. "I've got news for you, mister. The sister-city mosaic at Crossroads Park doesn't have a star anywhere in Scotland."

He narrowed his eyes. "And that troubles you, why?"

I sighed, disappointed, frustrated—outraged with myself for wanting more than a half-day relationship warranted. I moved to leave.

He grabbed my hand, held it. "Don't condemn me, Rylie, not about this."

I listened to the wind rustle in the trees, caught the rosy hint of nearing twilight through the leaves as day gave way slowly to evening.

"I know we've just met—" Closing my eyes, I leaned my forehead against his shoulder. Behind me, I heard Solo pick up Baxter and cross the street. "But when I have nothing left but memories, I don't want to wonder where the truth stopped and the lies began." I felt my heart squeeze at those crushing eyes when I looked up. "It's better to end this now."

"'Tis it not better to live in hope than die in despair."

"I don't think so—no." *You're running away again, Rylie.* "I want to have faith in you."

"But can't," he said dully, almost sadly. "I'm inclined to believe the granddaughter of a police detective must understand the need for discretion?"

"I do understand," I said. There wasn't any point in explaining the ruthless ache for trust inside me. "My mother and father abandoned me."

"Aye."

"All my life I've run from repeating their mistake."

He skimmed a thumb across my cheekbone. "A mistake not of your doing."

"But it shaped me." I knew I had mistakenly wanted one dependable man for years, and wasn't quite sure how to learn to trust another who seemed so uncertain, so risky, but—*God help me*—I wanted to try. "If only you would meet me halfway."

"With the truth?"

The birds hushed in the trees.

"Trust me," I said.

"Must we speak of this now, on a public street?"

I hadn't meant to be so demanding. This was another flaw, wanting what I could not have.

"We don't need to speak of it at all," I said, sighing. "I was wrong to ask. My grandfather refused to tell me about his work, lied about his duties, and the dangers he faced each day.. He said it was to protect me from harsh realities. Growing up I found the lies and silence terrifying."

Though still raw to remember, I couldn't fault my grandfather, not when he had sacrificed so much to raise me. But I could learn from it, from the sleepless nights, the endless after-school hours waiting for him to come home safe—alive. "I want more, Talon. I need more. I know we've just met, and that up until a few hours ago, I thought I wanted Zach. I guess he was—"

"Safe," Talon finished. "But that's not enough, Rylie."

"I know that now. But trust and honesty, those are a good way for us to begin." I swallowed my fear, and my need to know everything about him, gulping it down before it could resurface. "Tell me two things, only two things, and I won't ask for more."

He smiled at me and said, "All right."

"Are you working undercover? Does it have something to do with Lipschitz?"

He bent down, his crystal eyes searching mine. "Yes," he whispered against my hair.

I shifted, looked up at his face, into his eyes. One mountain climbed. The relief was almost touchable. Cars passed by and I took no notice. For this moment, I was somewhere else, somewhere unguarded, tender, and hopeful. I cupped his face with my hands, kissing him as I had never kissed before, without reserve, without suspicion—almost fearless.

"You baffle me, Rylie."

Solo came into view, walking Baxter toward us on the opposite side of the street, and the night birds began to sing in the twilight. A low seaplane flew overhead.

I brushed my mouth to Talon's, teasing, tempting. "I'll drive you crazy, too."

"Aye," he said.

It was another minute before we broke apart and crossed the street. I hadn't wanted the moment to end. Daringly, I'd taken some and given some. That step forward would have to do for now. Insecurity was a dogged master. I definitely wasn't *there* yet. Baby steps. I preferred baby steps, and the lasting confidence I hoped would come with each milestone.

"Uh-oh, incoming." Solo said on our approach. "Nosy neighbor alert."

Stooped and ancient Mrs. Bebitch stomped down her hill, brandishing her trusty trowel, and shouting, "Get that car off my private lane!"

She had a flushed glow to her weather-beaten face as she bore down on us. "What's with the shorter hair, Rylie? It makes your face look fat."

Talon flashed his badge under her bulbous nose. "Go away or I'll arrest you for disturbing the peace."

Outrage jumped into her creased eyes. "Well, I never—"

"Go," Talon ordered, his eyes dark and hard.

She stopped on her way uphill and looked back. "Your superiors will hear from me."

For the first time in what seemed like hours, I laughed. It felt good. "Here's the watch," I said, handing it to Talon.

His eyes sparkled. "That's all sorted, then. Now to find an attempted murderer."

A twitch of shock creased my brow. "Otto isn't dead? But how?"

"Nay, Otto Weiner couldn't be deader." Frowning, he draped the watch around his wrist and held it tight. "'Everyone is a moon, and has a dark side which he never shows to anybody.'" He met my curious gaze. "Mark Twain."

"Oh, I love Mark Twain." Solo petted Baxter as she snuggled contentedly in his big arms. "Interesting fact: he predicted his own death correctly."

"Interesting," Talon said.

"Isn't it? He was born when Haley's Comet was able to be seen in the sky and said he would die when it showed up next. And he did, seventy-five years later.''

"You don't say," Talon said.

"Gospel truth," Solo said.

I cleared my throat. "Guys, Otto Weiner, remember?"

"It was a heart attack," Talon said simply. Then he chuckled. "You're adorable when you frown like that. Though utterly fantastic, Otto died after a romping round of coitus."

"Sex?" I said, and he nodded. "Then that explains the discarded kippah."

"Oh, how so?" he asked, and I passed on Jane's revelation. "Any reason why Jane—"

"Gettelfinger."

"Would want to make Otto's death look like a homicide? I dare say the fall from the balcony appears to be for that reason."

"Jane wasn't with Otto last night," Solo said matter-of-factly. "She was sexing it up with Gilad Kupper under Rylie's house. It's true, Rylie told me on the drive over."

Talon burst out laughing. "Are you having me on?"

"Nope," Solo said. "Did you know Mark Twain also had nineteen cats as a boy?"

"That's mad," Talon said. "Did he also predict their deaths?"

I sighed, looking around, spying a fire truck parked at the hairpin bend in my driveway with what looked to be the coroners van behind it.

"I don't think so," Solo said. "But Hemmingway had over thirty cats."

"Don't be daft, thirty?" Talon said.

"Hello. The case," I said, frustrated. "And why is there a

fire engine down the driveway?"

Talon's laughing eyes met mine, and my knees almost buckled like a marionette. "Bloody inconvenient this traffic jam," he said. "As well as the spot of bother Lilith Desmont is having over her repossessed Mercedes and the fire engine keeping it from rolling downhill."

"What about my house?" I asked, worried.

"No structures were harmed, but the devil thrives on challenges, so it's going to be a while until everything is cleared, which brings me back to Otto. Someone gave him CPR last night," he said. "Not that you were ever in my mind as a suspect, but that clears you of any wrongdoing." He curved a gentle hand over my cheek. "Whoever worked on Otto knew what they were doing."

"Meaning?" Solo said.

"When Rylie gave Doris Oley CPR, her hands were wrong. They left impressions."

"Like fingerprints?" I asked.

"Had Doris not been wearing a shirt, yes. But in this case the imprint was indistinct, yet enough for the coroner to spot your hands had been too high and too far apart."

Imagine, judged innocent by reason of ignorance.

Then a happy realization struck. "If Otto wasn't murdered, then Leland is in the clear."

Talon shook his head steadily back and forth. "Regretfully, he is still a suspect. Booth Jackson was poisoned by painkillers added to his personal custom-made bottle of liquid vitamins," he said. "By his own admission, Leland retrieved his toupee from the box where those vitamins had been stored. And the tow-truck driver overheard bits and pieces of Booth and Leland's argument. Blackmail was spoken twice."

"So your hunch was right, Rylie. Booth's cash cow was Leland," Solo said and told Talon what we had overheard at the Hye house. "Can't you charge Booth with blackmail?"

"Only if someone admits to being blackmailed," Talon said.

"No, no," I said, remembering something. "I was wrong. Happy Hye said Leland was broke ass this morning at the station, so she knew, which means Booth had to have known."

"Possible. But it's just as possible Leland mentioned it to her—shall we say, in a conversational moment after intimacy," Talon said.

"We need to find out who this cash cow is. I think it's the key," I said. Paul Desmont's words came back like an echo. "Was it codeine in the vitamins that poisoned Booth?"

"No confirmation yet, but it looks like it. Codeine is in on his list of allergies," Talon said. "I'm awaiting a search warrant to search the Desmonts' house."

"It's a crime scene," I said. "Do you need a warrant?"

"Booth collapsed in their garage, and the house is a hundred feet downhill. A fine line, but I can't take the chance of the evidence being deemed inadmissible," he said.

"Lilith Desmont takes codeine," I said. "Paul said she buys the liquid form from Canada."

"And she has no alibi. Paul was asleep, possibly drugged last night," Solo said.

"And her motive for poisoning Booth is what?" Talon asked.

I searched my mind, shrugged. "I got nothing."

"Still it bears some thought," he said. "Her books are

riddled with deviant sex, one act in particular uses near suffocation to enhance the sexual experience. Motive outstanding, she could have gone too far and caused Otto's heart attack."

"And tried to frame Leland and me." I said it more as a statement than question.

He nodded. "Leland's fingerprints were on the plastic bag used to cut off Otto's air. It looks to have come from his garage office. It's the same ones used to wrap his liquid vitamins. I'll call in to see if I can find out if Lilith knows CPR."

"She was a Girl Scout leader. It's required even though she quit soon after—" At a sudden thought, I slapped my hand over my mouth. "Mt. Rainier. That's why she did it."

"Quit Girl Scouts?" Solo asked, looking lost.

"Poisoned the vitamins," I said. "Lilith must have wanted to bankrupt Leland so he couldn't build a Mc-mansion and block her view of Mt. Rainier."

Talon's lean face darkened in a frown. "Kill for a view of a volcano?"

"How about a two million dollar view," I said. "And I don't think she meant to kill Booth or anyone, just dose the vitamins enough to cause fatigue," I said. "Lilith is well-known, so if she let it leak that Leland's vitamins caused fatigue, no one would buy them. And those vitamins are all that is between Leland and bankruptcy."

I had expected Talon to ask for clarifications or more details as he had earlier at dinner, but instead he looked down, lips curved as he read a text message. "It was codeine in the vitamins." He showed us the text. "Not enough to kill Booth, but almost."

"Almost?" I said, stunned. "Booth isn't dead?"

"For crying out loud, hasn't anyone died today?" Solo asked.

I reminded him of the Oleys.

"Oh yeah, I forgot about them," he said.

"That was the second thing on my list of truths to tell you," Talon said, grinning like a confronted naughty boy.

I laughed. "Where is Booth now?"

"He refuses to go to hospital, so he's inside your house, resting. Hope you don't mind. He is weak, but willing to talk if I promised to retrieve the watch. Though the few things he has said so far have had no obvious relevance. Rylie, you should really lock your front door."

I will once I find the key. "He can't actually keep the watch, can he?"

"Hardly likely, considering its history. But there isn't any reason he should know that just yet," he said. "Quite fortuitous, but not altogether unexpected considering his health issues, but he carries a nasal atomizer of Naloxone for just such a reaction. It saved his life."

"You don't find that a little too convenient?" I certainly did.

"Aye, lass, it is rather opportune, which is why I've asked the medical examiner to keep him busy with health and safety inquiries as he rests."

"So let me get this straight, you're saying Lilith poisoned Booth's vitamins before Leland gave the box to Gilad last night to deliver," I said.

"That's the working theory," he said. "Leland said he retrieved the box from his garage office during the bonfire."

"And Booth left near the end of the bonfire," I said,

thinking hard. "Is it too wild to think he saw Lilith poisoning the vitamins? It isn't dark, dark until well after ten. Leland's balcony is easy to see from my driveway."

"I don't see Lilith tampering with the vitamins outside. In the garage, yes," Solo said.

My eyes popped wide. "But he could have seen her throw Otto's body over the rail," I said. "Mr. Singh said that after Otto couldn't get Leland's tram to work, he entered the garage. Omigod, what if he saw Lilith tainting the vitamins?"

"So then, Lilith is Booth's cash cow," Solo said.

Talon slipped his hand into mine and squeezed softly. "There's her motive. Great work putting it all together. Now I have the beginnings of a case against her."

I wanted to speak and couldn't. I wanted to smile. "I think it's time I had a heart-to-heart with my grandfather," I said.

"Aye," he said. "'Tis time."

"How about the muffin we heard Booth ate a little while ago?" Solo asked. Then he relayed what Tita had said about it being on the hood of Lilith's car.

Talon looked thoughtful. "I don't think Booth would have eaten a muffin. His medical alert bracelet says he has Celiac disease, intolerance to gluten, but I'll check it out."

I squeezed his hand. "I've gotta ask, what was the first truth on your list to tell me?"

He frowned at Solo. "Is she always this persistent?"

"Like a mule," Solo said and dodged my playful slap.

"I didn't track you via your phone," Talon said. "Though Alistair Barkley did keep me aware of your whereabouts." His eyes found mine. "I was concerned."

I smile at him in appreciation.

"I just had a thought," Solo said. "Was it codeine that

also poisoned the Oleys?"

Talon shook his head. "Preliminary report says foxglove seeds masked as poppy seeds."

A soft gasp escaped my lips. "Foxgloves?"

Unease crossed his face. "Rylie, I did run over your flowers. But to be honest, I was relieved when you openly admitted they were your favorites, even mentioned collecting seeds. Not the behavior of the guilty, which was enough to convince Lipschitz to ease up on you." One dark lock fell onto his forehead. "Of course, Lilith could have collected the seeds from your plants. Once I receive their genetic profile, I'll know which plants they came from."

"Lilith has used poisons and potions in her books," I said.

"Foxgloves?" he asked.

"Not that I recall, but I don't really read them. More like skim. They're a little—"

"Saucy," he said and laughed.

I nodded, my cheeks burning.

"Booth has foxgloves at the house he shares with Happy Hye and his stepdaughter Queenie," Solo said matter-of-factly.

"From what I gather, foxgloves are grown widespread in this area," Talon said.

"True," Solo admitted.

"You know Lilith mentioned knowing someone at Dragon, and it was a Dragon truck that ran me off the road last night. She said that she asked this person to remove a bad book review."

"The Oley's son is a Dragon programmer," Solo said. "He could remove a review, maybe even steal a truck."

"Well, then. I have enough to charge her," Talon said.

~Well behaved girls rarely make history~

The three of us stood alongside the fire engine and surveyed the scene below. As previously mentioned, a tow-truck with Lilith's sparkly Mercedes chained to its flatbed had broken down in front of my house. Two firefighters kept their eye on a steel rope suspended between the tow-truck's front-mounted wench and the hook under the fire engine's front bumper. They seemed untroubled as they discussed whether the roof would be closed during tonight's Mariner baseball game and whether Anderson would pitch.

A typical Lilith was inspecting the Mercedes for damage. She gave us a narrowed glance, but said nothing. Instead, she harassed the firefighter tinkering with the engine underneath the tow-truck, whirling around in fury, her caftan ballooning like a jellyfish.

Paul Desmont stood in his above-garage office window, on the phone and wiping his sensitive eyes as he watched Mackenzie standing outside at the railing near their tram platform. Dressed in the same clothes as this morning, she frowned across the lake to Mt. Rainier.

"She must have found out they're broke," Solo said.

"I think she already knew." I reminded him of her insistence this morning that Lilith write, as well as her peculiar irritation at Lilith's prediction of a new BMW in her future.

"Duty calls." Talon turned back slowly, smiled that smile of his. "We make a good team, Rylie, you and me."

I thought of how Zach had called Solo and me a team of trouble. I wondered what sort of team Talon and I would be. I couldn't wait to find out. "You're adorable when you talk like that."

I watched him stride downhill toward Lilith. He had such broad shoulders, such long legs. *Be still, my little plasma pumper.*

When I heard someone call out my name, I looked over to see firefighter Curtis Hobbs climbing from beneath the tow-truck and looking at Mackenzie. The back of my neck prickled when he strode to her, only to pull up short when she turned his way. "Sorry. I thought you were someone else." He turned uphill and our eyes met. "There you are, Rylie," he said. "I thought I'd heard your voice. Got a minute?"

He had mistaken Mackenzie for me, and the relevance of that error smacked into me like a tidal wave. I rushed forward, sparing Curtis a speedy promise to talk later as I passed him on my way to Talon. I caught him several feet from an oblivious Lilith, who was now standing beside Mackenzie and looking over the lake. Pulling Talon aside, I told him the significance of what had happened.

"You realize what this means, of course?" Talon said.

"That I should be nicer to Mrs. Bebitch?"

He laughed. "I wouldn't go that far. I suppose you're wondering why I'm standing here."

"It had crossed my mind."

"It's time for you to get your feet wet." He swept a hand toward the two women at the rail. "Go get 'em, tiger."

He went on looking at me in a captivated way with those stunning eyes. I felt wanted. I felt craved. "You wish for me to tell them?"

"'Tis only fitting. You are the one who reasoned it *oot*."

I frowned. "But I'm troubled by how Leland and I were framed. It doesn't add up."

"All the same, it will in time," he said. "Remember that ostensibly unrelated detail I received from Booth. It now has relevance. You start. I'll jump in later. Now, go on."

He was ready to trust me. And evading or pleading for help would let him down, so I squared my shoulders, though nerves jumped like grasshoppers. "All right, then."

"It's time," he said, gently urging me forward.

I took a step, searching the driveway. Just as I found what I was looking for, Solo hurried closer and poured the mandala sand the monks had given him into a run-off drain that flowed downhill to the lake.

"For good luck," he said.

"For good luck," I repeated.

With twilight in full flush, yet still light enough to see all around, the ample outdoor lighting glittered everywhere gold, the hillside, the foliage, and the homes. Normally I found it magical. Now I saw it as proof.

Lilith turned our way as we approached. The current flower at her ear was a red Zinnia, her earrings diamond chandeliers.

"Was it worth it?" I asked her, pointing to Mt. Rainier tinted rose by the bursting sunset. "If you had it all to do again, would you?"

"What are you saying?" One bruised hand rested at her throat. "I have no time for this. I need to write. I need to make money since others can't seem to do it." She threw a hard look up at Paul, who paced across his office window, a phone still to his ear.

It was the panic as much as the anger in her expression that had me remembering words my grandfather often said, *"Greed is a type of fear."*

It was ill timed, and utterly amateurish, but I laid a gentle hand on her arm. "I'm sorry."

"Take your hands off me," she said. "Just go away."

"Yes, go away," Mackenzie echoed. "We should build a fence, block out the riff-raff."

I laughed as Talon came up behind me, close enough to champion, far enough to set free. "But a fence would destroy your view of Mt. Rainier, much like Leland and Nava's mansion would do." I publicized to everyone her plan to bankrupt Leland.

She frowned, but her eyes were amused. "Ridiculous."

"Completely," Mackenzie said.

"You love your mother," I said to Mackenzie, "which is why you tried to protect her."

She closed her eyes for a moment, barely an instant, but I saw it. "I don't know what you're talking about," she said.

"I see. But, thankfully, neither of you killed Otto Weiner," I said.

"Of course we didn't," Lilith said sharply.

"Otto Weiner died of a heart attack," I stated.

Lilith's expression didn't change, but Mackenzie gasped.

"This comes as a surprise to you," I said to Mackenzie. "Not that I'm sure you hadn't wondered the exact cause of his death, but you knew who was involved."

Her shoulders tensed. "Ridiculous. This has nothing to do with me."

I brushed a fingertip over the gooey stain on her cuff, and touched it to the tip of my tongue. "Not marshmallow from the s'more you must have carried uphill for Zach. Only he went into work early and wasn't home. It's tacky, much like toupee glue. I guess some got on you when you covered Otto's head with the plastic bag, only to leave a s'more inside," I said. "An easy mistake, of course, considering your hands were probably shaking. Witnessing a murder would do that."

"There was no murder." Mackenzie tossed her head. "You just said so."

"But you didn't know that last night," I said. "All you could think about was the murder you believed your mother had committed."

"You have no proof," she said. "No proof!"

I smiled. "Funny thing, Mrs. Bebitch saw you at Zach's door." I said. "She thought you were me since our hair color is close, only your hair is longer since I recently cut mine. I didn't catch on until that firefighter mistook you for me. You see, I also knocked on Zach's door."

"Yes, I know. Zach and I were together—intimately," she added smugly.

I pushed my hair back, my eyes on her. "Mrs. Bebitch went to five o'clock mass. She never saw me since I was at his door just after five, but she saw you later on, during the bonfire. It isn't dark at ten, and his front door is easy to see from her house."

"You're guessing."

I held up the half-eaten licorice. "It's yours from this morning. You tossed it aside. Saliva on it will match the saliva on the half-eaten s'more. I'm curious, though. Did you bite into it at finding Zach not home, or as you watched Lilith seduce Otto in order to buy his silence?"

Mackenzie clapped a hand to her mouth. "She didn't!"

"Ah, you missed the seedy part," I said. "That explains why you missed Otto's heart attack. You wouldn't have tried to frame Leland had you known Otto died of natural causes."

Lilith was pale. "Lies. All lies."

I turned, studied her. "I gave someone CPR today. Only problem, I did it wrong. The coroner noticed the imprint of my hands. Otto's chest bears the hand imprint of the person who gave him CPR. Yours, Lilith." She looked at me as if expecting more. I grinned confidently and explained that Otto had been shirtless. "It's like a fingerprint. Forensics will match it."

"But I don't know CPR," she said quickly.

"Try again," I said and reminded her of her Girl Scout leader days. "You didn't have to try to save him. That will go in your favor at sentencing."

Lilith looked away, her bottom lip quivering. "Sex with Otto isn't a crime."

"It is to me," Paul Desmont said as he approached. "Tell me you didn't drug me last night. Never mind, I know you did."

Lilith rushed to him. "I — I had to do something. I cannot

lose my Mt. Rainier view. It wasn't so wrong. I take codeine all the time. Fatigue, that's all that happens."

He said nothing, just turned his back on her, staring out over the lake.

"But I didn't go through with it, Paul," Lilith pleaded with him at his shoulder.

"Because you got caught," he murmured.

"I had only doctored two bottles when Otto came in to use the phone. If Leland's damn tram had been working, none of this would've happened." She squared her shoulders, hissed. "So what if I used sex to silence him."

"He didn't want money?" Solo asked.

She bristled, whirling. "You think sex with me isn't enough."

Solo went fuchsia.

I was thinking fast, weighing my chances for more evidence since I wasn't certain the forensics would hold up. Mackenzie might not have eaten the s'more. She could have merely broken a piece off. And, of course, the impressions from Lilith's hands could prove indistinct upon further analysis. I needed to loosen some tongues.

"But then Mackenzie made it worse," I said finally. "Good thing Otto was small. It made it easier to toss his body over the railing. Bluntly put, you screwed up, Mackenzie. Ruined everything with your selfish desire to frame Leland for murder."

Lilith laughed. In fact, she laughed so hard that the air reverberated with it. "Mackenzie's involvement in this is ludicrous. She isn't that clever."

Mackenzie sparked as though electrified. "I am too that clever!"

Bingo.

"Oh, come on. You are not!" Lilith said.

Mackenzie's eyes went from mad to fuming. "It sure as hell looked like you killed him. Then when you heard Leland whistling his way up the hill you jumped into action like a crazy woman, grabbing the codeine and vitamins, rushing out the front door." She waited until she turned to me to wail, "I had to do something! Omigod, without her books we're broke!"

I took a ragged breath and focused on the evidence. "And you involved me to clear the way to Zach," I said. "Too bad it was all for nothing."

"Listen, Zach is mine. You don't stand a chance," she said.

She didn't know about the priesthood. "And since you worked at Leland's lab for a while you figured the incinerators would make an excellent place to dispose of a body."

"All wrong!" she cried. "I never touched Otto's body after I shoved it over the railing. I kicked away the kippah and left. I have no idea how his body got into your van." There was a moment, while she spoke, when our eyes linked I could see genuine confusion. "You gotta believe me."

I couldn't. Not with the evidence. But?

"So you have us," Lilith said with an alluring smile for Talon. "I'm guilty of not alerting authorities to Otto's death by natural causes, and my daughter of desecrating a body. Our records are clean. We will do community service. So what? People love a good story. My book sales will skyrocket, I'll keep my house—"

"Our house," Mackenzie corrected.

Paul hissed an oath, pushed a cell phone at Mackenzie,

and stomped up the stairs to his office.

"One sticking point," Talon said to Lilith. "You missed a bottle of tainted vitamins, Booth's vitamins, and he's allergic to codeine. Attempted murder is a crime."

"That can't be." Panic shot through her voice. "I know how many bottles I doctored. Hell, I had only had time for two, and I threw those away in the lake. Goddamnit. It's the truth!"

Talon ignored her, shifting to Mackenzie. "I understand you work at the Starbucks near Pikes Place Market."

"I did. I quit today," she said, her voice shaking, her eyes darting to her mother.

"Doris and Cokey Bill Oley lived in an apartment above that Starbucks."

"Who are they?" she demanded.

"Their son lives with them."

"So? What's that to me?" she asked.

"Victor Oley frequented the Starbucks where you work—worked," he corrected.

I gaped at him. "Victor?"

He nodded. "Miss Desmont, do you know this man?"

She shook her head.

"He sometimes goes by Big Vic."

Queenie's Big Vic?

The tension in her face relaxed a little. "Oh, sure, Big Vic. Vanilla latte, no foam," she said with *way* too much airiness to be worried about being linked to him. "He's shagging some black chick. Talks about her all the time. What's he got to do with this?"

It took me nearly five baffled seconds to remember Leland and Queenie's conversation from earlier at her house:

> Queenie: *"And Victor hasn't called me all day…"*
>
> Leland: *"Is he your boyfriend?"*
>
> Queenie: *"Love of my life. If Booth doesn't chase him off like the rest."*

I figured out what had been bothering me. I needed to sit down. I needed to stand. No, I needed to make a call. Slowly, furtively, I stepped away as Talon continued to question Mackenzie. I dialed, tapped my foot until Jaspal Singh answered. He vacillated over my question, but when I reminded him that he was also a father, he relented and hung up.

I shifted, opened my front door, and called for Booth to come out. He was cleaning his teeth with his tongue when he joined me beside the group.

"Have you got my watch yet?" he asked. "Cha-ching."

I had a wild urge to laugh. "All the good it will do you in prison."

"You drive me crazy," he said.

I caught Talon's smile. "Booth, it was you who framed Leland and me," I said.

He sneered, something dark wedged between his front teeth. "Prove it, greenhorn."

I checked my watch, saw the time was about the same as last night's bonfire, and silently thanked the mandala for excellent timing. "I understand you have an apartment you only occasionally use. Do you know what that tells me, Booth?"

Chin set, he shook his head.

"It tells me you want to keep a relationship secret, maybe from your wife."

Booth crossed his arms. "A man's gotta have some privacy, see. It's not a crime."

"No, it isn't," I said. "But blackmail is."

His squirmy brows shot skyward, but he managed to say coolly, "So."

"You saw Mackenzie throw the body over the rail last night. See how easy it is?" All eyes followed as I pointed to Leland's discernible balcony. "She didn't see you, though, but then she was busy," I said. "Paul Desmont would do anything for his daughter, and you planned to capitalize on that. Only problem, the Desmonts' are broke."

He jerked a shoulder, but his eyes had widened in surprise. "Why are you dragging me into this?" he asked. "I heard everything you said a moment ago, see. That girl framed you." He jabbed a gold-laden finger at Mackenzie. "She's guilty, not me. I even helped Detective Talon. I told him I'd seen her working at the Starbucks near the wharf."

Mackenzie rushed forward and pushed him. "You set me up. You bastard!"

"See how violent she is?" Booth straightened his coat. "She's guilty, her and her mother."

Mackenzie went to Lilith and hugged her, but received only a weak pat on the back.

I sighed, focused on Booth. "I figured you must have seen Lilith when she came home with the Codeine and vitamins last night?"

"This is insane," he said. "I didn't see anything."

"Let me spell it out," I said. "With Leland in jail for Otto's murder, you have a better chance of keeping the watch. With Lilith in jail for doping the vitamins, you get free rein to blackmail Paul to keep Mackenzie out of jail. Now framing me, that was just mean."

"I don't have to stand here and take this." Booth moved to leave.

"I think you do," Talon said, pulling him back.

I drew in a breath. "Booth, you dragged Otto's body to FoY's van. Those darn nettles, huh?" With my hands in my pockets, I fidgeted with the cross Zach had given me. "Then you poisoned Victor Oley after he tried not once, but twice to kill me. What did you do, promise to give Queenie and him your blessing in exchange for his help?"

He stared at me, beads of sweat on his upper lip.

"But still," I said, "you worried about looking guilty. After all, the police would connect you to Victor through Queenie. And, of course, everyone knew you left the bonfire before it ended. So you dosed yourself with codeine to throw off suspicion."

He was scratching the rash again. "None of this will stick."

"And the icing on this murderous cake was killing Victor Oley, and you were using Happy Hye's love for you as leverage to make Queenie agree to be with you," I said. "You're in love with your own stepdaughter."

"That's sick," Mackenzie hissed.

"Might be a book in there somewhere," Lilith said.

Booth's lips peeled back in a twisted grin. "Where is your proof?"

I stared at Talon, trying to put an unspoken message into my look. "The genetic profile on the foxglove seeds collected from Booth's house," I said to Talon. "Did they match the ones found on the muffins that killed the Oleys?"

"To the T," he said easily.

"Three murders, Booth. Not good. And if I were to guess, I suspect we'd find another muffin in a Starbucks bag on the hood of Lilith's car." I watched his eyes narrow. "After the second attempt on my life, you didn't plan on Victor leaving muffins in the panel truck for his parents to eat. You know we still have the death penalty in Washington." I smiled. "Tough luck, greenhorn."

Sighing, Booth bent to tug at his pant hem, fiddle with his sock. "Flower DNA. Ain't that something?" He came up with a pistol in his hand, aimed it at Talon. "Go ahead, Detective, put the safety back on your revolver. I'll be leaving now."

Sounds went on around us: Mackenzie's whimpers, Lilith's curses, Talon's warnings, Solo's subtle growls. Even the firefighters were chatting over the tow-truck, seemingly too busy to notice Booth had a gun. But it was all background noise to me. Even the fear that made my heart race didn't matter. Nothing mattered except I had to finish this, right here, right now.

Bracing my feet, I balled Zach's heavy cross in my hand, adjusting the sharp point to jut out my fist. I inched it from my pocket. Booth was smugly chuckling at my shoulder as Talon snapped the safety over his gun.

Arrogant asshat was my thought as I swung out and drove the cross into Booth's crotch. He whooshed out a huge breath, buckled. Talon grabbed his gun, wrenched it away, and pushed him to the ground, where Solo plopped down on his back, flattening him like a cow patty.

Lilith dropped down beside Solo. "They'll roll over if you don't sit on their ass. It is all about torque. Writers study these things."

I sighed in sweet relief, but it didn't last long.

Mackenzie screamed, staring at her phone, "Omigod. Zach is becoming a priest!"

She whizzed past me, running in the direction of my house. I heard what sounded like a hysterical promise to kill herself. I rushed after her. She was heading to the deck. As I neared, she was already at the edge, teetering where the rail should have been had my grandfather not taken it down for repairs. She was sobbing, staring at the ground, some thirty feet though the trees, a hundred foot rocky roll to the lake.

"Go away!" she said. "Just go the hell away!"

I was amazingly calm. I had just brought down a killer. I had saved my job, kept my family's home off the auction block. What's more, I was a trained suicide prevention councilor. I was ready, prepared. Composed. Gandhi in a woman's suit.

"Mackenzie, step away from the ledge," I said evenly.

"Go to hell."

I inched closer, faced her. I was okay with heights, but, *wow*, it was a long way down. With nothing else to hold onto, I grabbed the tip of a maple branch. "I'm sorry."

She rolled her eyes my way, and I got dizzy just watching her. "What are you sorry for, chasing Zach away?"

I paused and took an emotional inventory. Heartbeat a little fast, but not soaring. I was still in control. "Zach was never mine to chase away," I said.

"The son of a bitch couldn't tell me in person," she hissed. "A goddamn text message is all I got!"

"Did you know it takes years to become a priest?" I said, thinking ahead.

"Really?"

"You know, I think I can win him back." I lied as she

turned. "I'm sure I can."

"Over my dead body."

I eyed the drop below. "You can either clear the field for me, or fight me. Your choice."

In one giant step, she was away from the edge. "You haven't a chance, Rylie. I know things. Just so we're clear, I've had his cock inside me."

Go figure. I finally talked down a jumper, and now I wanted to push her off the edge.

"You got me there," I said.

She stared past me, sudden horror shooting into her eyes. Garbled words spilled from her mouth, echoed in the shadows. I turned my neck, shifting from confused to grim as hoards of bats exploded out from beneath the deck. In a whirling black wave, they tangled in my hair, scratched my face. The shock of it, the sting of it sent me spinning to slap them away.

I lost my balance, screamed. I flailed backward, grasping for something—anything. I caught hold of the maple, but felt it slip from my fingers. I slipped off the edge. Falling, a second scream froze in my throat. I hit a branch, managed to seize it with both hands, the abrupt stop nearly jarring my teeth from my mouth. I hung there, catching my breath, my legs dangling.

In a haze, I noticed the tree trunk only a few feet away. If only I could let go, just one hand. The strength of the other might hold me. It moved fuzzily through my mind that if I could grab hold of it, I could shimmy down the thirty feet. Maybe there was a way to inch over without letting go.

"Rylie." It came from behind, on the deck, half panic, half plea.

I turned my head, stared at Talon in silence.

"Lass, grab my hand."

But it seemed so far away. With my arms shaking, my strength failing, I slowly, deliberately, shook my head. "I can make it. I can reach the tree trunk."

He was silent now, but his eyes were pleading with me. It was not until I inched a hand toward the trunk that he ripped out an oath. "Jesus Christ, honey, trust me."

Then I turned back to him, my fingers freezing on the branch. "I can't. I can't reach you."

"Reach me?" He spoke gently now. "You've done so much more than that. Take my hand, lass."

For a moment, I stared. Then the weight of his words had me reaching out. Capably, calmly, he took a hold of my wrist, locked his fingers around it.

"Right, then." His hold on me tightened. "Now the other hand."

Somewhere on the lake music was playing. "I trust you, Talon."

I let go.

Then in a wild tangle of fingers, faith, and fear, our hands locked. The second he pulled me up to the deck, I began to tremble. He wrapped his arms around me, held me close while the sunset on Mt. Rainier faded to gray and the lake sparkled with night.

Hazy voices and footsteps sounded all around as my trembling turned to numb shock. Paul led Mackenzie away, soothing her with soft words. Solo popped his head around the corner, assuring us that Booth was tied up and going nowhere. I didn't look up when someone said my name, only forced myself when I heard it again. Curtis Hobbs stood over Talon and me, his mouth grim.

I smiled faintly, managed to say, "Thank you for sending the note to Lipschitz."

"Not that it did me any good." Curtis's mouth sunk deeper into a frown. "Who is this guy, Rylie?"

I introduced them, but Curtis refused to shake Talon's extended hand. Instead, he marched away in a huff.

"And his problem is?" Talon asked.

"I guess I wasn't thankful enough," I said. "I'll talk to him later. I'll make it right."

"Thankful for what?" he asked.

I explained the Bintliff note. "Solo and I think it refers to the gambler Shoeless Joe Bintliff. We think Lipschitz might owe him money."

"Lipschitz has many vices, but gambling isn't one of them. No, it more likely relates to Maxwell Bintliff, a recently fired firefighter."

I remembered the protestors outside the fire station. "I think I saw picketers holding up signs about that. Why was this Maxell Bintliff let go?"

"He was arrested last month at Crossroads Park."

"What for?"

"Disorderly conduct, public drunkenness, and indecency," he said. "Cross-dressing, thong bikinis, and two black wigs were involved."

"Two wigs?" I asked.

"The evidence suggests he had a friend with him who escaped."

I lifted my shocked gaze, met his laughing one. "Lipschitz?"

"Sounds like it," he said.

Lipschitz in a thong. *Ack.* "Will this new information help your investigation?"

He shook his head. "It's neither here or there, and best kept secret for now. More secrecy, I know, but trust me on this."

"I have a feeling you'll be asking that of me a lot."

His smile spread slowly. "What cannot be helped must be put up with."

"Another Scottish proverb?"

He nodded. "Chancy thing your friend Curtis did for you, but I'm pleased he did."

Help doesn't always come from who you expect, nor result in what you expect. Curtis had been protecting me, but it was Talon who gave me freedom to protect myself, who I wanted—wanted badly. Ironic. I would always appreciate Curtis's assistance, the chance he took by quasi-threatening a police detective, an under suspicion one at that, and I would convey my appreciation and apology for not returning the affection I suspected he felt for me.

"Lipschitz a cross-dresser," I said, imagining it. "That's wild."

"As to wild." He lowered his lips to mine, nibbled there. "Rylie Tabitha Keyes, I cannae wait for you to drive me crazy."

Acknowledgments

More than a few well-intentioned people warned that I'd never publish, citing the daunting disparity of books penned to books published. This pessimism stayed with me for many years, running though my mind, my heart, my hopes, and my dreams. I alone gave it power. The nagging need to pen stories broke through time after time, but I shut my eyes and paid no mind. I couldn't take the chance. I couldn't fail. Avoidance is insecurity's refuge. Others encouraged me, christening my attributes, spotlighting my resilience, while my pessimism only forged ahead impervious. Then I lost my mother and confronted a grief much worse than any sorrow that failing to publish could spark or ignite. So from death rose up strength, from heartache rose up determination, and from orphanhood rose up confidence. And now I write. But as with all endeavors of the heart, teamwork is what makes my work thrive. It is to these generous players I offer my never-ending gratitude. While to those participants I've unintentionally omitted, I ask forgiveness.

I am deeply grateful to my agent, Nicole Resciniti, and to Elizabeth Pelletier, my acquiring editor, and to Libby Murphy, my editor, for their unending love for the written word, their belief in this book, and their faith in me, an unproven fledgling. I am also in debt to Shannon Godwin, editorial director, and ultimate "voice of reason." I want to thank my publicists, Danielle Barclay and Anjana Vasan, who never baulk at my endless questions and work tirelessly behind the scenes. To my gal pals, who I list alphabetically to avoid sibling rivalry: Amanda Carlson, Marisa Cleveland, Jen J. Danna, Amanda Flower, Melissa Landers, Lea Nolan, Cecy Robson, Melody Steiner, Julie Ann Walker. Nothing can change our inception as "Nic's Chicks," though males in our mix would have been fun. "Nic's Chicks & Dicks" is priceless.

To Dr. Linda Seim for always being there and slogging through first drafts like a trooper.

To Deborah Drake and Sharon Barber for the friendship and laughs. Long live the Crossroads Hamsters.

To Gene for being you, your patience and support, and for loving me. To Sierra for listening when I chatter about plots and characters, but also for hearing me as no one else can. To Daniel for never being too big or grown up to hug and kiss your mother. To Blane for always being close when I need you. To Brian for enduring my youthful mothering even though I didn't know what I was doing. I love you all.

Get a sneak peek of Delicious Mischief, Book Two in the Rylie Keyes Mystery Series. Coming May 2014!

˜Mean people suck˜

When one hatches a last-minute plan, there are those who are in, those who are out, and those who just happen to be in the car. The septuagenarian riding shotgun seat beside me belonged to the latter bunch. As far as senior Jane Gettelfinger knew, I was hanging a u-ey to snag a Blizzard from the nearby Dairy Queen. However, my real aim was to track down a scumbag for my new boss at Snoop Investigations, a longtime Bellevue, Washington P.I. firm, where I'm a highly underpaid (i.e. diddlysquat) intern.

My name is Rylie Tabitha Keyes, and I hold down two other jobs in order to keep my ailing grandfather in our ancestral home on Lake Sammamish. So far, I've kept at bay the pesky tax assessor, who would love nothing better than to auction off our rundown lakeside cottage for some measly back taxes. Yet, however successful my efforts have been, they're only a work in progress, as my two paying jobs reward me with barely poverty level compensation. One job, with Baconnaise, because they only give me eight stinking hours a week, and the other, Fountain of Youth Retirement

Home (FoY), because it's cash strapped due to the owner, Leland Rosenberg, losing everything in a Ponzi scheme run by a Rockefeller imposter of the Egyptian persuasion.

Most wonder how a con artist who was so obviously not a New York blueblood with French Huguenot ancestry could've duped our fearless leader at FoY. But not me, I suspected if asked for help, my kindhearted-yet-gullible boss would have led the hungry wolf to a tasty Red Riding Hood. So in order to put Jelly Bellies into our tummies, my grandfather and I have taken in a roommate, my friend Solosolo Namulau'ulu—Solo for short—who also works at FoY. But rather than schlepping seniors to doctor appointments, churches, or Indian bingo as I do each day, Solo helps them stay active with exercises like Wii Fit, salsa dancing, and the occasional home-wide search for the TV remote control. While in his spare time, Solo—in conjunction with his 350 pounds of rawhide Samoan muscle—trains to perform someday on a circus bike for Cirque du Soleil, of which his first audition is in just seven days.

Truth is, both Solo and I have career goals that fly in the face of our loved one's expectations, but more on that later. Right now, I needed to figure out how to handle this quick detour from my original destination: senior Jane Gettelfinger's newly restored, yet so far unoccupied, mansion. Without pissing the old girl off.

"I'd been meaning to ask," I said to Jane. "Are you planning to move back to your own home soon?"

She flashed me an eye, a bit miffed. "Someday."

The same answer as always, but I persisted—some might say rather nosily—because I found it bizarre that anyone would live in a modest retirement home when they owned a million-dollar house. "That must have been some remodel job. You've been at FoY, what, two years now?"

"If you say so." She stared down at the fingernails she'd spent the last five minutes filing with an emery board and shook her head. "I don't have a memory for things like that."

"Now that you mention it, I think it's been three years."

"I didn't mention it," she said, a hint of annoyance in her voice. "I could've driven myself, you know? I'm not senile."

"Of course you aren't," I said, glancing sideways at her with admiration. She was really a physically fit senior. "Complications happen sometimes."

"Not to me they don't." She dropped the nail file into her purse and hauled out her iPhone. "Cataract surgery is supposed to be simple. Clouded eye. Damn nuisance — and don't tell me setbacks builds character like Elsa did yesterday. Not according to my book. Moral fiber is earned not endured."

"Speaking of earning," I said. "You've lots of people helping set up your party tonight, right?"

"Are you insane?" She huffed and fixed testy eyes on the phone clenched in her bejeweled — as in ice — hands. "Of course, I have help. Peons do everything for me."

Smooth. Insult peons while in the company of one. Nevertheless, I persisted to get on her good side. "Remind me how it was you came to be so rich," I asked, referencing one of her favorite subjects.

"Seat warmers." She jabbed a finger at her cell, clearly typing a text, but looking more like an act of murder. "One gave me a yeast infection back in '66. I took the car company to court and won a boatload. Suckers."

"Oh, that's right. Leland said you sued the pants off

them."

She barked a shifty laugh. "Fitting, Rylie, very fitting." Then she sucked in a sharp breath. "What a boring pack of old farts and fuddy-duddies, all of them."

Aside from money, Jane mostly talked about men: how to get them in the sack, how to ditch them when they got too clingy, the hit or miss dimensions of their manhood, and her appraisal of their carnal performances. Not a big shocker. Jane is a nymphomaniac, psychologically speaking. Or a sex freak, in slanguage.

"My God, it's one thing after another with these idiotic men," she went on.

I said nothing, only concentrated on putting my last-minute plan into action by maneuvering down the street alongside the Unemployment Office. Driving slowly, I looked for signs of the after-hours security guard through the large plate-glass windows, but came up empty.

"Don't they realize?" Jane's attention was still on her phone. "That nothing says amour like me under moonlight?"

"Problem?" I asked finally.

"Problem is an understatement." Her voice was as brittle as her bleached blond hair. "Not one male FoY resident is coming to my party tonight."

"Not true," I countered. "Gilad said he would be there."

She howled another laugh. "The impotent ones don't count."

I imagined Charles Darwin said that very same thing. Along with "No hard feelings, huh? Welcome to extinction."

Cruising on, I finally spied through the plate glass the after-hours guard chomping through what looked like a mega calzone, while Jane only continued to snarl at her phone.

"How can they not come to my party?" she said. "There will be agony for each and every one of those old pansies, believe you me."

Oh, I believed her, all right. Jane scared the bejesus out of me, especially when she jumped all over my ass after my split with Detective Thad Talon. For the most part, it wasn't much of a break up, because when I demanded (asked, really) Talon to confide in me his real identity, he only smiled and kissed me goodnight. Turns out, that kiss was our last.

The unemployment office's back lot was empty when I pulled in and checked my watch. Twenty past five pm, right on target.

Blah, bleak, bland Pacific Northwest rain snaked down the windshield, and even with the cloud-shrouded Autumn sunlight fading on the western horizon, I could see nearby trash Dumpsters were crammed with soggy orange and black party favors, a vampire cut-out, and those stretchy spider webs typically strung up for Halloween.

Jane bounced in her seat, at long last looking up from her cell. "What's up? Why are we here?"

I stared at the thin line of her lips. "Is your question one of anger or excitement?"

"Anger, of course," she said. "Only men get me excited."

I took a deep bolstering breath. "Jane, I've got a problem," I began. "I'm behind the eight-ball on an investigation—"

"Geez Louise, Rylie, spare me the PI lingo." Despite two facelifts, she glared at me from under deeply hooded eyes. "Plain English, please."

So much for that 99-cent e-book. "Look, if I don't find this guy." I took a picture from the center console and handed it over. "I'll lose my internship."

"Bullpucky." She scanned the photo, then let it drop into the drink cubby. "Never seen him. Wake up, doll face. Come to the real world of favoritism. That PI boss of yours is a friend of your granddad. He won't can your ass."

"But there's another intern, a son—daughter—of my boss's cousin."

"Which is it, a son, or daughter?"

I thought a moment. "Well, Sherwin Blank was a guy, but now he's a she."

"Sex change?"

I nodded.

"So he's a he-she." She eyed me hopefully, expression bright. "Do his man parts still work?"

I rolled my eyes. "Look, this is serious. My boss has time to train only one intern. Bottom line, whoever finds Andre Rostov first keeps their job."

"No sweat. Just ask Talon for help," she said. "That man could find Elvis."

"I can manage on my own," I said, pouting a little. Talon probably could find Elvis. I, on the other hand, can't locate my car keys most mornings.

"Suit yourself." Jane leaned back, her thinning hair scrunched against the headrest, her light eyes staring off in the distance. "You know, it just might do you good to lose this internship. You'll have more time to reconsider your break up with Talon."

"But—"

"Oh, I know," she cut me off with an irritated wave of the hand. "All you've ever wanted to be is a PI. But damn, doll face, that man is so, so—"

Sure, Talon was too babelicious for words, but as I'd feared from the moment we'd met last summer, I needed something more. Something resembling honesty. A moral accessory, Talon possessed in short supply.

"The key to relationships is openness," I said.

"Openness be damned. The key is sex." She squinted at me. "The sex was good, right?"

Heavenly. But her next question saved me from answering.

"What exactly is he not open about?"

I swallowed hard. I'd stupidly turned our conversation down a waterway I couldn't navigate without divulging that Talon had a secret identity. "Just stuff," I said, shrugging.

"What kind of stuff?"

I turned my neck to look out the windshield. "His past loves. Things like that," I lied not swiveling my head.

"Ha!" she barked. "Is that all? Doll face, you need to grow up. Past loves are nobody's damn business. Now, what's this Andre what's-his-name done? The one in the picture?"

"Insurance fraud," I told her, relieved by the change of subject.

"And he works here?" She looked around again. "Isn't this the unemployment office?"

I nodded. "Rostov quit months ago, but the after-hour guard knows him. Though so far, he's been uncooperative."

"And you've got a plan to make him talk?"

Vaguely, but still I answered yes.

"We will not be late for my Halloween party," she insisted. "Are we clear on that?"

"Crystal."

Jane and I were both decked out in costumes. Hers: a

spot-on depiction of a seventy-five-year-old Lady Zorro. As for my get-up, well, at least for tonight it double dutied as a costume, while four other nights a week, it made do as a uniform for my part-time job with Baconnaise. Swathing me from neck to knees were two rectangles of thick foam fused together at the top and sides, with an opening for my head at the top, while two slits at my shoulders freed up my arms. And gallivanting down the front and back were long, alternating stripes of russet and beige, while stamped across my chest and ass was my employer's slogan: EVERYTHING SHOULD TASTE LIKE BACON. I'm their Eastside spokesperson. I earn minimum wage eight hours a week as the freckled-faced redhead who waves to Bellevue, Washington rush hour drivers from the corner of 148th NE and NE 24th Street, where I often stand beside a pleasant, but crazed woman who dances while she shouts out rock bottom mattress prices for a nearby store. People frequently toss us money out of pity and at times a delectable like Filet 'o Fish sails from a car window. I scurry after those puppies, posthaste. Merely to show my appreciation.

Tonight was Halloween, and as mentioned, Jane was hosting a big bash for who I hoped turned out to be oodles of big tippers. It was a much-needed chance for me to earn extra moolah parking cars, and I needed all the dough I could scare up. I was currently experiencing a more than usual debtage after the '72 Pinto station wagon I recently bought from a friend and co-worker broke down not once, but twice this week.

I checked my watch again. Time to rock & roll. As I jockeyed the Pinto in between the back wall and the two columns supporting the overhead carport, the rear door whooshed open hard and whacked the left front fender. It happened just as I'd intended, only the hit was more forceful, surely making a dent in my car. Damn.

The calzone-eating guard's flushed face squished out through the thin gap between the door and jamb, his skin stretched bloodless, an unlit cigarette stuck between his lips.

Awesome. My hasty plan was working. As for knowing the security guard's routine: eating first, then smoking at 5:30pm. That was easy. Even at the spry age of twenty-four, I was a seasoned user of the unemployment office's job finding services. And though they know my name by heart, the staff calls me 'The Career Chameleon.' Very amusing. However, I'm done with all that flakiness now that my retired police detective grandfather has given his blessing to my private investigator dream, albeit grudgingly. I guess he just figured he had no choice after I solved a murder a few months back.

Rolling down the Pinto's window, I caught an earful of the after-hours guard's warp-speed Italian. Two lone words stood out: mutha fucka. Even garbled by his squished cigarette and thinned lips, some catchphrases were Swarovski clear. This guy was hopping mad.

He wormed out an arm between the door and frame. Swift hand gestures followed. None of them nice. "I gonna tell you what I tell you before. I no remember so much about Andre Rostov," he said.

"I know what you said. Now tell me the truth," I told him.

"How come you no read Idiots Guide to People Finding? Blocking me inside here is no way to get what you want. Italian men get ideas when they see a needy woman. There, what did I 'a tell you? I just got another one. Excusee, if you no mind me asking, what color are your panties?"

Big sigh. "Wake up," I said. "I already told you. I'm not sleeping with you for information."

"I might," Jane chimed in with an abnormally jolly hee-haw. "I'll have you know that back in '52, I spied for our Green Berets, swapping coitus with North Korean officers for military secrets. Funny how life shows us our strengths. I must have banged a hundred men that year."

"I've got this handled," I told Jane, and tried again to explain to the guard. "He used to work here on the weekends."

I gave the guard my most excellent dopy-eye look. When his expression lifted from pissed to sympathetic, my heart leapt north to my tonsils. Was I about to finally solve my first case for Snoop Investigations? Could it be that I was actually going to hold onto my internships?

"Everybody loves mall Santas," the guard said. "Not me. I hate the little sonnawabitches." Then he tried to light his cigarette, but dropped the lighter. Grumbling, he bent to pick it up. Only instead of getting a hand on it, he smacked his head on the doorknob. Loads more kvetching spilled out his mouth.

"Santa Claus?" I said. "The man is a mall Santa?"

"And flexible as hell."

Jane and I exchanged stumped looks. I asked him what he meant, but my question was drowned out when he whacked the door repeatedly against the Pinto's front fender.

"Look, lady, I gonna call the polizia," he shouted. "Let me out of here."

Jane clambered over me and stuck her head out my window. "Not until you spill the beans, buddy-o."

"Mind your own damn business, you old bag." The guard sidled between the door and jamb, trying to squeeze his fleshy body into the narrow opening like Play-Doh through a Fun Factory. Hindered by the doorknob gouging a whopping crater into his big ol' belly, he spit out a loogie in frustration, missing Jane, but not my much.

"Hey, you could use some pointers on how to treat a woman," she yelled, then gasped. "Oh, look at you. Such a naughty boy. Your fly is open, and my-o-my you're going commando. Well, I'll be. So it's true. The bigger the nose, the smaller the penis."

"Kiss off," he told her. "I think maybe you so old you no remember what an eccellente penis looks like. My mistress says I'm a stallion."

With her knees digging into the tops of my thighs, Jane climbed out my window even farther and flicked his equestrian do-hickey with a casual finger. "What a big talker. That doodad is nothing more than a Shetland pony."

His lips thinned even more. He reached up and seized one of the overhang's rickety crossbeams affixed above the partially open door, hung from both hands, and squirmed up, trying to squeeze his body outside. Problem was, he managed only to wedge part of his thick trunk into the opening over the doorknob. The man was stuck like Chuck.

"Sir," I said. "Just tell me which mall Andre Rostov works at. I'll move the car."

"He's—" The guard broke off, however, as something loud, a lot louder than a moan or even a groan, rumbled from overhead. Then he looked up, to the overhang above the Pinto, his eyes growing wide, and wider, then bulging like a squished guppy. "Oh, no," he gasped.

I stared at his petrified face. "What is it?" I asked, as the groaning from above got even louder. "What's wrong?"

But his attention was fixed on the overhang as he wiggled his big body out from between the door and jamb, then drop down to his feet inside the building and slammed the door.

Jane stretched to look out the windshield. "What's was that all about—"

Her mouth had dropped open, eyes staring up. A second later, I knew why, as a hair-raising snap shattered the soupy air and one corner of the overhang broke free from the building. Then it all happened fast, too fast to move or react. A squeal flooded the car, as nails affixing the overhang to the two support columns on Jane's side of the car surrendered to the downward weight and started to twist out. Frozen in horror, I watched the overhang rock backward and forward before the columns buckled, and the nails stripped free entirely. The remaining corner fastened to the building gave way, then, under the pressure the overhang collapsed onto the Pinto with an earsplitting bonk.

Jane and I locked eyes. I tried to beat down all thoughts of panic. No use. I gave into panting. Jane merely tugged on an unseen mustache hair, eyes relaxed. Cucumber cool.

"Oh well," she said, sighing. "I'm way too much woman for him. I bet he'd have popped an artery or something. I like ape sex."

I squinted in the dim interior to examine the Pinto's roof, hoping, praying it would continue to hold until I got Jane out of the car. The overhang didn't seem to want to stop moving. It went on rocking, only now up and down. With my side of the car too tight for an escape, I released my seatbelt and reached over Jane for the passenger door handle as though in slow motion, as if my body was fighting against my brain. The car's interior spun a little from my fast breathing, tilted, but I got a hand on the handle, pulled down and pushed. The door wouldn't budge. I spied the small knob for the lock. Found it up. Still, my second try to open the door was no better than the first, the third just as useless.

Jane stretched her spry five-foot body and peered out her side window. "It's a good bet we're trapped. It seems one of the columns fell against the door." Then she lifted her cell phone and punched a few numbers. "Look," she said into the mouthpiece. "You listen to me when I talk to you. I said I want pineapple and Canadian bacon on my pizza. I am too being serious," she added and hung up.

I was halfway into believing that a phantom blow to my head had knocked me silly when I realized she was, indeed, serious. "Pizza? Now?"

She nodded. "I must say, Rylie, I like you. I'm not sure why. Oh, that reminds me. I need to pick a bone with my next-door neighbor."

I stared at her as she dialed yet another number. "Can't that wait?" I said. "We're stuck in here. The police are probably on their way. And the roof could collapse."

She shrugged rather testily and ignored me. "Come on, Dil; pick up the phone, dammit. Okay, have it your way," she said, and I recognized the automated sounds of voicemail. "Here's the deal. Your cat climbed into my yard yesterday and pooped all over the place. Stinks to high heaven, too. Honestly, what the hell kind of crap are you feeding him nowadays? Smacks of bargain basement shit. You know, I put my money on your new security guard. Probably buying cheap and pocketing the rest. If I were you, I'd take a hard look at him. Just last week, he got his nose all out of joint when I told him to get your trash bins out of my roses. Hard to say, but I'm betting he left off the cat's invisible fence collar on purpose to piss me off. Dil, I'm telling ya, you better see that pussycat doesn't escape again, or I will, hear me?" She hung up, took a breath, and turned to me. "Okay, where were we?"

Now positive I was brain-injury cuckoo, I tore my bulging eyes off her and took another glance around for a way out. Of course, I realized now that we might have a chance to escape through the back seat door, especially since the overhang had stopped wobbling.

And then I heard it, a deafening whoop, whoop, whoop coming from over our heads. "What's that?"

"A helicopter," she said with a blasé jerk of one shoulder. "I mobilized it to help us."

"You called for a helicopter? When?"

Somehow, I knew the answer before she said it.

"When I ordered the pizza. Pineapple and Canadian bacon is code for big trouble. Huh, is that thick expression on your face because you think we're in extreme jeopardy? Well, I guess I could have ordered anchovies and black olives, but calling out the National Guard seems too much. It's only a silly patio overhang, not terrorists."

My mouth dropped open when an Asian guy in a classy blue suit suddenly appeared at Jane's window, freed the passenger door of the offending column as if it were a mere toothpick, and signaled for Jane to roll down the glass. A tiny wire snaked from his ear to mouth, and his eyes were incredibly dark, dangerously dark. Half my spit dried up just looking at him. He was uber ripped and smoking hot, in an Incredible Hulk meets Tim Kang sort of way, but with the added oo-la-la of long, sinuous black hair. Square chin. Statuesque. Not that I was in the market for a man. No sirree bubba. After all the grief they'd caused me lately, I'd sworn off things with penises. Still, I'm no man-hater. Frustrated is more the somber truth. I'm two for zero in the love department, more if being honest, but why talk numbers now. But before Detective Thad Talon, there had been Zach O'Neil. A great guy. A former cop. He was my first real love. But also my best friend. And one kiss from me drove him straight to the priesthood. Major ego killer.

"We'll have you free in a moment, Miss Gettelfinger." Incredible Hulk raised his voice over the noise from the helicopter. "Anyone hurt?"

We shook our heads in rapt unison.

"I brought a blanket." He produced one that looked like cashmere. "In case of shock."

"You silly boy, you shouldn't have," gushed Jane at full volume, though I noticed she grabbed the blanket and brought it to her nose. "It smells like you, Luke. All male."

"Yes, ma'am." He smiled, revealing a slim keyboard of perfect teeth. "I'll need you to roll up the window now, for your own protection."

Luke stepped back and turned away to cough. He gave a scarcely noticeable shake to his head and looked our way. "Sorry, ladies," he called out. "Dry throat."

Jane frowned and buried her head in her whale of a purse. After several seconds of rummaging, she produced a cough drop. "Here, suck on this." When Luke hesitated, she added at the top of her lungs, "Don't make me spank you, darling boy."

He bent to her level. "Thank you," he mouthed, coughing a little, smiling less. I reckoned Luke wasn't a fan of cough drops, or was it Jane for which he lacked a taste?

Luke moved away, seized one of four hook-ended ropes that had dropped from above and out of sight. I paid way too much attention to his powerful hands as they nimbly fastened each hook to evenly spaced points on the overhang. Still staring, I yelled to Jane, "What's going on?"

She exhaled another deep breath into the blanket and rolled up the window. The outside racket lessened, but only by a little. "Don't you just love how he throws himself into his work?" she shouted. "That's why I permit him to be my bodyguard."

"He works for you?" I shouted in a choked voice.

"Tasted and approved," she barked and smacked her lips. "I'm gonna have to ask you to keep quiet about this," she added, eyes hard. "Can I trust you to do that, doll face?"

She shifted her attention to Luke and wiggled her fingers when he looked over.

"Sure. Why not," I muttered. "A helicopter, a hunky bodyguard. What's to tell?"

Luke moved around to the front of the Pinto and did a thumb-up motion to the unseen helicopter pilot. If Luke was gorgeous before, it was nothing to how he looked with his long, flowing Jesus-hair blowing wildly by the rotors. After a quick scoot up to the dashboard, Jane cupped her chin in a propped hand. I couldn't see her face, but I swear I saw her mouth form a moan.

"Relax," she called out to me. "Luke will take care of everything, even the security guard."

After that, we sat in silence. The helicopter lifted the

overhang. We watched, rooted to the spot. Luke looked in top form, so it must have been persistent dryness causing him to cough into his sleeve as he grabbed the fourth metal hook. The overhang swung over the Dumpsters and the wind from the rotors sent Halloween party favors flying all around like vivid shrapnel. Luke scurried, collected, crumpled the soggy stuff into a huge wad, and threw it away. He used up a few more minutes prying up and over the rusty Dumpster lids to keep more trash from blowing out.

When the helicopter lowered the overhang to the asphalt just ahead and to the right, Jane, as I was doing, clapped and cheered. Turns out being rescued was sort of a rush. Luke waved for me to drive off, and as I did so, I saw two things in the rearview mirror: Luke disappearing inside the unemployment office, and a better view of the helicopter— gaily painted in alternating stripes of yellow and gray—as it touched down at the rear of the lot. But still, there was no sign of the after-hours security guard from inside.

My head had a pulse as I thought about how I might be in deep shit. Suppose he'd already called the police from inside the office then insists they charge me with unlawful restraint once they arrive? Suppose Talon was called in to drag my sorry butt to jail? Suppose my being locked up in the pokey caused me to renege on a payment to the tax assessor, only to make Granddad and me homeless.

Hello, God. I'd like to leave now.